Zoë Beck
Fade to Black

Translated from German by Rachel Hildebrandt

German version published under the title Schwarzblende, published March 2015
Copyright © Zoë Beck, 2014

First English Edition
2017 © Weyward Sisters Publishing
ISBN 978-3-95988-025-1

Second English Edition
2023© Clevo Books

Translation: Rachel Hildebrandt
Editor: Pippa Goldschmidt, with additional editing by Aumaine Rose Smith and Cathryn Siegal-Bergman
Cover Design: Ron Kretsch

All rights reserved. No part of this publication may be reproduced or transmitted in any form or by any means, electronic or mechanical, including photocopy, recording, or any information storage and retrieval system, without permission in writing from the publisher.

Published in 2023 by
Clevo Books LLC
530 Euclid Avenue Suite 45a
Cleveland, Ohio 44102
www.clevobooks.com

*This is a simple story of good and evil,
light and dark, black and white.*

—Hofesh Schechter Company, "Sun"

FADE TO BLACK

WEDNESDAY

1

People don't walk through London with machetes.

Unless Niall counted the two men passing him just then. He'd already wrapped up taking pictures of the spot where the Effra River had once emptied into the Thames when he saw one of those men glance back at him. The man's gaze lingered a split second too long, his eyes offering an invitation. At least, that was what Niall thought. Perhaps the man wanted to challenge him, defy him, like "Hey, look what we can do without anyone trying to stop us in this city that bans all rubbish bins anywhere near government buildings out of fear that someone might plant a bomb in them." As if bins were the only places people left explosive bombs.

Niall had preparations to make for his shoot next week. He needed to decide what he was going to record, which camera angles would work best, and which scenes would make the most sense. Then, he needed to visit the grocery store and head home. But he nevertheless began trailing the two men, their machetes making him both vaguely uneasy and a little curious. Besides, an underground river was hardly going to up and disappear on him.

They strode down the southern bank of the Thames and under the railroad bridge before turning left and walking a short distance along the edge of a park. They seemed to be in no particular hurry. They passed other pedestrians, but nobody paid them the slightest attention. Everyone was focused on their own thoughts, their own lives.

Actors, Niall decided, on their way to an audition or a film shoot. But why would actors be carrying their own props? They were part of a small acting troupe, perhaps. Or showoffs with something to prove. Or maybe it was a dare, like the ones for bachelor parties, just with a less silly theme, something with weapons? There had to be a reason. Should he call the police? He wondered. Or should he wait a bit? After all, they weren't bothering anyone and didn't seem that dangerous, despite the machetes. In any case, they were carrying the weapons confidently, as if they weren't dangerous. Maybe they weren't. Niall snapped off surreptitious photos. Nobody would believe him later if he didn't have proof.

They looked like brothers from behind: same height, similar build, both in jeans and sneakers. As far as Niall could tell, they both had short black hair, dark brown skin, and neatly trimmed beards. One of them wore a green t-shirt, the other a blue one. Nothing else distinguished them, at least, not from behind at this distance.

They turned into the park before coming to a halt. They were chatting, as they had been doing off and on the whole time, occasionally laughing. They even looked back at him once to make sure he was still there, which did not seem to bother them at all.

Niall was still holding his phone, ready to call the emergency number at any moment, but nothing happened. The machete men just stood there cheerfully, as if waiting on someone. Niall guessed they were somewhat younger than him, though not by much. Mid- or late-twenties, both physically fit. The one in the blue shirt was quite attractive: an open face with large, watchful eyes. With his thinner lips and more closely set eyes, the one in the green shirt looked more secretive.

Two joggers were wheezing their way through the park while a young woman pushed a stroller alongside another woman of about the same age. A boy, twentyish, strode past Niall and cut across the grass.

Since nobody else seemed worried about the machetes, Niall decided they had to be fakes. The men were probably meeting in the park for some kind of role-playing game, and their friends would show up any minute with more toy weapons, perhaps even in costume. All of it would, no doubt, be harmless. Good thing he had waited to call the police, he considered, since he would've just made a fool of himself. Niall snapped more pictures of the men before turning and walking off.

He had almost reached the edge of the park when he heard someone start screaming, followed by voices yelling all at once. Niall spun himself back around. The machete men were threatening someone: the boy who had passed him so resolutely. His hands were thrown up, as if in surrender, and he kept crying out, "Leave me alone."

Although he was much taller than the other two and as fit as they were, he seemed off-balance, vulnerable. He was alone against the two of them, and they were armed. They were using their machetes to keep him at bay: one in the front, the other behind, their knees slightly flexed as if about to jump. With their arms spread out and their weapons as extensions, they looked as if they might embrace each other.

The joggers had come to a stop close to Niall, and they were also watching the three men.

Niall still gripped his phone, but instead of calling the police, he tapped the camera symbol.

"Call the police," he said to the joggers.

They both reached for their phones.

"What for?" one of them asked, as his companion dialed, "you're already holding yours."

"I'm recording," Niall said.

"Jerk," the other one snapped.

The man in the blue shirt lunged, aiming for the boy's throat, but he ended up striking his upraised left arm. With a howl of pain, the boy fell back a step and doubled over, trying to press the bloody gash on his upper arm closed with his right hand. The man in the green shirt was also recording with his phone, and Niall heard him urge his friend, "one more time. You're not done yet." It was as if he were supervising a motorcycle repair job.

"I've got this," the one in blue replied before kicking the injured boy in the back of the knees so he crumpled into the grass. Between sobs, the boy cursed his attackers, then the man in blue bent down and started stabbing.

The one in green cheered him on, "yeah, that's right. You're doing great!"

"I know." The other one said, sounding annoyed. Even after the victim's agonized screams broke off, the attacker continued stabbing, though with less enthusiasm than before.

"It takes a while," the one with the phone remarked.

"I know," the other man repeated, his movements growing sluggish until he was just jabbing the body with the tip of his sword. His friend circled the two of them, recording. The attacker finally gave up and lazily slashed his machete through the air, blood dribbling from the blade and down his hands. His shirt was covered in blood splatters, and on his face, beads of sweat mingled with the boy's blood.

The man in green lowered his phone, nodded encouragingly at his friend, and slapped him on the shoulder before glancing over at Niall, the joggers, and the other people who had gathered around them. Spectators. Fascination with someone else's death was always stronger than fear of one's own.

"We have an audience," the man in green commented.

The murderer followed his gaze and straightened up to his full height. "Good." ▯

2

"Hey," the man in green shouted at one of the joggers.

"Hey! What are you doing with your phone?"

The man who had just called the police dropped his phone before raising his arms. "Nothing."

The man in green picked up his machete and walked toward him. "Nothing? You fucking kidding me? Did you call somebody?"

The jogger wet himself, and his companion groaned, either in horror or shame. Instead of helping his friend, he took three steps back.

"Calling is shit. Show a little respect, okay?" He stopped right in front of the jogger. "You're supposed to watch what we're doing, got it?"

The jogger whimpered.

Niall said: "He didn't do anything. I was watching." He kept his camera trained on the man with the machete, but he was starting to feel dizzy.

"You!" the man in green shot back. "You were paying attention, huh?" He lowered his machete. "Did you record everything?"

Niall nodded.

"All of it?"

"Yes."

"Good. Wait a second, don't go anywhere." He pulled something out of his pocket, a piece of cloth he then unfolded. Niall saw a black rectangle, white Arabic letters in the upper half and a white circle underneath with even more letters. The flag of the Islamic State. The man walked back over to his friend and the corpse, positioned himself in front of them, and waved the cloth back and forth.

"Did you get that? Did you?"

Niall nodded, frightened. Despite his first impulse to run, he could not help wanting to see what happened next.

"Come over here," the one with the flag ordered.

Niall obeyed. He was not one bit better than the others who had chosen to hang around, but he also sensed something else: a feeling of obligation. He had recorded everything, so now it was his duty to distract these two men from the joggers, from the other people who had joined them, and from the women with the stroller who were still there though they should have taken the child to safety. Niall focused on his fear, knowing he needed to channel it the same way actors use stage fright.

"You're fighting for the Islamic State?" he asked.

"Yes!" the other man responded proudly, continuing to wave his flag energetically.

The man in blue pushed past him, leaving a bloody handprint on his shirt. He walked straight up to Niall and stared into the small phone camera. Niall struggled to stay calm, battling his flight instinct as best he could. He had seen predators through his lens before, recording them as they slaughtered their prey, but he had never been this close to one. He spread his feet further apart to project the illusion of stability and grasped the phone with both hands. He could not stop trembling, though.

"We've killed a soldier." The man pointed his bloody machete at the body in the grass, and Niall's gaze and camera tracked the gesture. The boy on the ground had very short, neatly clipped, light brown hair and was in his early twenties, at most. In any case, he was younger than Niall and the two men. He wore civilian clothes. Nothing about him showed that he was in the military, except perhaps his haircut, but that could have meant anything. Just as their beards didn't necessarily carry any specific meaning.

"We killed a British soldier because we're at war."

"What war? You mean jihad?"

"We're at war against everyone who doesn't acknowledge the Islamic State."

"Are you jihadists?" Niall's hands were steadier now, but his voice cracked a little.

The green one raised his right pointer finger and grinned into the camera as the blue one replied: "We're killing your soldiers because you've killed ours. We're taking your women because you've taken ours. We're turning your children into orphans because you've done that to ours." He shifted slightly, throwing a quick glance at his friend, who nodded back.

The blue one continued: "We support the establishment of an Islamic caliphate and follow the orders of Abu Bakr al-Baghdadi. We want to fight for him, and we demand the liberation of all Palestinians. You occupied Palestine and then allowed the Jews to settle there. They invaded our land and have killed women, children, and civilians, so we're killing your soldiers. This man," he gestured at the body with the point of his machete, "killed our women, children, and civilians, which is why it's okay for us to kill him. It's our duty."

"Did you know him?"

"He was a soldier."

"How do you know that?"

"He was a soldier," the blue one repeated, taking a step toward Niall.

Niall lowered his camera.

The man with the bloody machete declared: "Everyone needs to see this. Upload it."

"What?"

"On YouTube," the one in green added.

"Okay," Niall replied, swallowing hard once or twice as pressure built inside his ears.

"Keep recording," the one in blue ordered.

Niall pointed his phone back toward the men.

The one in green paced back and forth in front of the body and waved his machete at the jogger. The man was surrounded by a group of concerned onlookers.

I have to keep them talking, Niall thought. That way they won't focus on the others. He was still considering what to ask when the one in green shouted something.

"Takbīr!"

"Allāhu akbar!" the man in blue responded.

Niall quickly cut in: "Where are you from? London, right?"

The man in blue hesitated. Niall studied his face on the small display, too scared to risk looking at him directly. He seemed perfectly normal, calm, relaxed. He had dark skin and black hair, possibly Arabic. Then again, maybe he wasn't. He spoke with an unmistakable South London accent.

"Palestine," the man in blue finally said. "We were occupied and oppressed by you Brits. You stole our land."

"You're both from Palestine?" Niall could hear police sirens in the distance. "Your friend, too?"

"We demand the establishment of an Islamic caliphate in our homeland."

"He's from Palestine?"

"Turkey," the one in green called.

"Turkey?"

"If the Turkish government continues controlling the waters of the Euphrates and oppressing our brothers in the Islamic State, we'll have to liberate Istanbul!" He waved the black flag and stood beside his friend.

"We're at war against unbelievers. Against all infidels," the Palestinian explained. The man in green handed him the flag, then walked back to the body and nudged it with his toe.

"Come here," the Turk called to Niall. "I want to show you something. Hurry up, and don't stop recording."

Niall shuffled forward cautiously, making sure the Palestinian did not close the gap between them. He took care to keep both men in his frame, though there was no real need to worry about them going anywhere. The Palestinian stopped beside his friend and lifted the flag with both hands, like his comrade had done earlier. Blood-smeared fingers gripped the black fabric with white symbols. He continued to clutch the crimson-stained machete in his one hand, so it looked as if the flag were tied to it. The archaic triumph of a man who had just killed for his faith, for his country, for himself, he marched up and down beside the body, personifying victory, power, superiority. It was an awe-inspiring image, a horrifying echo of every war since the beginning of time.

The man in green positioned himself close to the dead boy's head, legs apart. He clenched the machete tightly in both hands, swung it back, and swept it down on the corpse's neck. Blood sprayed in all directions. He struck over and over again, shouting to his God with every blow.

Niall forced himself to hold his phone steady so the scene stayed in the frame, but he could not bring himself to watch. He tried to imagine himself miles away but was unable to block out the screams from behind him. More and more people were coming, clustering into small, tight groups, staring in horror and disbelief, hands over their mouths. Some of them were vomiting, and one man had passed out.

Niall shut his eyes for one long heartbeat, and when he opened them again, the man in green had finished decapitating the boy. He pushed the boy's head a short distance from his body with his foot, as if it were a soccer ball, before bending down and picking it up.

"Did you get that?" he called to Niall. "That's what we'll do to all enemies of the Islamic State." He then turned to his friend: "Police."

Niall thought this would finally be the point they would make a run for it, but he was wrong. They stood their ground, watching, though they did set the boy's head back on the ground.

Niall saved the video sequence, his hands clammy and cold. The touchscreen on his phone could barely register the commands he was trying to enter. His hands trembled so much he kept clicking the wrong things. He had to keep rubbing his thumbs on his pants, repeating commands, undoing his mistakes.

The police drove up in a small army of vans, cruisers, and rescue vehicles. As a group of uniforms tried to press the bystanders back, Niall stood rooted beside the Palestinian, though he had begun recording the special forces officers in full protective gear: black uniforms, helmets and guns. One of them yelled: "All weapons on the ground. Hands where we can see them."

The two men tossed the machetes at their feet and raised their arms out from their sides.

"We're at war. We've killed a soldier," the Palestinian called.

The police drew closer and surrounded them. "Everyone's hands up!"

Niall finally realized that many of the police officers were pointing their guns at him. He lifted his hands, still holding his phone.

"Hey, I'm not part of this," he shouted, looking around. "Tell them I'm not with you!"

The Palestinian refused to make eye contact. The Turk shrugged with a grin, then glanced down and reached into his right back pocket, the way someone does when he wants to get his phone after a message has just come in. He pulled out his phone.

"Weapon!" someone cried.

Shots.

Niall saw the Turk collapse, two large, dark spots spreading across his shirt. The man in blue screamed and ran to his friend, but the officers were quicker. They converged on him and threw him to the ground. Somebody knocked Niall down as well, sat on top of him, and bound his arms and legs.

"I had nothing to do with this," he wheezed, but there was no reply.

Paramedics ran to the man who had been shot. Niall could not tell if he was dead or if they were trying to save him. They were all ignoring the boy, both his body and his head.

The man sitting on top of him stood up. Once back on his feet, he kicked Niall in the ribs. Two other officers grabbed him under his shoulders and yanked him off the ground. He saw that his face had landed only centimeters away from a pile of dog shit, but his phone had not been so lucky.

FADE TO BLACK

"My phone," he implored.

"Ours now," somebody in black declared. "Just like you are." ▯

3

They shoved him through the back door of the police van. He fell to the floor, where they left him. All he could see were the boots on the feet of his guarding officers. He tried asking more than once where they were going, but they said nothing. They just kicked him until he shut up.

The drive took about an hour. From the floor of the van, he was unable to make out much through the bars on the back window. Although he did not think they had crossed the Thames, it felt like they were heading east. Greenwich and beyond.

The officers remained silent, but he could hear the driver and front-seat passenger murmuring indistinctly. Niall felt a stab of pain each time he inhaled. He tried to shift his position, so he could breathe better, right before a boot struck him in the back.

"Oops," someone said, possibly the same person who had kicked him earlier. Somebody else snickered. That was all Niall heard for the rest of the drive.

Once they reached their destination, a couple of officers grabbed him under his arms, hauled him out of the van, and dropped him on the pavement, his head cracking hard against the concrete. At that point, the kicking resumed, each officer delivering a swift blow as they walked past. One stopped walking long enough to kick him several times, until someone called out, "That's enough."

Niall still couldn't see more than booted feet at the end of black pantlegs. He tried to lift his head, but someone slammed it back down. They left him lying there for a while before he was picked up and dragged into the prison. The officers handed him over to the prison personnel like a sack of garbage.

In the block for pre-trial prisoners, neither the guards nor the doctor said more than the barest minimum to him: Get undressed. Open your mouth. Bend over. Cough.

"How did you get hurt?" the doctor asked.

Niall told him. The doctor did not reply, simply took pictures. Niall kept repeating himself. "I had nothing to do with it. I just happened to be there." Nobody cared what he said. They were only interested in Niall's blood, urine, hair.

He said, "I want to make a call. Don't I get an attorney? What about my rights?"

No one even looked at him.

After being given a prison uniform, he was taken to a solitary cell. As the door closed, he shouted: "Carl Davis. He's my uncle. You have to talk to him. You can't just keep me here without telling someone. Carl Davis, he works for the Ministry of Health. Please!"

The door slammed shut before he got the last word out. Niall pounded and kicked it, yelling for someone to talk to, then pleading for help, finally settling for profanity. He eventually gave up, exhausted. His head buzzed, his ribs ached from the beating, and his backside felt sore where the doctor had poked around. His voice completely gone, he dragged himself to the cot, stretched out on the blanket, turned to his side and stared at the wall. Then he stood back up, went to the sink, let the water run over his hands, and washed his face. The scrapes he had gotten from falling down smarted, but the bleeding had stopped.

He rinsed his mouth, then finally went back to his position on the cot and stared at the wall some more, too afraid to close his eyes. He did not want to see the boy being beheaded again, but the severed head kept surfacing in his mind.

Niall tried to think about something else. About how his uncle would surely get him out. His Uncle Carl had a solution for practically everything. He was an older, conservative man, stuffy and a little pompous but very congenial and, above all, helpful. He knew his way around bureaucracies, being a civil servant himself, and was acquainted with hierarchical structures from his years in the military.

Carl was not actually his real uncle. He was a cousin of Niall's mother, but as a child, Niall had always called him Uncle Carl.

Niall needed to somehow get to a phone. He was in Great Britain after all, not South America. Citizens have rights here, don't they? He thought. He kept telling himself that everything would be alright.

He wasn't convinced of that for much longer. In Niall's mind, the head kept rolling across the field and he couldn't stop thinking about how much it resembled a kicked soccer ball. Getting back up, Niall started hammering on the door again, refusing to stop until someone came. Suddenly, the door opened and Niall was shoved backward by a pair of hands, then thrown to the floor. He landed on his side. He tried to protect his head with his arms and pulled his knees up to his chest as somebody drove the end of a truncheon into his shoulder.

"If you don't stop, we'll stick you in a very different cell, asshole," a voice growled. As the footsteps moved off, Niall risked lifting his head and looking. He saw two men in uniform with no distinguishing markings. He lowered his head back down and decided to stay put on the cell floor, curling up even tighter into a fetal position.

For the first time, he wondered: What if I never get out of here?

Hours later, somebody finally brought him something to eat. Whatever it was, it only bore the loosest possible resemblance to food. Niall asked once more if he could place a phone call. Again, he received no answer.

Although he was exhausted and cold from being on the floor, he was unable to fall asleep on the cot after eating. He had no sense of where he was. Was he still in London? How late was it? When would it get dark? He heard roaring and whistling in his ears. Were the sounds coming from outside or inside his body? He knew he had not been locked up for all that long yet.

Keeping him awake were the images that kept appearing before his eyes. The Palestinian, blood dripping from his hands and down the machete blade. The Turk, as he sliced and hacked off the boy's head, before proudly hoisting it as a trophy for the camera.

Why had they not killed him instead? Or one of the joggers? Why the boy? The Palestinian in the blue shirt had called him a soldier. Maybe they had met him earlier? Or followed him? Perhaps they had arranged to meet up with him. The boy had walked past Niall with purpose. There was no way he had known he was going to his death.

Had he really been a soldier? A young man walking unsuspectingly through a park—murdered because a couple of fanatics wanted to prove something to the world. Why had they not killed Niall? He couldn't help but wonder again. It was possible that they had been about to, that they would have killed him if the boy had not come along.

And now what? He thought. Niall was sitting there because the police thought he was a terrorist since he had been there for the attack and recorded it. His guards succeeded in making him afraid of being badly mistreated by them again despite his innocence. In their eyes, he was part of an Islamic terrorist group and a participant in an Islamist attack. Could he really blame them? What else were they supposed to think? He had remained there, standing as his camera recorded the blood-soaked murderer calmly giving him an interview. Of course, they beat him.

Niall was gradually coming to terms with his situation. Since being seized in the park, the normal rights enjoyed by every British citizen no longer applied to him. He had no right to an attorney. He was allowed to be held longer than normal without arraignment, much longer even than someone suspected of murder.

Earlier in the doctor's office, he had been able to read a location from one of the files: Belmarsh Prison.

After the 9/11 attacks, Belmarsh was where any suspected terrorists were sent. They were held indefinitely without arraignment or trial until the Lord Justice had decided that practice qualified as a human rights violation. Belmarsh had been called the British Guantanamo, but the laws were revised one way or another, more than once.

They could currently hold someone for twenty-eight days without an arraignment. That was twenty-eight days in which the prison authorities could do whatever they wanted. Without even the slightest hint of irony, Niall concluded that he was lucky. At one point, Parliament had considered setting the limit at ninety days.

While he sat in his cell, they were examining his clothes, his bodily fluids taken by the doctor, his apartment, his computer. The detectives would be establishing his whereabouts, or at least those of his phone, which would be made all the easier because the GPS was always on and he was registered on all the major social networks, which posted his location without any extra effort on his part. They would check out his call log, his emails, his internet searches, his browsing history. They would go through the calendar on his Google Dashboard, finding there an hour-by-hour record of his movements. They would analyze his photos and scan his Facebook posts and Tweets for suspicious comments. They would comb through everything the government agencies had on file about him ranging from his birth certificate to his latest tax return. And the investigators had more leeway to dig around in his personal life than they usually did, since his was now a case for the domestic intelligence service, MI5.

Niall felt dizzy. The rushing in his ears grew louder, and he could feel his heartbeat all the way down through his fingers and toes. They would come across something, somewhere. Various trips abroad, including to Middle Eastern, Islamic countries they could easily use against him. They would see that he had taken the same route from the bridge to the park as the attackers and would wonder why he had spent so much time on the bridge. They would discover that he had repeatedly explored that area, which was also home to the foreign intelligence service, MI6. Besides that, they would soon realize that he had been tracking the course of an underground river, which would look great, he imagined, to paranoid terrorist investigators.

He would not be getting out of there any time soon. Would they even give him a chance to defend himself, or would they simply leave him locked up there without an arraignment? Niall considered what he knew about Guantanamo and British prisons like Belmarsh. He thought about the photos of the US soldiers who had abused their prisoners of war in Iraq. The ones who had desecrated the bodies of their enemies and taken pictures of it all. About how some people turned into sadists when the laws no longer applied to them. How they were changed by the power they suddenly wielded over other people, especially when they themselves did not have to face accountability for anything they did.

Twenty-eight days without any rights or protections. For those outside his cell, he was nothing more than the person who had held the camera. What would they do with the two attackers? After being shot, was the Turk even still alive? Had they beaten the Palestinian on the drive over to the prison as well?

He had watched them senselessly butcher that boy. Niall did not care what happened to the two of them, but he had not done anything. Although those two men deserved their punishment, he did not. It was all so clear cut to him.

His anxiety gradually cooled down. The more he thought about it, the more convinced he felt that everything would turn out alright. Niall had never made political statements, and there were no connections between him and the attackers. He could explain everything if they would let him. His Uncle Carl knew good attorneys, and as soon as he learned what had happened to Niall, he would intervene. Besides that, Niall did not fit the profile of an Islamist terrorist or a Western convert. He came from the white English middle class. The investigators would definitely take that into consideration. Good grief, he realized how easy it was to be racist when his own freedom was at stake!

Breathing more evenly, Niall tried again to go to sleep. It was too bright, but he could do nothing about the light. Despite the darkness outside, the bulb still blazed in his cell. His cot was supplied with a stinking wad of cloth that counted as a pillow and an equally foul blanket, rough and thin. He wouldn't pull either over his face. He covered his closed eyes with one hand, but it didn't help. Still wakeful, he remained sprawled on his cot as his exhaustion grew.

His fear pendulum swung back up with increased time. What if nobody out there actually cared about him? What if his uncle was not allowed to hire an attorney until the twenty-eight days were over? What would happen to him over that time? Would they beat him even worse than they had just because they could? Would they stop feeding him? He recalled what the one guard had said about there being a very different cell. Niall had no idea what he'd meant, but he imagined a dark hole without a toilet, without a sink, without a cot. Three square feet. Him, sitting in filth for the next four weeks.

He wondered if something like that really still existed. He thought about Guantanamo. The conditions there had been made known. Anything was possible.

Niall was scared. He liked his life, his freedom, the opportunities he had. He was thirty-one years old and a long way from achieving everything he hoped to. He was still making boring documentary films, and these films were even duller than the ones he had made years prior. Things in his industry were not looking all that rosy. Then, there was the fact that he had been very publicly fired from a production two years earlier, thanks to a moment of extreme stubbornness. The news had made its way around. But back then, he had been in a bad place.

What Niall wanted to do was make important, interesting films. To uncover injustice. To tell the stories of people in need. To analyze politically significant topics. But he seemed stuck with animals and landscapes. Once a person had a reputation for something, he knew, it stayed with them forever. Animals and landscapes. Exotic animals and landscapes.

His next film was going to be about London's forgotten underground rivers. He could already see himself sitting behind the camera for a cooking show. He wondered momentarily if perhaps he had deserved to land in jail after all, but he shook off his self-pity. He had to get out, back into life. There was still too much to do out there. No, he didn't wish for death. And especially not like this.

Niall stood up and started pacing. His heart was racing, and he wanted to keep moving until it slowed back down. He felt as if he were about to have a heart attack.

When you get out of here, he told himself, you're going to apologize to all sorts of people. To your father, because you were so stubborn and refused to talk to him. To your ex-girlfriend, because you walked out on her without an explanation. To your buddies, because you hardly go out to the pub anymore and use work as an excuse. When you get out of here, you'll do things differently. You won't take on any more jobs you hate, only those that will further your career. When you get out of here.

Over and over, he tried counting the steps from the cell door to the opposite wall, back and forth, back and forth. He tried to chant, "Everything will be okay" as a mantra, and then, because it was not working, "We all have to die sometime."

He stopped in the middle of his cell. He finally understood how religion worked. Of course, there was no sense to human existence. If more people realized that and could accept that there was no afterlife, they might stop killing each other. Live and let live. In the end, we are all the same, Niall thought. We simply stop existing.

But the minute someone claims that some people are chosen or special, then other people want to be part of that. In this case, it was in order to achieve life after death. A good life after death. A better one. Clear enemies, rigid rules, fear of punishment, the concept of an afterlife as a reward for obedience. Religion was a very clever invention to counteract the fear of death, to make people submissive for their entire lives. The only problem was that Niall did not believe in a god.

4

He woke up to the sound of footsteps outside his door. The steps drew closer, then stopped. He heard metallic scraping, then the steps receding. The pattern repeated itself. Niall thought he had been dreaming, but now he was awake, he was firmly convinced that what he had heard had been real. Niall had no idea what time it was. The garish light was still burning overhead, and he had no sense of when he had laid down.

He tried to go back to sleep, but the footsteps returned only minutes later. He sat up and listened. Somebody paused outside his door, and he heard the scrape of metal, two bursts of it, one after the other, followed by the sound of someone walking away. Was he under suicide watch? That would explain why they had left the light on in his cell. They wanted to keep an eye on him to make sure he did not kill himself.

He took this as a relatively positive sign. They still needed him. Or were they just worried about negative headlines? "Suspect Hangs Himself in Pre-Trial Detention" wouldn't look all that great. He wondered what had made him think about hanging. He glanced around the cell. Table, chair, toilet, sink, wardrobe, bed. No doorknob. The window had bars mounted on the outside and could not be opened. There was no way anyone could hang themselves in there.

He got up and went to the window. Day was just dawning, so it was still quite early. He lay back down on the cot and turned over on his side. He heard the steps approaching.

"I'm still here!" he called. There was no response as the steps retreated.

He felt tired but could not fall back asleep. The images had returned of the decapitated head and the blood on the Palestinian's hands. Niall sat up and waited for the steps to return. He started counting in an effort to distract himself. He could not stand the visions of blood anymore.

He finally heard the steps again.

"Hello?"

Silence. So, he stood back up, walked over to the door, and knocked loudly. When nothing happened, he pounded harder and kicked, which he regretted instantly since he was not wearing shoes. Niall yelled in pain and hobbled back to the cot, cursing as he sat down. He examined his right foot, touching it gingerly and hoping he had not broken anything.

Someone must have heard him. The door swung open, and a man in uniform stepped inside, looking around but saying nothing.

"I have to talk to someone," Niall said.

The man turned to leave.

"I need my medicine. It's critical," Niall called after him.

The man paused, but only for just a moment, before slamming the heavy steel door hard behind him.

Niall slumped back onto the cot. They were not going to respond to anything, regardless of what he said. They just wanted to keep him alive, no more than that.

Though perhaps, he thought, something would happen now that he had mentioned medicine. He would just have to wait. Niall touched his foot again and slowly wiggled his toes. Everything seemed alright, but his foot still ached. He would be more careful next time. He finally knew how to get their attention.

He stayed stretched on the cot, even though it was growing light outside. At some point, they would bring him something to eat. Despite not feeling hungry, he would have to eat, otherwise he wondered how he would he be strong enough to face what was coming next.

His thoughts turned to the dead guy, though this time not to his corpse, but to the way he had eagerly crossed the field.

Where had he been going? A date? What about his family, his parents? Did he have siblings? A girlfriend? Their world had to be collapsing. Niall felt angry at himself for only just then thinking about the people the dead guy had left behind, but then he heard footsteps back at his door, and like before, it swung open. The guard from earlier stepped inside, followed by someone in civilian clothes. It was the doctor who had examined him after his arrival.

"Which medicine do you need?" he asked, wasting no time on niceties.

"Ibuprofen. Everything aches from yesterday."

"It'll get better."

"I can't sleep either."

"That's to be expected. Nobody can sleep on their first night in jail."

"I'm having panic attacks!"

"Like I said." The doctor turned to leave.

"Come on, just one. I mean, who beat me up after all? The police, right?"

"All you will get from me is what you need to survive. Like, if you were a diabetic, I'd give you some insulin." He stepped closer to Niall, placed his hand on his wrist, and took his pulse against his watch.

"Regular and strong." He then bent over and gently pulled down Niall's lower eyelid. "Looks fine." He turned to go.

"Please give me an aspirin, won't you?"

"Relax. Do a few yoga stretches or something like that. You aren't going to die."

"I have bruises everywhere, and my ribs hurt whenever I breathe. And…" The doctor turned to the door.

Niall got to his feet and followed, reaching out to keep him from leaving. The guard grabbed his arm, twisted it behind his back and pushed him to the floor. Niall cried out as his head cracked against the edge of the wardrobe.

"Hey, what are you doing?" The doctor sounded angry as he knelt beside Niall. "Let him go, for God's sake!"

"He was about to attack you."

"Really?"

"Yes, I saw him."

"Get off him. His head is bleeding, and I need to take care of it."

"I have to secure him first," the guard insisted, snapping cuffs around Niall's wrists. Niall cried out again from the excruciating pain in his shoulder.

"Did you dislocate his shoulder? Bloody hell, were you a wrestler or something?"

"Hey, doctor," he said as he got to his feet, leaving Niall where he was lying. "You know better than most what kind of people we deal with here. And this one," he aimed a kick at Niall, "earned it."

"Help me get him up again. Now." They lifted Niall from the floor and lugged him onto the cot. The doctor examined Niall's forehead. "We'll be able to staple that, won't need stitches."

"Want me to take him to the infirmary?"

"No. To my office."

"Doctor…"

"Go get my things."

The guard did not move.

"Today, if you would be so kind."

"I can't leave you alone." The guard pulled out his radio and asked another guard to bring the medical bag.

"Why can't I go to the infirmary?" Niall rasped. The latest kick in the ribs had brought back yesterday's pain, which, contrary to his claim, had actually faded some.

"Security measure," the doctor explained. "You would have to be worse off to make it to the infirmary." He pressed a tissue to Niall's forehead. "I'll just disinfect that spot and staple it together. It looks worse than it is. You didn't pass out so I don't think you have a concussion, but you need to watch out for any symptoms that may arise over the course of the day, such as nausea or a headache."

"If that happens, will I go to the infirmary?"

"You don't want to go there. Just be happy you have a little space for yourself here."

"You have no idea what you're talking about," Niall murmured.

"And you don't know your fellow inmates," the doctor replied.

"Are you worried about my condition?"

"Don't expect too much from me. I won't give you anything for your insomnia or your fear. You just have to accept that. I can only give you what's on the list."

"What list?"

"The one of the medicines inmates are allowed."

"There's a list?" Niall groaned as the doctor fingered his shoulder.

"Lift your arm."

"It hurts."

"Yes, but lift it, very slowly."

He obeyed, very slowly.

"Great. May I?" The doctor carefully bent Niall's arm back and forth. "Not dislocated. Something was probably torn. We'll take a good look at this."

The guard talked into the radio again, checking on the other guard. The door opened a moment later, and the doctor's bag was handed inside. Niall could not see who had brought it. The guard took it and passed it to the doctor before positioning himself, legs spread, in front of the closed door, as if suspicious Niall might try to make a run for it during the treatment process.

When the doctor was finished, Niall asked, "Can I at least have some Ibuprofen for my shoulder? That guy over there almost ripped my arm out, and the cut on my head…"

"I was here, and that's not what happened."

"I'm in pain."

"I'm sure you'll manage."

"Is it normal to…"

"Listen," the doctor interrupted. "Consider where you are. And why. Did you think this was going to be some kind of resort?"

"I had absolutely nothing—"

The man cut him off again, but this time he spoke fast and low. "I'm a doctor, not a public prosecutor or even a judge. It can't make any difference to me what you've done. Just be happy that they even let me in to see you. It would be best if you kept your mouth shut from now on."

Bag in hand, the doctor turned around and knocked on the steel door. Someone opened it from the outside. The guard threw Niall a distrustful look before leaving the cell. The door quickly closed behind them.

Niall stared at the steel surface. He was supposed to be happy that the doctor had even come. What were they doing with the Turk, he wondered, letting him just die from his gunshot wounds? Niall had watched the man decapitate a corpse. Only two hours ago, he could not have imagined feeling anything even remotely like sympathy for him and the Palestinian. But his perspective had begun to shift as his fear of the guards changed to anger. They had beat him because they could, because nobody was watching them. But it was more than that: The whole system was inhumane. The silent treatment of prisoners. Not letting them sleep. The continuous checks. The refusal to offer medical aid. It was institutionalized torture.

Still, these were softer measures than the ones used at Guantanamo, Niall knew that. The doctor was right. He should be happy things had worked out for him as they had. He would keep his mouth shut from then on.

FADE TO BLACK

THURSDAY
5

A different guard woke him up.

"Can I have something to eat?" Niall asked. He must have nodded off, since he had no sense of how late it was.

"Follow me."

"I'm hungry."

The guard just looked at him and pointed at the open door.

"What time is it?"

The man still said nothing.

"Will I get my clothes back?" Niall asked. No response. "May I call an attorney?"

He no longer expected responses but asked just for the sake of asking. He was led silently through the corridors and the security checkpoints to the prison yard, where a transport van was waiting for him. Two men sat in the cab, while two more were waiting to guard him in the back. A sense of unreality was slowly setting in, the one that signaled an approaching anxiety attack.

"Where are you taking me?"

No answer.

During the drive, Niall tried to catch sight of recognizable landmarks through the barred window. He saw nothing familiar for a long time, and the words on the signs they passed remained illegible. However, he thought they were headed toward the city. In any case, they were not leaving London.

Niall finally got his bearings as they passed Greenwich Park. He recognized the Old Royal Navy College and the National Maritime Museum on the other side of the greenspace. He recalled his last visit there, some time ago. He had gone for a walk with his girlfriend. Correction, ex-girlfriend. That had ended because of his unwillingness to talk to her about the things that had bothered him the most.

"What day is it?" Niall asked.

"Thursday."

He was surprised someone had answered. He had only asked to break the silence, in the vague hope of verifying that he had spent just one night in the prison. He risked another question. "What time is it?" The light made him suspect it was late afternoon. The days were slowly growing shorter now that August had arrived.

"Five o'clock."

He began to feel a little carsick. When had he last eaten? They had not brought him any lunch that day, though he might have slept through it. His blood sugar felt low, and he was thirsty. He mentioned this, but the guards did not reply.

An hour later, they reached Westminster Bridge, where he caught sight of Big Ben and the Houses of Parliament: a picture-perfect view, if bars had not been in the way. MI5 was located one bridge downstream. MI6 was only one bridge further, and the Vauxhall Pleasure Gardens were right behind it, the park where the boy had been beheaded. Niall wondered if the terrorists had intentionally chosen their location because of its proximity to the intelligence agencies.

"The Met?" Niall asked.

One of the men glanced up and seemed to blink affirmingly.

The van made a right off Victoria Street and came to a stop at the guarded driveway to the New Scotland Yard compound, a tall, blocky structure clad in smooth, reflective panes of glass. The driver said something to the officer at the barrier, the bars swung open, and they parked in front of the building.

His guards stayed seated, waiting. Niall did not hear the men in front get out either, but he did not bother to ask why they were waiting. The guards seemed relaxed, so everything had to be running according to plan. The two of them knew what counted as normal routine around there. Niall noticed that one of them was fiddling absentmindedly with a box of cigarettes in his pocket.

"Feel free to smoke," he said. "I don't care."

"No." The guard answered.

"Suit yourself." Niall had meant the offer sincerely, but then he felt insulted.

They continued to wait in silence. After a while, he grew restless. With his hands and legs cuffed, he was on the verge of a headache.

"I didn't have anything to do with it," he began. "It was just a coincidence that I was recording those guys." He knew there was no point, but he still felt the need to say something.

Neither guard said anything. The one with the cigarettes just sniffed a little disdainfully.

"Alright," Niall continued. "I know you're just doing your job."

Voices drifted in. The van shook as the driver got out and slammed the door. The guard without the cigarettes bent forward, as if to hear better what was going on beyond the van walls.

"After we get back," Niall remarked, "can I talk to the doctor again? He said I was supposed to tell him if I started feeling bad or got a headache."

The non-cigarette guard did not make eye contact as he asked, "Do you need to throw up?"

"No, just dizzy."

The man laughed, shaking his head.

Someone knocked on the back door of the van before it swung open. Niall recognized the driver, but it was the first time he had seen the blonde woman in a suit beside him.

"Mr. Stuart," she said, nodding at him. "DI Helen Gilpin. I apologize for your long wait." She held out her hand to shake his.

Niall blinked hard and slowly got to his feet. "I'm sorry, but I can't…" He twisted slightly to show her that his hands were cuffed behind his back.

"Oh, of course." Gilpin turned to the guard with the cigarettes. "Could you please…" She waved her hand vaguely, while Niall's guards blinked just as dazedly as he had seconds before.

The van driver interrupted: "Today, boys," clearly some form of authorization. Even if they did not trust Gilpin—whether because she was a woman or because she wanted the handcuffs removed—the guards were willing to obey their colleague.

Freed from his hand and leg cuffs, Niall jumped down from the van and stood uncertainly in front of Gilpin. "Hello," he said.

She smiled widely. "Mr. Stuart." She once again held out her hand, and this time he could actually shake it. "What happened to your head?"

"Oh, that." He touched the bandage and glanced over at the guards. They watched him tensely, waiting to see if he was going to rat out their co-workers. "It's nothing, really. I fell."

"Ah, I see." Gilpin studied the guards for a moment.

"DI Gilpin," Niall mumbled, as he rubbed his aching shoulder. "I, um, didn't have anything to do with what happened. I know that's probably what everyone says, but it really was just a coincidence that I was—"

"Please follow me. We'd like to talk to you." Again, the smile.

Niall felt wretched. "Sure," he said, though he would have preferred to just get back in the van. His silent escorts seemed less menacing than the smiling Helen Gilpin. The guard with the cigarettes had begun smoking, looking up at the building, eyebrows cocked. His three companions were talking quietly amongst themselves. The man who had been in the passenger seat was holding some papers and showing them to the others. As if at a secret command, all of three of them glanced over at him simultaneously. Niall took a step back, startled.

"See you later," he said uncertainly to the prison guards.

They exchanged looks he could not decipher.

The van driver finally responded: "We won't be seeing you again."

6

Niall followed Gilpin into a small, not especially modern elevator. They rode up to the third floor, walked partway down a long, bright corridor past a row of closed doors, and entered an interrogation room with an observation window, where two men and two unoccupied chairs were waiting for them. A round table held a coffee carafe, cups, a microphone, and a surprisingly clunky digital recorder. Two notebooks were also carefully positioned in front of the men. They nodded at him, mumbled a greeting, and acted as if they did not notice his prison uniform.

"This is Mr. Stuart," Gilpin introduced him as she gestured at one of the chairs. "Mr. Stuart has kindly agreed to answer our questions."

"May I possibly call an attorney now?" Niall asked.

"You don't need one at this point," the younger of the two men remarked. His suit was nicer than his colleague's, but the older man gave the impression of being the more self-assured and senior inspector.

"I have a feeling it would help to have somebody with me who knew their way around—" he plucked at his overalls, helplessly, "—things like this."

"You'll be getting your clothes back. Your phone, too," Gilpin assured him.

"Right now?"

"You'll have a chance to freshen up and change later," the younger man said. "Mr. Stuart, I'm Detective Inspector George De Verell. It's nice to meet you. Is it okay if we go ahead and start? As you can imagine, we're under some pressure on this case."

"That's fine." Niall's gaze took in the three impatient faces. "Let's start."

"Would you mind if we recorded our conversation?" De Verell pointed at the recorder.

"Not at all." Niall studied the little group. Gilpin was in her late thirties. Her hair was pinned up tightly, and her makeup was subtle. De Verell was about Niall's age. Interestingly, he had the same rank as his older female colleague. He must be ambitious and driven, Niall thought. Either that or he knew the right people. He acted like the leader, but Gilpin's chilly sidelong glances showed that not all was smooth sailing on their team.

Their colleague was in his late forties or early fifties, and he seemed to be the only one who had nothing to prove. He was leaning back and playing with a pen, taking in the scene with watchful eyes and a placid face. De Verell turned on the recorder and introduced everyone in the group. The older man went by DCI Hodges.

"Are we ready to start?" De Verell asked doubtfully.

The relaxed DCI balanced a pen between his thumb and forefinger as he said, "You know what this is about. We saw your video and know you followed the two men from Vauxhall Bridge all the way to the Pleasure Gardens. If you could answer a few questions for us, we'd be grateful. Why did you follow them?"

"Because of the machetes."

"Why didn't you notify the police?"

Niall anxiously scanned De Verell's and Gilpin's faces, hoping to read his answer there. "They both looked pretty relaxed, actually. I thought the swords had to be fake and the two guys were on their way to a role-playing game or something like that. I mean, who runs around London with real machetes?"

"Obviously, the two of them," Gilpin interjected. "You followed them."

"Yes. I felt a little concerned and wanted to see what they were up to."

"And you? You didn't have anything else to do?"

He hesitated. "Yes, I did."

"So, you were concerned, but you didn't call the police. Right?" The man leaned further back in his chair, still playing with his pen though not taking any notes. De Verell doodled in his notepad and shot occasional glances at the recorder.

Niall felt lousy and had no idea what to say next.

"Why were you in the area? Your apartment's in Brixton."

"I was out for a walk."

"A walk." The man leaned forward and set his pen down on the table.

"Yes, I was following the course of the Effra, which runs through Brixton, practically past my back door. It flows into the Thames underneath the MI6 building."

"And why were you following this particular river?"

"We're making a documentary next week about London's forgotten rivers. The Effra is one of the largest."

"Who is we?"

"I'm working for a small production company."

The door opened, and a short-haired woman walked in carrying a clear bag holding Niall's clothes. She went to the DCI and whispered something to him. The man just nodded as she turned toward Niall.

"Your things, Mr. Stuart." She placed the bag on the table in front of him and left.

"Thank you," he said, surprised.

"So, a small production company hired you to scout out channels running underneath the foreign intelligence building," De Verell summarized.

"It sounds a little fishy if you put it that way. I always check out the film locations beforehand to get a feel for the atmosphere and what I might want to shoot. I also take pictures of my sites, which is why I was up on the bridge."

De Verell frowned for a moment. "And then you were distracted by the two men with the machetes, so you followed them. Did anything else catch your eye?"

"Besides the machetes? No, they both seemed quite relaxed. They were chatting and laughing like normal people."

"Good. However, you still wanted to know what they were up to."

"Yes, I…" He trailed off.

"Would you like to add something?"

Niall nodded slowly. "One of them looked at me, just for a second, but he looked me straight in the eye as they walked by. Do you know what I mean, when a person looks at you just a moment too long?"

"But he didn't say anything?"

"No."

"He didn't give you a sign or some kind of gesture?"

"Nothing."

"Alright. So, you followed the two of them to the park."

"Yes, and nothing happened at first. They just stood there. I thought they were waiting on someone. Like I said, for a role-playing game or something like that. I was just about to leave when the boy started screaming."

De Verell stopped doodling and looked at him curiously. "You don't know if he said something to them or the other way around?"

"No. I thought that if nobody else cared that two weirdos were wandering around with machetes, then perhaps I had just imagined it all, and they were just toys." He gnawed on his lower lip, which had started quivering. "I'm sorry," he mumbled.

"It's not your fault," De Verell commented, his tone belying his remark.

"A famous father can be a lot to live up to," Gilpin declared suddenly.

"What does that have to do with this guy's murder?"

"We're just getting to know you. Small talk, that's all."

Niall crossed his arms. "My father died two years ago, and I'd rather not discuss it."

"So, a film about…what was it? London's forgotten rivers? Charming. A film like that isn't exactly the most thrilling project, though, if you want to make a name for yourself in that industry, is it?"

"What are you getting at?" Niall asked, though he could guess. They had spent the last thirty-six hours doing nothing but screening his background. By that point, they knew everything about his family, his friends, his career. They also knew that the films he had shot as a camera operator over the previous two years had not exactly been the pinnacle of creative achievement. Perhaps they assumed he wished he was doing something different.

"Maybe," Gilpin surmised, "you knew all along those two men were up to something."

"I didn't know them! How many times do I have to tell you that?"

"You followed them in the hope of filming something spectacular."

Niall shook his head. The smiling Helen Gilpin. Yes, she really was more dangerous than the prison guards. At least with them, he knew the lay of the land. "No, I really didn't think that…"

"That's why you didn't call the police," she interrupted. "You wanted something to happen."

Niall leaped up. "Are you totally crazy? What are you trying to say?"

De Verell was at his side like a shot, grabbing him by the shoulders. Niall groaned in pain, and the man released him at once.

"Sorry," he said, raising his hands to indicate he had not meant to hurt him. "I just wanted to calm you down, Mr. Stuart. Please, sit back down. My colleague is simply doing her job." Niall sat down slowly, rubbing his injured shoulder. He watched Gilpin, who in turn threw dirty looks at De Verell.

DCI Hodges continued: "We were talking about what happened. You heard the screams and turned back around."

"Yes. Who was that guy anyway? The men said he was a soldier, but was he?"

"He was an Air Cadet in the Royal Air Force."

"How did they know that? Had they met him before?"

Hodges studied him. "Did it seem like the three of them knew each other?"

Lost in thought, Niall rubbed his shoulder again. "I have no idea. I can't even tell you if the men went to the park on purpose or if it was a coincidence. All I know is that that guy rushed by me like he needed to get somewhere. That doesn't mean he was on his way to meet the two of them, though. Maybe he was just in a hurry and heading in their direction." He paused. "What's happened to the man who got shot? Did he die?"

"He's still in intensive care. What happened to your shoulder? DI De Verell didn't grab it all that hard."

"What? Oh, it was already hurt. I can tell you that now. One of the prison guards threw me down on the floor to cuff me. That's how I got this as well." He pointed at the cut on his forehead.

"I'm sorry," De Verell muttered. "I had no idea."

"Why did he do that?" Hodges inquired.

"He thought I wanted to attack the doctor."

"Did you?"

"No, I just didn't want him to leave. He had refused to give me something to help with the pain." The three others exchanged silent, questioning glances.

"You don't know about that, right?" Niall stood up and took off his shirt. "Do you see the bruises? Some of them are from the arrest, but afterward, on the drive to the prison, the guards kept kicking me. See that on my ribs?" He turned to the side and raised his uninjured arm.

Gilpin kept her eyes down as she scribbled something on a piece of paper. The two men briefly examined the spot.

"I'm sorry they treated you like that," Hodges responded. "I hope you'll be feeling better soon. Would you like to see a doctor right now?"

"A painkiller would be a great start. And I'd be grateful if a doctor could take a look at me. The one in the prison said that it wasn't so bad, but he only looked at it. No x-ray or anything. Also, um, if you possibly have something to eat here, I haven't had a real meal since yesterday. And may I have a glass of water from over there?"

FADE TO BLACK

Hodges stood up, poured him a glass, and placed it on the table. "Niall, we'll take care of things. Since you have already undressed, I propose we take a short break and give you some time to freshen up." ▢

7

Two hours later, as the sky dimmed to twilight, Niall had finally eaten enough. He had also been given a fast-working painkiller, and the good news was that his shoulder had not been dislocated. The bad news was that it was going to continue to hurt for quite some time. After showering, he changed his clothes and found the three detectives back in their seats, watching him with somber eyes.

"Are you feeling a little better now, Mr. Stuart?" Gilpin asked, back to acting friendly, as if she had never accused him of being an irresponsible sensationalist.

"Yes, thank you."

"You could have told us what you needed."

"Well, you said you were in a hurry." He glanced over at De Verell.

"Do you feel well enough to answer any more questions?"

De Verell was not looking at him.

Niall was always suspicious of anyone who was overly polite to him. At that point, he knew he was being jerked around.

"Isn't that why I'm here?" he answered curtly.

De Verell fell silent.

Hodges took over. "Did you upload the video right away, there in the park?"

"Yes, to my YouTube channel."

"You have your own YouTube channel?"

"I'm a cameraman. I post work samples there, so yes."

Gilpin bent forward, speaking quietly: "You posted those clips to your work samples?"

"Yes, to the samples, because the only people who look in that file are the ones I've sent the link to. The two men demanded that I upload what I'd recorded. Should I have argued with them?"

"I wasn't accusing you of anything, Niall," Hodges declared, though that was exactly what he had done. "You did the right thing and provided us with some valuable footage as well. It was quite brave of you."

"Brave?" Niall snorted. "I would have been brave if I had tried to help that boy."

"You couldn't have done anything."

"Whatever. DI Gilpin is right. I should have called the police earlier. But I…" He fell silent, then continued: "I should've at least tried to stop them."

"All you'd have done was put yourself and possibly others in danger, and we would have had more than one body on our hands. Niall don't beat yourself up about this. You did the right thing." It only then dawned on Niall that they were not treating him like a suspect.

Hodges noticed. "We've had enough time to check into you and analyze the data. There's no indication that you were in contact with those men."

"Ah, good. Well, I guess I don't need an attorney then. Although I really would've liked to have had one in the prison."

"They told us you didn't want one." De Verell looked at the others. "Didn't they?"

"I didn't want an attorney? I kept asking for one, and for a chance to place a phone call. Sure." He laughed. "I didn't want a lawyer. Brilliant."

The three detectives studied him, processing this new information. When they said nothing, he added: "Alright, so for the record, I definitely wanted an attorney. And I didn't volunteer to be beaten up either. Okay?"

"Well, that's outside our jurisdiction, but we will, uh, follow up on it." De Verell scribbled something down.

"Ah, I understand. You mean that under the circumstances, I shouldn't have expected anything else, right?" Niall looked at the man expectantly, but his expression was unreadable. "Suspected terrorist and all that? They come down harder on that than, say, your average armed robber. What happens to rapists? Are they castrated on the spot, if that's what suits the guards, or do they at least wait until the charges are made?" Now that he was feeling much better—and above all, safer—he was furious.

To get things back on track, De Verell asked: "What else happened?"

"They left the light on all night and kept sending someone to make sure I wasn't going to kill myself. But the main thing was that they wouldn't talk to me or answer any of my questions. They wouldn't even tell me what time it was. Although—" He almost had to laugh. "Wait, they did finally tell me that on the ride over here."

De Verell said: "You're free to discuss this with an attorney."

"Sure. Now," Niall mumbled. "I don't know any attorneys. I also don't know if I can afford one, but I have an uncle who works for the Department of Health. He might know someone since he moves in those kinds of circles."

"Your uncle?" Gilpin flipped back in her notes.

"My mother's cousin. I just call him my uncle. It's not all that important."

"Be sure to ask him," De Verell remarked. "But don't get your hopes up too high. The anti-terrorist laws are—"

"—the harshest in Europe. I know."

De Verell nodded. "Is there anything else you can think of? Something that perhaps didn't seem that important before now?"

"Are we talking about the prison or the attack?"

"I mean, what happened in the park."

Niall thought for a moment before slowly shaking his head. He then glanced up again. "Are we done? You have everything from me and know what's in the video. I don't know any more than that."

"You'll have to sign the transcript of this conversation," Gilpin commented. "You can do that tomorrow. When it comes to a court case…"

"When? Don't you mean 'if'?" he interrupted.

"As soon as it comes to a court case, you'll need to give a statement."

"Of course." He looked around, clearly searching for something. "My phone? Am I really allowed to have it back?"

De Verell stood up. "If you'll come with me."

Niall also got to his feet, but Gilpin and the DCI stayed seated.

"We're not quite done, Niall," Hodges said.

Niall stared at him. "This was all just a joke, right? I'm really being arrested?" He laughed, but it sounded nervous. The DCI's eyes were serious, and he fell silent.

"Niall, we have two problems."

"Two."

"Number one. You might be a target among supporters of the Islamic State. We're not sure. We also don't know what contacts the two men may have to other jihadists or how organized they are. We still need some time for our investigation, so until we wrap it up, it would be best for you to not return to your apartment. Is that possible?"

"Not even to pick up a few things? I mean, I can't afford to replace everything. I don't have the money."

"Sure, you can get some things. We'll send someone with you. Could you stay for a few days with friends, somebody you trust?"

"But why—"

"Think about it," DCI Hodges urged. "One more thing. The enterprising national tabloids have figured out your identity."

"How?"

"The video went viral yesterday."

"But I only uploaded it to my YouTube channel. Nobody…Oh, shit." He shut his eyes and sighed. He had changed the settings. An acquaintance had encouraged him to do so: more personal advertising via social media platforms. Producers poked around places like those when looking for people to hire, which was why he had changed his YouTube settings so that anything he uploaded automatically went out on his Facebook and Twitter accounts. He had forgotten all about that.

"Yes. You are now blocked from both Facebook and Twitter, as well as by YouTube."

"What—"

"That's what happens these days. Anyone who shares content like that gets blocked."

"Shit," Niall repeated. His entire virtual existence was gone. Maybe not his email address, though, he could only hope. But there were people with whom he was only connected on Facebook. He did not have email addresses or even phone numbers for them, and it was going to be tedious to try to reconstruct those contacts. What a brave, new, virtual world.

"Your connection with the video was only visible for a relatively short time before the content was removed. But before that happened, other users were already sharing the video. All it took was a couple of intrepid journalists nosing around to figure out who was behind it. For the past hour, your name, along with a photo and a still from the video, has been accessible on all the major tabloid portals. They're also on the major newspapers' websites, though the coverage is at least less lurid. It'll be all over the print media by tomorrow, so you need to get used to the idea."

"Are they saying that I had something to do with the murder?" Niall's head was threatening to explode.

"No."

"Good." He turned to De Verell. "Let's go get my phone."

"Niall," the senior detective cut in.

"There's a third thing?"

"I wasn't done."

"You really aren't making this easy for me. What else?"

"A photo of you. Your name. Do you have any idea of who all is going to want to talk to you?"

"The entire English press corps."

"And then some."

"I suppose you mean this is another reason for me to go hide away somewhere."

The man nodded at De Verell. "Take care of our hero."

FADE TO BLACK

"Which hero?"

The senior detective sighed, "Niall, you really have no clue what's waiting for you out there." ◻

ZOË BECK

FRIDAY
8

The two DIs took him home. For Niall, the equation was quite simple. If the journalists were hanging around, the jihadists probably would not hack him to pieces in front of them.

"A running camera won't stop them," Gilpin reminded him. "Quite the opposite. Don't forget that."

"I'm not a soldier. I'm a civilian and probably less interesting. And they don't seem to care much about getting rid of witnesses."

"True. They prefer to abduct journalists and keep them as hostages for a few years," Gilpin responded drily.

"Anyone who is down there, that is. But not from London. That would take too much effort."

"Are you a hundred percent sure?" De Verell parried. "Do you really think you know what you're doing?"

"No, but I'd like to go home now."

DCI Hodges had been right. A mob of journalists were gathered in front of the apartment building and had obviously been waiting for some hours. The story about his imprisonment had clearly made the rounds.

"Have you come straight from the prison?"

"How did they treat you?"

"Did they apologize?"

"How long were you in jail? Until just now?"

"When did the police realize their mistake?"

"How are you feeling?"

"Did you have any contact with the two attackers?"

"Weren't you terrified?"

"Do you think you're safe now?"

Gilpin positioned herself in front of the crowd and spoke eloquently about ongoing investigations, individual rights, and the inviolability of personal space. During this monologue, De Verell maneuvered Niall into the building, and they hurried up the stairs.

"My colleague will take care of this. She likes to talk to the press."

"You're a little younger than she is but have the same rank."

De Verell nodded. "I'm an overachiever. I also don't enjoy talking to the press."

"In other words, she didn't keep her mouth shut."

"And she was passed over for promotion. She was even suspended from duty for a while."

Niall unlocked his apartment door but only opened it a crack. He was reluctant to invite De Verell inside. He could not help feeling ashamed of his tiny, messy place.

The detective noticed his hesitation: "I've already been in there."

Niall opened the door and let him inside.

Considering they had searched everything in his studio apartment, it looked decent, Niall thought, not much messier than usual.

"I'm bad at keeping things picked up," he mumbled.

"If I weren't married, my place would look just like this."

Niall studied De Verell more closely than he had before. The sleek, expensive suit, the perfectly ironed shirt, the polished shoes—Niall would have guessed he had a good laundry service, maybe a maid. De Verell read his look and laughed.

"I'm a conservative overachiever."

Niall glanced around. His laptop was missing.

"When will I get it back?"

"Do you have another computer?"

"No."

"Then we'll bring it back as soon as possible."

"That'd be good."

De Verell checked the kitchen and the bathroom to see if everything was in order. "You have our number in case something happens. Be careful. These people are insane."
"You mean the press or the jihadists?"
"Both."

After De Verell left, Niall collapsed onto his sofa bed and tried to get a little sleep. His phone had other plans. He answered automatically, realizing too late that it was probably the press.
He was right. It was somebody from a morning talk show. How would he feel about being on the program and talking about what had happened to him?
"Nothing happened to me," Niall corrected. "The boy is the one who died. Do you happen to know his name?" He had failed to ask the police for his name, as well as the names of the attackers. Names would transform the figures in his mind into actual people. He was uncertain if he was ready to conceive of the dead boy as a person and not just a victim, but he could only avoid it so long.
"Paul Ferguson. His friends called him Paulie," offered the woman on the other end of the line.
Paulie. He could still see the beaming, healthy young man. Paulie Ferguson. "Thanks," Niall replied.
"Will you come?"
"No."
"Why not?"
"I don't want to be on TV, and I haven't done anything remarkable. Why are you calling me anyway?"
"You're a hero, and you should tell your story."
"I'm no hero. All I did was film something with my phone. If you consider the fact that I'm a professional cameraman, it really wasn't anything exceptional."
"But in this situation?"
"It would have been better if I had developed superpowers, so I could have done something useful." He gulped. He did not say that he wished he had thrown himself in the fray and risked

being killed in Paulie's place. It would have been a lie, after all. "I wish I could've helped him. I'm more of a coward than a hero."

"You could talk about that."

"I could also just leave it alone. Listen, I should be hanging up right now. I shouldn't have answered the phone."

"We'll pay you if you come. And I don't just mean a reimbursement for the drive over to the studio."

"You pay? Since when?"

"Ah, there's always a separate budget for special guests. That is, if we get an exclusive. Would you be willing to offer us an exclusive interview?"

"I actually hadn't planned to talk to anyone."

"Is that a yes?"

"How much?"

"A thousand."

"Two."

"Paulie's parents would like to meet you."

Niall choked. "What?"

"They'll also be there."

"On the program?"

"Yes."

"Why?"

"They feel a need to."

"What for?"

"The two of them want to find out what happened to their son. And that's why they want to talk to you as well."

"With me. They've asked for that specifically?"

"Yes."

"You aren't lying to me, are you?"

"No."

"I don't believe you."

"The Fergusons really do want to meet you."

"Why?"

"If you come tomorrow, you'll find out."

"Your powers of persuasion will take you far," Niall sighed.

"What time do I have to be there?"

"At four."

"Four a.m.?" He added strong emphasis to the letters.

She laughed again. "It won't be the end of the world if it's ten past four, but you'll have to let me know if you're coming in that late." She gave Niall her number and explained where he needed to go. Her name was Laura. Niall could hear a buzz of voices in the background.

"Laura, is there a chance you're standing right outside my building?"

"I waved, but you didn't look my way."

"What is your position with the station? Office blackmailer?"

"I'm the assistant producer for the morning show."

"For now. Give it a few years, and you'll be calling the shots. I hope you never go into politics."

"I promise. We said a thousand, right?"

He sighed. "Good grief. That'll work."

"Then I'll see you tomorrow around four."

After she hung up, Niall disconnected his landline and shut off his cell phone.

By the time the alarm went off at three, he had neither slept much nor particularly well. Niall took a shower, got dressed, ran to catch the night bus, and arrived fifteen minutes late at the television studio, located north of Oxford Circus.

"Four-thirty would've been fine," Laura said with a grin as she led him into the opulent Art Deco lobby.

"Then why did you say I had to be here by four?"

"Because at this hour, everyone runs late. Nobody ever gets here at four."

"You're pretty sneaky," he said, impressed.

"I know."

Laura looked familiar, but he had no idea why. She was short and chubby with dark blonde curls and mild acne concealed beneath heavy makeup. He could tell that her looks would not help her work her way up the professional ladder, so she would need to leverage her skills and intelligence to draw attention to herself.

Niall hoped she would find a way to do that. The television industry was cruel when it came to moderately attractive women, and intelligence was not always an asset, not even behind the camera. He felt a need to compliment her, but nothing came to mind. To girls like her, people always said things like, "You have a great voice." Or a great personality. A pretty smile. Lovely eyes. A good sense of humor. Laura was too smart not to see through comments like that. If he asked her if they knew each other from somewhere, she might take it the wrong way. He hoped he would eventually remember on his own.

"Are Paulie's parents already here?" he asked.

"No, they're coming later and won't stay long." She pointed at his forehead. "What's that?"

He cautiously touched the stapled wound. "Long story." Too long for a morning show interview.

She took him to the guest lounge, where food and drinks were already set up for him, before leaving him on his own for two minutes. Sipping a cup of coffee, Niall walked around and tried to wake himself up. His thoughts turned to his prison cell, which had been smaller than the lounge. He was eying a tuna fish sandwich that was beckoning to him from the table when Laura returned and announced that it was time for him to go to makeup.

There, he was powdered and coiffed before being microphoned by Laura and introduced to the team. Nobody seemed to be interested in him. They just nodded curtly in his direction and went back to whatever they were doing. It was now 5:30, and in thirty minutes, the show would be on the air, live.

Hero, my ass, he thought, recalling the conversation with the Scotland Yard DCI. No one cared who had made the video. Nobody ever cared about the person holding the camera because everyone thought that holding a camera was the easiest thing in the world to do. Anybody could hold a camera, just like anyone could push the switch on a coffeemaker. Just press the right button, and the machine takes care of the rest. As usual, a mild wave of irritation washed over him.

"You can wait back in the lounge," Laura commented.

"In other words, get out of here. You're in the way."

"Finally, someone who really gets me," she retorted. "Your fifteen minutes of fame are almost here, and actually you'll be getting more than fifteen. Drink up on the coffee and grab a sandwich or some cookies. Once you're on the air, you won't be thinking about food."

"You think so?"

"I know so. Go on now." She smiled cheerfully and pushed him toward the lounge. She grew serious, though, once they were inside.

"Paulie's father isn't coming."

"No? He's changed his mind?"

"He's in the hospital, had some kind of breakdown."

"Shit."

"But his mother's still coming."

"Why? She should stay with her husband. This will just make her more upset."

Laura nodded slowly. "She doesn't want to miss this."

"Do you think that's alright?"

"It's her decision." She glanced up at the large clock over the door. "I'll be back to get you in a few minutes. You aren't going on right at six, so you've got another half hour of peace and quiet." With that, she left.

Niall opened a plastic bag and extracted a tuna fish sandwich. As he ate, he checked his email on his phone. His Uncle Carl had written, suggesting they meet for lunch. Friends and acquaintances had been checking in. Since his father's death two years ago, his relationships with some people had been neglected, which was completely his fault. But now they were touching base. Some of them because they actually cared, others because they wanted to use this opportunity to tell him he was a fucking loser. The latter group included his ex-girlfriend. True friends, he thought. At least none of them were pretending to like him just because he was now all across the media.

He skipped most of the messages, especially the ones from people he did not know. He pulled up the station's home page and clicked through to the page for the morning show, but it did not have any particularly useful information. Maybe he was looking in the wrong place. He had never really watched the show.

Sometimes, if he fell asleep with the TV on, he would wake up in the middle of the show and watch it for while. Or when he was traveling, he would occasionally turn it on in his hotel. He had never seen more than occasional bits and pieces. The show featured a mixture of extremely repetitive news reports, astonishingly thorough weather reports, interviews with studio guests, and film clips related to contemporary topics that had no real news, entertainment, or educational value. He thought they sometimes did cooking demos and animal shelter features on dogs in need of new homes, too.

He could feel the unmistakable early jitters of stage fright. Niall did not enjoy being in front of the camera; he belonged behind it. His palms were growing sweaty as his pulse quickened. What he really wanted was go home. What had he actually thought he needed to say on the program?

Laura walked in, and suddenly he recalled where he had seen her.

"It's time," she said before he could say anything. "Is everything alright?"

"Yes, of course." He stood up.

"You look a little pale."

"Despite the makeup?"

"Compared to just a few minutes ago. Excited?"

"You could say that."

"Your first time on live TV?"

"My first time in front of the camera."

9

The two moderators were already waiting for him in the studio. He had his pick among multiple sofas, which looked comfortable on the screen and perhaps actually were for the others. Niall felt like he had landed on a waterbed.

"We still have a minute to go," the female moderator commented. Shirin, he remembered. Her colleague's name was Brian. No, Dylan. Or Colin? He was drawing a blank, his anxiety approaching borderline panic. He hoped they were about to say something directly to him. After all, they were supposed to ask him questions, not the other way around. Regardless, the line of thought helped distract him from the fact that he had forgotten the man's name. What nonsense would he start babbling once the cameras started rolling?

Shirin flexed her back and flashed her brightest smile while her colleague loosened his cramped position and leaned back with practiced nonchalance. Niall had missed the countdown. They were live. Shirin kicked things off with some upbeat comments, and Niall tried his best to imagine that the cameras were encouraging spectators. His thoughts turned to his cameras back home and to the subterranean rivers, but then he heard his name. He snapped back to the studio.

"Hi," he said cautiously. "Good morning." He nodded vaguely in the direction of the camera that was transmitting, indicated by a red light.

"You have just survived two turbulent days," Shirin remarked. "We'll talk about that in a minute, but first let's discuss the reason you're here. Dear viewers, Niall Stuart was the man who filmed the vicious murder of Air Cadet Paul Ferguson. We're only going to show you a short clip because of the brutal nature of the incident and out of respect for the deceased."

The clip started, and on a nearby monitor, Niall could watch what the viewers at home were seeing: heavily edited images that only hinted at the horror. The clip ended with the man in the green shirt waving the flag and the one in blue talking about the Islamic State. You could see the blood on his hands, the dripping machete. Niall was relieved that they did not show Paulie.

"Niall," began the moderator whose name he could not remember. Robert maybe? "How did you happen to shoot this film?"

Niall considered his response and obviously took too long for a live show, since Shirin cut in before he could even open his mouth.

"It must have all been so terrifying. What did you feel as it was happening?"

"I don't know. Of course, I was scared. All I could think was that I had to film the two men so there'd be evidence for later. I had no idea…" He broke off. "I mean, they had those machetes, but…nobody pays much attention to things like that. At least, I didn't."

Shirin leaned forward and patted his arm, moving deftly so she did not block the light while also staying in the camera's sightline. Niall knew this gesture was intended to show the morning show audience how sorry she felt for him, and he gazed in distaste at the moderator's slender, perfectly manicured hand. "You could have run away."

"Yes, maybe, but…" He shook his head. "It was like a reflex."

"Occupational weakness."

Brian, Niall thought. It suited him. Or was it Colin, after all? "Possibly."

"And the way you talked to the attackers. Unbelievable! You recorded their confession. The authenticity of your film is undisputed and will carry weight in the trial. The attackers actually gave you their permission to make the recording, right?"

"They even demanded that I upload the video."

"You did the right thing." Shirin was back to sounding sympathetic.

"Well, it was supposed to just be on my personal YouTube channel. I thought that no one would see it there, but at least I would have uploaded the video in case the guys wanted to see proof that I'd done it. But I forgot that I'd—"

"Yes," beamed Brian-Colin, "the web never forgets! Once it's online, the whole world knows about it. Speaking of the world, it's time for us to check in with Fiona: What's going on in the world right now, Fiona?"

Fiona, the news anchor, greeted the moderator and called him Harry. Harry and Shirin relaxed a little once the cameras swiveled away from them.

"That was very good," Harry said to Niall. "We'll now move on to what the men said to you."

"Alright."

"You're doing a great job." Harry claimed a coffee cup from the small table that stood between the sofas. "Want one?"

Niall shook his head. "I already had some."

Shirin submitted to a makeup touch-up, and Harry gestured for someone with hairspray to come his way. Niall tried not to suffocate in the ensuing fog.

"The red cup's mine," Harry declared.

"Got it."

"Thirty seconds," someone called.

The moderators resumed their positions, and Niall tried to make himself more comfortable. He felt like he was listing to one side, so he leaned forward and rested his arms on his knees. It struck him that he had assumed the brace position recommended for airplane travelers during an emergency landing.

"What did they say to you, Niall?" Harry asked, once the cameras were back on them.

"They said that they were at war, and that was why a soldier had to be killed. One of them stood there and waved a flag."

"A flag, right," Shirin commented with a smile. "Did you recognize it?"

"Yes, it was the one used by the Islamists, from the Islamist, uh, Islamic State?" Niall's nervousness had settled down during the break, but it was back in full force. He scooted a bit forward. "What exactly is on the flag?"

"We wondered that, too, and pulled a little something together about it. Watch." A schematic was pulled up, and Shirin read from the screen. "This is a variation of the flag for the Islamic State, although I have to add that this is not a legitimate 'state' recognized by international law. This is an organization. Many governments have gone so far as to label it as a dangerous Salafist-Islamist terrorist group. The upper part of the flag shows the Schahāda, the Islamic profession of faith. In English, it reads: 'There are no gods except Allah.' The symbol at the bottom is the Prophet Mohammed's seal."

The director switched back to the three of them in the studio.

Shirin smiled once more, but her mouth had grown tight around the edges. "That's what the men said to you, right? That they were supporters of the Islamic State?"

"The caliphate, yes," Niall answered uncertainly. He felt annoyed at himself for not having prepared more for the interview. His knowledge was superficial, limited to what he had heard on the news and read online. Laura had said nothing about supplying political commentary, just morning show chitchat.

"Abu Bakr al-Baghdadi is the leader of the ISIS organization, which was recently renamed IS. The group has several thousand members, and the organization is growing through an influx of people from all over the world. More and more young men from the western nations are converting to Islam, and they are particularly susceptible to the influence of the Salafists." Harry mouthed his text fluidly, his concerned eyes turned toward the camera. "Trust me, you don't want your sons to be involved with this group. Twenty-six-year-old Frank Holeywell was one of those who hoped to find their destiny in its ranks."

A photo of the man who had killed Paulie was shown, only in this picture he was clean shaven. His hair was a little long, and he was smiling shyly. Niall only recognized him at second glance.

"Since his conversion to Islam, he has called himself Farooq Kaddumi al-Engeltra. A totally normal young man from South London, he was radicalized."

Niall had no idea if he was allowed to interrupt, but he did it anyway. "He told me he was Palestinian."

"No, according to our sources, he is a British citizen. Frank Holeywell sounds very English, doesn't it?"

"Yes," Shirin picked up the thread of conversation. "His accomplice, Cemal Bayraktar, twenty-four, was seriously injured in the arrest, and has been in intensive care since then."

"The Turk," Niall added. "At least, that's what he said."

They put up a photo of Cemal Bayraktar. Grinning confidently into the camera, he had somebody's arm draped around his shoulders, but that someone had been cut out of the picture. Like Farooq, Cemal had no beard in the photo. "Cemal Bayraktar was born in London. His grandparents left Turkey back in the sixties." Shirin gazed gravely into the camera. "Not only did Niall Stuart film the two perpetrators during their brutal attack, he also interviewed them afterward and kept them distracted long enough for the police to arrive. A full-blooded journalist you could say, a professional, and that would be the truth. He is a camera operator and documentary filmmaker by career. Niall," she turned back to him. "Your courageous intervention prevented an even greater bloodbath and enabled the police to arrest the two men. That was amazingly brave of you."

"Oh? I don't know about that."

"You're accustomed to extreme situations. As a documentary filmmaker, you travel around the world with your camera." Assuming Shirin did not intend to explain his work to him, Niall figured this information was probably meant for the viewers.

"My specialty is animals. And landscapes," he clarified.

Harry was already interrupting: "Is this a talent you inherited from your father?"

Niall needed a moment to respond. "My father? He ran a nursery," he said. "Or do you mean my preference for beautiful scenery? I've never looked at it that way."

"But your father—"

He was not going to let Harry dictate the conversation. "—died two years ago, that's true. I took his death pretty hard. It's terrible to lose someone so close to you. I can imagine what Paulie's parents are going through right now." Goaded by his anger at Harry, Niall's words tumbled out quickly. "How old was Paulie? Did he have any siblings? It's hard for me to accept the fact I couldn't do anything to save him. I can still see him when I close my eyes. It's horrible."

Shirin waited for him to pause to breathe before cutting in quickly: "Paulie's mother, Valerie Ferguson, will be with us shortly." She turned to the camera that was broadcasting. "We will now turn to Carol, who will tell us what the weather will be like over the next few days. Carol, what should we expect? Will it be warm and sunny again today?"

Shirin kept smiling until she was sure the camera was off her. She then looked questioningly at Harry, who responded with a shrug.

"Don't ever do that again," Niall growled.

"What?"

"I will not talk about my father, got it?"

"How was I supposed to know?" Harry turned away, pretending to fiddle with his microphone.

"That's private," Niall replied. "You can't just ask questions about my personal life."

Shirin answered for Harry, who was acting like he was deaf. "He admires your father a lot."

"That has nothing to do with the attack. It was a shitty thing for him to do."

"You're right. He should have asked you about it beforehand. Please excuse him."

"He should ask me himself," Niall mumbled softly. Glancing back over at Harry, he saw him talking to Laura. It seemed to have something to do with Paulie's mother, who had shown up earlier than expected and was ready to appear in front of the cameras.

"Bring her over," Harry said, waving at a woman who was standing back in the wings. "Come here, Mrs. Ferguson.

Please." He stood up and walked over to her. "My condolences. All our condolences. Your Paulie did not deserve that. How is your husband doing?"

Valerie Ferguson acknowledged Harry's greeting with a mute nod. She looked around, a little confused as she squinted into the spotlights.

"This way," Laura declared.

"How much time?" Harry asked in the general direction of the invisible director.

"In twenty. Hurry, please," came the response via the loudspeaker.

Laura dashed out of the studio, and Harry motioned for the woman to sit down next to Niall. Shirin bent forward to murmur her sympathy as well.

Niall studied the woman from the side. She might have been in her early forties. At her age, some women were still having children, while she had just lost hers.

"Mrs. Ferguson," he began, as Shirin leaned back and screwed her smile in place for the camera. "I'm Niall Stuart. I'm so sorry about everything. I wish I could have—"

"Thank you, Carol," Shirin responded. "It should be a marvelous weekend for anyone not living in Wales. Dear viewers," her face grew serious, "we now have in the studio the mother of Air Cadet Paul Ferguson, who was killed on Wednesday in the terrorist attack in Vauxhall. Valerie Ferguson, we are very grateful that you have taken the time to join us on this program. How is your husband doing? He was taken to hospital last night after a fainting episode."

Valerie Ferguson was still squinting, obviously unsure where she was to be looking. "Who is this?" she asked.

"Who do you mean? The man next to you? That is Niall Stuart, the man who made the recording and prevented anything worse—"

Valerie Ferguson had stopped listening. She got up and stood in front of Niall, who was gazing at her in confusion.

"You watched my son be slaughtered and didn't do anything!"

FADE TO BLACK

The woman screamed so loudly her words were incoherent. A feedback screech emanated from somewhere, and out of the corner of his eye, Niall saw Shirin and Harry leap to their feet. Unfortunately, though, they were not quick enough to prevent Mrs. Ferguson from punching him in the face. ▯

10

"Still don't want a doctor?" Laura asked.

"Nope," Niall replied, continuing to press the ice pack against his cheek. "You really don't need to check on me every few minutes. I'm a big boy."

"May I take a look?"

He lowered the pack, and she frowned.

"She almost hit your eye."

"But she didn't."

"Or your forehead, and then your wound would have re-opened."

"Nothing bad happened. Has she calmed down yet?"

"Yes, but only thanks to the doctor. By the way, he's out in the hallway if you—"

"No. Really."

"What if you have a concussion?" She sounded truly concerned.

He was surprised at how much she honestly seemed to care, and he suspected this came naturally to her. Regardless of what she did in life, she seemed like she would always give it her all. And then some. She was an unusual person and a bad fit for the superficial world of morning television.

He smiled. "Laura, I'm alright. Honestly."

She eyed him skeptically.

Niall knew that Shirin had grabbed Paulie's mother from behind and shoved her off the set, a maneuver that needed immense physical strength since Valerie Ferguson was obviously committed to pounding Niall into a state of unconsciousness. He never would have thought the slender Shirin had it in her. While this was going on, he heard Harry offer a soothing apology to the transmitting camera, all while taking baby steps that moved him away from the altercation, shifting the drama out of the viewers' direct line of vision. Laura had guided Niall to the lounge, and since then, he had been sitting there icing his face.

"Is the program still airing?" Niall asked.

"Of course. The two of them are total professionals. They would keep chatting if a spree killer broke in here."

"If that ever happens, call me. I'd like to watch."

"Will do." She held out a glass of water.

"This should help with the shock."

"I'm not suffering from shock. I was just taken off guard."

"Drink it anyway."

Niall took it. "I now recall where we met."

Laura smiled as she raised her eyebrows quizzically.

"Three years ago. I was making that film about Botswana. You were the intern in the London production office."

"Yep."

"Why didn't you say something?"

She brushed it off with a wave. "Nobody remembers the interns. Besides, we only crossed paths a few times." What she meant was that only the pretty ones got remembered.

"I remember."

"But it took a while."

He protested in fake outrage: "In my condition, it's a miracle I can recall anything at all! What's my name again?"

Laura chuckled.

He recalled her laugh. It had left an impression years ago: a true, sincere laugh. "I know that your boss Rick was very impressed with you. Reliable, smart, fast, resourceful. He said you'd make it big one day."

She blushed. "He put in a good word for me here. I finished my degree and then got this job, thanks to Rick."

Niall nodded. "He came through nicely, but don't stay in morning TV too long."

He was just taking a sip from his glass when the door opened.

"Good morning." A tall, slim man around seventy with a full head of graying hair stepped inside. Niall's water suddenly went down the wrong way, and he started choking.

"Good morning, Mr. Huffman," Laura said, sounding both surprised and excited. "Have you...Did they send you here for the program? I'm afraid nobody told me. I'll get right on it—"

"No worries," he said, smiling at the production assistant.

Niall wiped his mouth and noticed how flushed Laura had become.

"I just wanted to look in on our young friend here. Niall, how are you doing?"

"Thanks, just great."

"Your forehead, did that—"

"No, it's older."

"Ah."

They fell silent. Huffman smiled, Laura began to fidget, and Niall leaned back and closed his eyes, holding the ice pack back up to his cheek. He was still shivering and hoped that by the time he opened his eyes, he would be alone again with Laura. Or just alone.

Leonard Huffman, the legend. The great war photographer whose pictures over the past thirty-plus years had both written and documented history. About five years ago, he had officially retired from photography and had shifted his focus to helping organize exhibitions of his photos around the world. He worked for the television station in an advisory capacity, but Niall had not calculated on running into him.

"Um, I'll just go make sure that everything's alright out there," Laura remarked into the silent void.

"No, stay," Niall replied before Huffman could nod her out the door.

"Are you sure?" she asked.

He could not tell if Huffman was annoyed that she was staying. He treated her with flawless courtesy, inviting her to sit down, and even handing her a cup of coffee, as if she were his guest. He knew how to endear himself to people, Niall thought. Laura's face was still bright pink. Niall considered the advisability of handing her his ice pack.

"Niall, I'll speak with Harry later. He shouldn't have pried into your personal affairs that way."

Niall shook his head dismissively, avoiding eye contact with Huffman.

"But that isn't why I'm here," the man continued when Niall did not respond. "I would like to talk to you about a project."

"Not interested, too busy. Sorry."

"What are you working on right now?"

"Something here in London. Local history," Niall offered, intentionally vague.

"Is this project very important to you? Or unusually well paid?"

Niall sighed. "Fine. What do you have in mind?"

Huffman smiled. "Thank you. I've been talking with various program managers and directors, and there's some interest in making a documentary about the two attackers. Of course, you came to mind."

"I did? Uh-huh. Sorry, not interested. I'll be perfectly happy if I never have to see either of them again." He tried to keep his voice calm but failed. It sounded raspy and unsteady.

"You would be the right one for this. The only one."

"Since I do such a great job with those nice landscape and animal shoots? Sure."

"You've always wanted to do something different. Something with depth and meaning."

"Until two years ago, that is."

"Niall, we need to…"

"Who says that my next film won't be challenging? Or are you just assuming I'll walk away from it?"

"The forgotten rivers. That really can't be all that interesting."

Typical. He already knew everything. Niall shook his head and glanced over at Laura, who was listening intently to everything and not even trying to hide her admiration. He breathed deeply.

"Listen," he said to Huffman, "why don't you just find someone else?"

"Because you were the one they talked to."

"They would have talked to whoever happened to be holding the camera." Niall felt exhausted.

"But they happened to talk to you. They know you now." Huffman smiled slightly.

"Considering the adrenaline rush they had to be feeling, they'll hardly remember me."

"Niall, please give it some thought. We want a critical, comprehensive background story. What led up to two young Englishmen joining an Islamist terrorist organization and killing a person in broad daylight? This is a huge story, and you've already gotten it started. Besides, you care about what happens to them. This is exactly what you've been looking for, that much I know."

"Wow," he heard Laura gasp.

"I'm too busy."

"Is that your final word?"

"Yes."

The man stood up and nodded at Laura. As he moved toward the door, he added: "Just think about it, okay? We'll talk again later."

"I said it was my final word. Is that really so hard to understand?" Niall called after him.

Once Leonard left, Laura and Niall sat in silence. Laura needed time to fully recover from Leonard's visit before her face returned to its normal hue. Niall was glad for the silence. His lower lip still trembled each time he opened his mouth: an unhealthy mixture of excitement and exhaustion.

"Wow," she finally said.

"What, wow?"

"You know each other pretty well, don't you?"

"No, not really."

"But...it seems that way."

Niall shrugged and immediately regretted it, rubbing the sore spot. "How is Mrs. Ferguson? Any better?"

"Should I go check?" Laura stood up but then hesitated. "I see, you want to get rid of me. You should just be upfront and honest. I'd prefer it that way."

"I'm sorry. No, please stay. I'd appreciate your company. It's been a bit much today, the past few days." The ice pack had grown room temperature, so he set it aside. "But don't you have to be somewhere? Doing something? Whatever it is that production assistants do?"

She glanced at the clock. "I still have some time." She joined him on the couch.

"Thanks."

"It's in my job description. You shouldn't think I'm just blowing something off."

Niall chuckled. "I don't think you're lazy. Don't worry."

She nodded contentedly. "How's your cheek? It doesn't look like it'll swell up too much. Good thing we iced it right away."

After a moment of silence, Niall finally said: "Go ahead and ask."

"It's none of my business."

"Ask, if you'd like."

So of course, she did. "Why don't you want to make the documentary? It sounds like an amazing offer. Besides, the station pays really well."

"I know, but I'm already working on something."

"And you can't get out of it?"

"I don't want to."

Laura stood up and started pacing the length of the lounge. Her cheeks were flushed again, but this time, not due to self-consciousness. "But you could talk to the production company; maybe they could push the filming off a bit. Surely, they'd understand that something more time-sensitive has popped up. It would be a really good opportunity for you."

"Laura, I have another film to work on. I can't just—"

She refused to let him distract her, "you said you don't want to do it. That's something else completely."

He studied her from the side. She was young and enthusiastic, lacking the egotistical ambition clear in most people working in her industry. In her industry? He corrected himself. In all of them. Laura had managed to preserve her sense of empathy, and it seemed to Niall as if she were the kind of person who would not so easily lose it. Her enthusiasm for Huffman's offer was sincere, and he felt like he owed her an honest explanation. Perhaps because he instinctively trusted her, perhaps because his nerves were worn so thin, he could no longer keep his despair bottled up inside.

"The short version or the long one?" he asked.

She studied him, then smiled. "I'm curious."

"I'll have to give you the backstory. You might not have enough time or patience."

Leaning back, Laura pulled her knees up and cradled her coffee cup in both hands as she gazed at him encouragingly: "I enjoy a good story."

"The truth is that I'm scared. Because it's such a big project and because Huffman is the one who offered it to me."

He explained to her how even as a young boy he had been enthusiastic about photography and film, interests his parents had only reluctantly supported. His father had owned a nursery, and his mother had worked beside him until Niall turned twelve, the year she was diagnosed with terminal breast cancer. After a year full of despair, she explained in a farewell letter that it would be for the best if she ended it all. Niall's father never remarried. He took care of his son and finally threw himself behind Niall's passion for the visual arts, buying him a video camera. He paid for a summer course, where Niall learned how to run a camera and edit his own films. And when Niall decided to leave school at the age of sixteen to work on film sets and learn how to run a camera, his father supported him, one hundred percent, even when it proved challenging: poorly or unpaid jobs, distant shoots, and long, hard hours. Pete Stuart stood beside his son, encouraging and backing him in every possible way.

By his early twenties, Niall was specializing in documentaries, and he had started traveling around the world. His father suggested he take a class to flesh out his academic qualifications. He had even saved up some money, but Niall refused, declaring that he would make his own way. Although he really did want to advance his career, there were two things holding Niall back. First of all, he was uncomfortable with the idea of his father investing so much money in the course. The nursery had hit hard times, and he really needed every penny for himself. Besides that, Niall simply could not imagine going to college. He imagined that the people there would look down on him because he had never attended college before and had been accepted to the course on his professional qualifications alone. When he had quit school, he had walked away before completing his A Levels. The odds were good he would end up something like a second-class student, so he decided to gamble everything on his wits and skills without a degree. However, his career trajectory was proving challenging and slow, despite the fact he was good at what he did. He kept being hired for the same niche: animals and landscapes.

His father had died two years ago. The scant inheritance that remained after the nursery and house had been sold and debts paid off was quickly consumed. Now was truly not the time to think about starting a university program or to strike off—and self-finance—his own project. Niall accepted anything he could get, regardless of its quality. He did have one firm standard though: He refused to sink so low as to run a camera for a cooking show or a reality TV program. Not yet, anyway. And now? Huffman had come and made him the kind of offer that he had been waiting on for years. It was just that it was impossible for him to accept it.

Laura studied him, processing what he had just told her. "You don't like him. Why?"

"Oh, I've admired him my entire life. And feared him, too."

"In other words, you're worried that you'll disappoint him?"

"He disappointed me."

Laura raised one eyebrow. "Huh?"

Niall leaned toward her. "I respected him, just like everyone else. He created the most inspiring, incredible works, and I wish I had the talent to express in film what he has conveyed through photography."

"But?" She had been so caught up in his story that she had forgotten to drink her coffee. After quickly checking how hot it was, she set it down. "Keep talking. Please."

Mere days after his father's burial, his will had been read. There were no surprises. As the only son and only living relative of Pete Stuart, Niall was the sole beneficiary. The only strange highlight of the whole affair was a single sealed letter that bore Niall's mother's handwriting. The notary explained the one stipulation tied to this document. Niall's mother had wished for Niall to personally deliver the letter to Leonard Huffman, who was supposed to open the letter in Niall's presence. Niall asked why Huffman had not been invited to the reading of the will.

"As far as I know, Huffman is not inheriting anything, so there was no reason for him to be here. It is up to you whether you give him the letter or not. There are no conditions tied to this request, but your father asked me to communicate your mother's final wish to you this way." With these words, the matter had been closed for the notary.

Niall felt as if he had landed in a bad film. He'd racked his brain about what his mother had hoped to achieve with the letter. More than once, he found himself about to open the letter, but each time, he managed to curb his curiosity at the last moment. The only reasonable explanation was also an embarrassing one. Perhaps it was some kind of request. A dying mother asking a prominent figure to take her son, who admired him so greatly, under his wing and mentor him. Nonetheless, if this was what his mother had wanted, this was what he would do.

On the day he came to his decision, Niall searched online to see if he could figure out where Huffman was that day, and he discovered that the photographer was opening an exhibit in the Keller Gallery in London's West End. On his way there, Niall thought about his mother, how she had never shown any interest in art or photography, not even films. She had invested her body and soul in running the nursery with his father. She had not just helped him with the bookkeeping, but she had been practically as knowledgeable as her husband about plants. She had supplied excellent advice to customers and arranged gorgeous bouquets. Niall imagined Leonard Huffman walking into the nursery one day to buy flowers. And then what? Had she told him about Niall?

 By the time he reached Oxford Circus, Niall's palms were sweaty, and as he descended the steps from Oxford Street to Ramillies Street, he kept having to assure himself that he was not dreaming. He could still recall staring up at the giant white letters for the Keller Gallery that ran vertically down the tall, brick building, partially clad in smooth, black slabs. After entering the gallery, he was not allowed to go inside because he did not have an invitation. However, as soon as Leonard Huffman came down and Niall gave him the letter from his mother, everything was alright.

 That was the night Niall learned that his parents had lied to him for twenty-nine years. Pete Stuart was not his biological father. Leonard Huffman was. The man had smiled at him, shook his hand, and said: "So, you're my son, Niall." His parents, his three parents, had made the decision not to tell him the truth before that moment. When he had lost both his father and mother, he was supposed to finally know about his real parentage.

 The only problem was that, since that day, Niall had wished he had never been told.

11

Niall was waiting in front of the Keller Gallery cafe when it opened.

"Wow," the waiter remarked. "We never have a mob like this in the mornings."

The West End was always sluggish before noon, as if the neighborhood needed to collectively sleep off its high from the previous night. Niall had fled the station right after finishing his story. Once she finally grasped that he was the son of a legend, Laura's face precisely mirrored his fears from the previous two years, the ramifications of standing in the shadow of the great man, of being an indisputable failure not even half the man his father was.

For the past two years, he had struggled with the question of whether his unnamed birth father had been the reason his parents had responded so unenthusiastically to his passion for photography. He even occasionally wished they had managed to stop him from pursuing it.

This, however, was not the only reason Niall was so angry. It was everything all jumbled up. Learning that his own parents had lied to him for decades. That the father he had loved was not his father—not his "real" father—although that was exactly what he had been. He had been a real father, better than anyone else Niall could have wished for. Still, everything Niall had with him had been taken from him in a single blow. His identity, his basic trust, his foundation. This had made it hard for him to truly mourn for his father, Pete. What he'd gone through was a kind of double mourning. Niall missed Pete greatly, but he was also disappointed in him, as well his mother.

It was the man he had admired so much—the same way others looked up to actors or authors or athletes—who had told him that Pete had first met his mother when Niall was already two months old. Niall recalled asking his parents why they had first gotten married a year after he had been born. His mother had simply shrugged and said: "We didn't care about conventionalities, and that's just the way it happened."

Two years before, in that very gallery, Leonard had explained further: "I thought your mother was an amazing woman, but I couldn't have a family, and she understood that. She absolutely wanted to have you, even if I wasn't going to be there for her. We made the decision together."

After that revelation, Niall had refused to have any contact with Leonard, though the older man had never given up trying to open up lines of communication with birthday cards, Christmas cards, a call or email every few weeks, postcards. He had even suggested that they get together to chat. Niall had rejected all these attempts to get to know Leonard. He'd wished the Christmas cards and the attention had been spread out over the previous twenty-nine years.

Niall had even gone so far as to throw away every one of his volumes of Leonard's photographs. He'd no longer wanted them and hated himself for ever admiring the man. He had almost wished he could have tossed out all the memories of his parents as well.

That was probably the reason he had come to be sitting in the gallery in the West End, drinking coffee and considering what it all meant. Two years had passed. Two years of defiance, anger, wall building. All because he did not want to be his father's son.

He ordered another coffee and pulled up the internet on his phone to see what was being said about the debacle during the morning show. What he found was an entire bandwidth of responses, from sympathy for the poor woman who had overreacted to speculations that Niall's presence at the scene of the crime might have been more than coincidental. He also discovered that Laura had emailed him, asking if he was doing alright. If he wanted to talk some more, she would be glad to listen whenever he wanted to chat. She thought he should seriously consider the offer from the station to make the documentary. She still thought it was a good idea.

Niall stood up, nodded at the waiter, and stepped into the gallery's bookshop. He wanted to buy one of Leonard's photography books. No particular one, just whatever they happened to have on the shelf.

Of course, they had all of Leonard's books, those from him and the other great photographers: Margaret Bourke-White, James Nachtwey, Dorothea Lange, Lewis Hine, Steve McCurry, Robert Capa, Elliott Erwitt. Even Vivian Maier and Marchand and Meffre's book about the ruins of Detroit. There were no cheap photographs anywhere in sight, no London picture books for tourists.

Only two years before, Niall would have felt like he had landed in heaven there. He would have spent hours meandering through the shelves, paging through books, browsing. He would have overdrawn his account, buying more books than he could afford. Now, he missed that enthusiasm and fire.

Leonard had published a total of five titles. Niall studied the prices on the back covers, trying to roughly estimate what he still had in his account.

"If you take two of them, I'll give you a discount," the woman behind the register called over to him. She was struggling against the heaviness of her eyelids, fighting to stay awake. She held a mug of something hot, and Niall hoped she had not seen the morning show.

Niall mumbled something about not having enough money with him. He was thinking about postponing his plans, if not abandoning them entirely, when she said: "Ah, it's you."

"Dammit! I was hoping you didn't have a TV. Or hadn't turned it on, at least."

She looked confused. "I don't know you from TV. I'm sorry. If you're in some series or news show, I'm afraid I don't keep up with things like that." Her accent seemed to indicate that she was Canadian.

"Didn't you just say, 'Ah, it's you'?"
"Yeah. You were here for one of the exhibits."
"Two years ago."
"With Leonard Huffman." She pointed unnecessarily at the books he was still holding.
"You remember that?"
"You're his son." She smiled, her eyes still a little drowsy. "He told you?"
"Is it a secret?"
Niall hesitated before returning the volumes to their places on the shelf. "It was to me, for about twenty-nine years," he said softly. Before she could respond, he asked: "Is this your gallery?"
She nodded and came out from behind the counter. "Annie Keller." Annie stuck out her hand, and he shook it. "I've known your father for at least thirty years, from when he was still the photo editor at Time magazine. That's where we met."
She looked younger than she had to be, more like she was in her mid-forties. Her long hair, dyed black, had been pulled back in a braid that was looped over her shoulder. Her makeup was minimal yet effective, and she wore snug, black clothes, which suited her lean physique nicely.
"I'll come back again soon to see one of your exhibits," he commented evasively, backing toward the door.
"Don't you want to buy a book?"
"Oh. No. I just wanted to look at them."
He could tell she did not believe a word he said. "Alright," she said.
He felt like he needed to add something more. "I just happened to be in the area. I…" Niall's words failed him.
Annie walked back to the counter to reclaim her steaming mug. The scent of coffee wafted Niall's way. "You don't owe me an explanation," she replied.
He forged on anyway. "I had all of his books, except the last one. It was coming out around the time I met him. After that, I threw them all away. Now, I'd like to buy one as a replacement. One or two."

Annie shook her head, chuckling quietly. "Threw them away, huh? Pick out a book and take it with you. My treat."

"What? No, I can't accept it."

Annie cocked her head a little, staring slightly past him. She seemed to be considering something, her coffee still cradled in her hand. Niall decided not to interrupt her thoughts. He waited a minute, but then the silence grew uncomfortable, so he grabbed the volume that stood closest at hand. Diane Arbus of all people. A young man in curlers stared up at him, his gaze resembling the one Annie was sending across the room.

"Niall," she said finally.

"Oh. You even know my name."

She put her mug down, stifling a yawn before getting back to her feet. "Come with me. I want to show you something."

"What?"

"Unpublished material. Come on!"

He followed her through the shop and gallery to a back door. They went up a staircase and along a narrow corridor to an office stuffed full of shelves holding mountains of books and binders. Despite these, the room did not seem messy, just very full.

The woman made a beeline for a certain shelf and reached up for a binder that stood on the uppermost level to the far right. She was tall enough that she did not need a chair for added height. Niall could not tell any difference between this binder and the others, but after quickly flipping through the pages, she found what she was looking for. She asked him to sit down and wait. He heard her move down the corridor and enter the adjacent room. After five minutes, she returned with several black-and-white photos in the A4 format. She placed one of them on the desk: a trench in which a seemingly endless line of soldiers was standing. Not a single face could be seen, only steel helmets. A tank was parked on one side of the trench.

"The armored regiment battle of Susangerd. Iran-Iraq War," Niall commented.

She fanned the other photos out on the desk. An entire field of helmets, as if the soldiers had yanked them off their heads and thrown them aside, saying: 'That's enough, we're leaving.' Soldiers celebrating in front of tanks. Soldiers dead in front of tanks. A very young soldier, who looked like a child, with wide-open eyes and missing legs.

"I know these photos," he declared. She had said something about unpublished material.

"Leonard was there when it started. He wanted to be there for the whole war."

"I know." He was gradually losing interest.

"He was injured at Susangerd. Did you know that, too?"

Niall shook his head.

"He never made a big deal about it. He and some other journalists found themselves caught in the line of fire. One of them threw himself in front of him, enabling him to reach cover. Leonard took a bullet and spent several weeks in the hospital. The one who saved him died, shot through the head."

"Bloody hell."

"A journalist from New York, early thirties. Younger than Leonard was at the time. But unlike Leonard, he was married and had a daughter."

"Ah, I see where you're going."

"Whenever a war photographer is shot, people usually make a big deal out of it. But Leonard didn't want that, because the other man had died for him," she explained. "It affected him in other ways. He was not prepared to do that to a woman. Or to a child. He loved his work, which may have been the only thing in this life he could and can fully love."

"How did he cope with all of it?"

Annie shrugged. "I have no idea. He's the only one who can answer that. All I can tell you is what he once said in an interview, which you've probably already heard: He absorbed all the horror and agony he ever saw or heard or smelled. There was no room for anything else inside of him."

Niall nodded wearily. The images that Leonard had captured in his pictures were only a fraction of what he had actually experienced. The photographs represented nothing more than what he was prepared to share with the world. Any thoughts about what had been going on in his mind as he shot the pictures were nothing more than conjectures. But what did this have to do with Niall, he wondered, with the fact that they had hidden the truth from him? Were humility and gratitude the only acceptable responses to the fact that he was Leonard's biological son? Maybe he had a small army of other children out there who were also unaware of their link to Leonard. Maybe…

"One more thing," Annie broke into his thoughts. "The young man who saved him during the war—his name was Niall."

She placed the final picture in front of him. The unpublished photo she had mentioned showed a blonde man in his thirties wearing a bulletproof vest and a helmet. He was lying on the ground, his arms flung wide, and his legs bent at strange angles. A single gunshot wound was visible over his wide-open left eye, and blood was streaming down his face and neck.

"I'm sure you've heard this quote from Leonard: 'I take pictures of the most horrifying things that people can do to each other, and I do that so we'll never forget, so we can finally realize why we have to stop.'"

Niall nodded. He knew the quote. Everyone did.

"We can go back downstairs now. Take his books with you. All of them. And don't ever throw even one of them away."

He had no idea what to say. He felt ashamed and upset, also furious, but this time at himself.

He followed Annie back to the shop, where they stopped at the shelf holding Leonard's books. She gathered one of each title, then pulled two large bags out from under the counter, slid the books into them, and held them out to him. Niall handed her fifty pounds in return. It was all he had on him, but there was no way he was going to walk out without paying Annie something.

After he said goodbye, he went back to Oxford Circus. As he waited on the tube platform, he came to the decision that he would give Leonard and his project a chance.

12

In reality, he was giving himself the chance. This was exactly the kind of project he had long wanted to do--a socially relevant film, a statement. He had already met both terrorists and was connected to the subject. It was his subject, and he would be foolish to let it slip away.

Niall called the production company that had hired him to make the documentary about the underground rivers. He had hoped they could postpone the filming, but the producer refused, although the team that would be affected was quite small. The only possible way for Niall to get out of the contract was to find a replacement. "And make sure it's someone who can actually hold a camera, alright?!" the man had demanded.

Niall placed call after call, until he reached a woman who had just had a baby and was grateful for any shoots that did not mean she had to travel. The producer was unhappy, although the woman had a good reputation. "Not as good as yours," he growled. "Her name isn't all over the newspapers."

That was the moment Niall realized he had made the right choice. His next call was to Leonard to accept the job. Thirty minutes afterward, he was again on the subway on his way back to the station.

Leonard met him in the lobby. "I'm glad you—"

Niall interrupted him. "Let's not make a big deal about it, okay?"

His father nodded, but he could not keep the corners of his mouth from twitching. Amusement, perhaps. "And your other project?"

"I found someone else to cover it. I'm sure she'll do a much better job than me."

Leonard looked as if he wanted to hug Niall, but fortunately, he was able to stop himself. "Let's head upstairs. I've told the editorial team about your decision. We're already in the process of putting together a team."

He followed Leonard into a conference room: giant screens, pleasant space, pale, inviting furniture. A variety of drinks were spread on the table: juices, lemonades, sparkling beverages. Fruit, too. Three men in suits and a dark-haired woman in jeans and a t-shirt were already waiting at the table, their phones and tablets arranged in front of them.

The group had curious, interested faces. It was a very different feeling from the one he had experienced at New Scotland Yard, and a very different setting. Niall's thoughts turned to how he could play these distinct atmospheres off each other in the film editing process, the kinds of lighting he would use.

One of the men was the station's program director, while another handled the political team, and the third one was in charge of nonfiction programming. Niall did not fully grasp the distinction between the men's positions, but it seemed that the three of them would not play much of a role in the daily filming process. Leonard would act as the editor. The name of the woman with the somber, somewhat brooding gaze was Beth Sagan, and she was the film's producer.

Niall was told that his team would also include three research assistants and a production assistant. He would have at his disposal any technological tools he needed, and the entire post-production process would be handled by top-notch people at the station. He would also have a camera assistant, who would take care of the sound, as well. It would be a small, agile team, they said. Niall asked if Laura could be brought on board as the production manager.

"Laura who?" the program director asked.

"From the morning show. She's their production assistant," Leonard explained.

"Ah, the—"

"She has a lot going for her," Niall cut in. "And is too good for what she's doing right now. Besides, I've known her for some time." He stretched the truth a little, in the hope of increasing the odds that they would assign her to his project.

"I didn't think your request had anything to do with her looks." The man laughed, but nobody joined in. The producer, who was an attractive woman around forty, grimaced, as if she were having to watch a crow play with roadkill.

"What's your plan?" Leonard asked. "Do you have any ideas about how you'd like to start?"

Niall said: "I would like to shoot inside the prison. I'd also like to interview Farooq and Cemal as soon as he's in a condition to talk. As for the background story--family and friends, how the two of them grew up, which mosques they attended, other radicals…"

Beth nodded. "We can get started on those details right away."

The small group dispersed. Niall wondered what would happen to the fresh fruit and drinks. No one grabbed even an apple on their way out.

Beth led him to a large office. Three young men who looked like college students introduced themselves as the researchers. Books on Islam, Salafism, Palestine, the Arab world, the Islamic State, and al-Qaeda were piled up around their computers. They explained that they had been working with that constellation of topics for a long time and that they had already pulled together some material for him.

Beth gave him a tour of the building: the old part of the recording studio, which was protected under historic preservation laws, and the newer, more avant garde part where he would be doing most of his work. She invited him to her office, which was large enough for two. It was rather dark and was crammed full of electronics, almost its own post-production studio. She explained that the windows were soundproofed and faced north, so it never got too terribly hot there, unlike the offices with southern exposure.

Beth's office lacked personal touches. Niall thought there might have been things in the drawers or the closet, but nothing sat visible. She pointed him toward a computer before calling the IT department, which set him up with a password and a personal email address. An hour later, his head was buzzing. When Laura stepped into the office and grinned at him, he felt pure relief.

She blushed a little as she said: "Thank you, Niall. I'm so happy to be part of this!"

Niall nodded at her and then looked across to Beth: "Do you know each other?"

"Just in passing." Beth greeted Laura with a nod.

"I wouldn't even be here if it weren't for Laura," Niall admitted. "She convinced me to do this."

Beth cocked one eyebrow but said nothing.

Laura jumped in quickly, "We've gotten permission to shoot tomorrow in the prison."

"That fast?" Niall asked.

"They're quite anxious to show that the prison conditions are acceptable."

"Acceptable? Right."

"Leonard called them personally."

The prestige of the station. The power of famous names. Niall was uncertain if he was supposed to feel impressed or disgusted. He decided not to say anything, opting instead to ask Laura about the filming schedule. She sat down on a chair against the wall by the door before explaining that Cemal was finally stable but still in intensive care, so they would chat with Farooq first.

"Our shoot in the prison is subject to certain constraints. Heightened security checks, but also increased security around our work. At first, they wanted us to 'submit our material for inspection,' which won't be happening. As usual, they'll still let us in. Our appointment is for eight tomorrow morning."

"Then we'll need to leave around six," Beth commented.

"Six is perhaps a little late," Laura rejoined.

"Come on, Laura. Don't ask us to show up half an hour early just to get us there on time," Niall cut in.

"I'm serious. I only ask studio guests to arrive early. The drive will take us at least an hour, and then we'll have to get through the security check. You always have to assume that something could go wrong along the way. Five-thirty."

Beth shrugged, a wisp of a smile playing around her lips. "Well, Niall, this is the way you wanted it. She's the boss."

Leonard was standing in front of Niall's building, looking as if he had suddenly found himself in an open-air museum. His hands were shoved casually in his pockets, and he had moved his head back to study the building's facade. It was a seven-story building, clad in washed concrete slabs, punctuated at regular intervals by very small windows. The newer, similarly sized, multi-family buildings constructed nearby had slightly nicer facades and considerably larger windows. Even the balconies were bigger. Niall had no idea what the apartments were like on the inside, but they had to be a step up from his own.

"Seen enough?" he asked Leonard, who spun around.

"Oh, there you are. I wanted to talk to you, in private, without the others around."

"Why?" Niall sidled past him and unlocked the exterior door. Cold air, reeking of food, alcohol, nicotine, and sweat assailed him. It was always colder in the foyer than outside. The smell never changed.

"May I come in?" Leonard asked.

Niall hesitated. He had asked without any trace of entitlement in his voice. "Would you leave if I said 'no'?"

Leonard nodded, his hands still in his pockets. "Too bad. I'll just get going. But we need to chat tomorrow, whenever it works for you." He turned around and headed toward the street.

Niall called after him. "It's okay, come on in."

His father turned back around. "Are you sure?" He seemed happy.

"Come on, before I change my mind."

Leonard hurried back and followed Niall up to the fifth floor. Niall rarely took the elevator, and that day was no exception.

"Most of the time it stinks in there," he explained. "Trust me, you don't want to know what it smells like."

Leonard did not reply, and Niall felt like he needed to offer an excuse. "I can make the rent for this apartment even when things aren't going so well, financially speaking. Besides, Brixton isn't a bad neighborhood. Not anymore. And the transportation connections to the city are good. I like it here."

"I didn't say anything," Leonard remarked.

"Just in your head." Niall opened his apartment door, mentally running through his options for quickly dealing with the worst of the mess.

"Let me pick up a little," he said.

"You don't need to."

"But I want to. It's embarrassing."

"It looks worse over at my place." Leonard offered the socially expected lie.

"Give me a few minutes, okay? Just sit down over—" He broke off when he saw that the photo books, he had gotten at the gallery were lying on the armchair. Huffman picked up the pile to clear some space to sit, and then, unsure what else to do, he balanced them on his lap.

Niall grabbed them from him and piled them on top of other photo volumes on his bookshelf. He then gathered his scattered clothes and stuffed them into the washing machine in the bathroom before hurriedly clearing all the dirty dishes into the kitchen. Last of all, he made his bed, then took a seat on the couch. "Sorry. I don't get many visitors."

"No worries." Leonard smiled at his son.

"So," Niall continued, "what can I do for you?"

Leonard pointed at the bookcase. "You have all my books."

Niall shrugged. "You're not here to make sure I've done my homework."

"I wanted to thank you for taking on this film."

"You arrange a job for me and then thank me for it? It should be the other way around." Niall shook his head. "Is that it? You're here so I can thank you for this?"

< 90 >

Leonard looked hurt. "I'm sorry you'd think that of me. For the two years we've known each other, I've tried to make it clear that I'm not your enemy."

"Yeah, I know that. 'You wouldn't have had such a wonderful childhood if I'd been your dad. You were really lucky to have the father you did. I'm not the kind of person who would be good in a family,' etcetera. We've been through all this."

"Niall, your mother also thought it was better that way. Even your father, your other father, wanted this."

"Would it really have been so bad if I had at least known?"

"You might have missed out on something. What if I had died? How would you have coped with that?"

"I don't know. For various reasons, I was never given a chance to find out."

The older man exhaled slowly. "Three adults come to a joint decision and think it's the right one. In the end, it isn't as good as they thought it was. That happens. Now two of them are gone, unfortunately, and all I can do is try to sweep up the shambles we managed to leave behind. I've been trying to do this for two years, and I will keep at it as long as I live. I just wish sometimes that you'd at least give me a chance."

Niall said nothing.

"I'm here to thank you. Honestly. For the sole reason that I happen to know how hard it must be for you to accept this project because of me. If someone else had offered it to you, it would have been easier for you."

"Probably so."

"And you walked away from another project to take this one, which couldn't have been easy either. You had a contract."

"Yes, but it's all worked out. Anything else?"

"I wanted to tell you that I believe in you because I can see how talented you are. But you don't capitalize on that."

"And now you want to help me do that. So, you are here for me to thank you after all, right?"

"No!" Leonard himself seemed surprised at the intensity of his reaction. He continued more calmly. "I know you're afraid of being compared to me, but you've accepted this project anyway. I thought you might at least shake my hand."

Niall gazed out the window which faced the green strip that the apartment managers pretentiously called a park. The strip divided the apartment building from the road. "It's simply what I want to do," he said, wearily. "That's why I agreed."

Leonard leaned forward, propping his arms on his knees. "Niall, you're going to make a good film. I know you will. However, you could make something incredible out of it. In the end, a finished film is worth more than a college degree."

Niall studied him, suspiciously. "What do you mean?"

"Pete and I used to talk sometimes."

The fact that Leonard had always taken an interest in his life did not make things any better. Quite the opposite—the vision of his two fathers secretly talking to each other about him hurt. He turned away and fell silent.

Leonard continued. "Niall, listen. You have the technical ability, as well as the talent, and you want to do this. You could make something amazing."

"Amazing, huh? And what if it's not? What if the film's a flop? Gets bad reviews? Doesn't win even a single prize from any of documentary film festivals around the world? What then?"

"Then nothing! Except I can't imagine that you—"

"Stop. I can imagine it just fine. They'll say, 'Oh, Niall Stuart's films fall far short of his father's photos. Leonard Huffman's got to feel sorry for his son." That's exactly what I can imagine! You know what, this was a shitty idea. Let's just call it quits. Right now."

"Niall!"

He flinched. His father had yelled so loudly his ears were ringing. "Wow," he said. "You'd think I was sixteen and had screwed up something."

"Yes, that's exactly how you're acting! Obstinate and childish and stubborn—"

"I think obstinate and stubborn are synonyms."

Leonard stared at him, jaw slack, but didn't say anything. He rubbed his face and shook his head. Then he stood up and stepped into the kitchen without asking, returning with a glass of water. "I've earned this," he said, draining the glass in a single gulp. "We probably would have handled this better when you were sixteen." He sounded calm and subdued again, as was typical for him.

Niall did not respond.

"There's nothing worse than parents who wish their child was different than they are. Or who want mini copies of themselves, of their ideal selves. I'm not interested in that. I've achieved enough in this life. I don't need children whose photos I can show off to other people. I have a son, and I'm proud of him. Because he's talented and a great person, from what I can tell and from what his parents have told me about him. Now he has a chance to make an important, major documentary. I can give him this chance. And I think he should stick with it. Niall, do it. You'll just be punishing yourself if you walk away."

Niall gulped. He felt ashamed and tried not to show it. "I can't," he said.

"Sure, you can."

"Why do you think that?"

"I'm old enough to recognize who's got the spark and who doesn't."

"Aha. Well then."

"You realized right away what Laura could do, didn't you?"

Niall nodded.

"Alright, then listen to me. You can do this. You just have to decide what's important to you and what you want to tell. I have seen things nobody could ever put into words, and even if someone had tried, those words never could have been as powerful as the pictures I took. You can do even more. In your film, you can combine the most penetrating words with the most powerful pictures, with your pictures. Forget my work, forget everything else. Do your own thing. Show everybody out there what is really going on in this country. Now get on with it."

ZOË BECK

SATURDAY 13

The next morning, Beth, Laura, and a lanky boy with blonde, shoulder-length hair named Ken—the production van driver and Niall's camera assistant—beat him to the meeting point. All he had to do was climb into the van, and they set off. Laura was proven right in her careful planning. They had to wait a long time before they were admitted inside the prison. The security control officers were meticulously thorough, and by the time they were led into the pre-trial block, it was almost eight o'clock. The cameras ran the entire time, because Niall wanted to capture the long walk through the prison complex. They would have to blur out the faces of the guards and alter the voices, but the guards mattered less to him than the building itself-the depressing corridors, the intimidating bureaucracy to which the visitors had to subject themselves, the austere walls, the bleakness of the entire apparatus.

He had slept very little the night before. The conversation with his father had upset him, and he had tried until long past midnight to prep for the filming with Farooq. At some point, he had abandoned the summaries from the research assistants because he could not concentrate, and he felt like they were not helping. He kept seeing Farooq in his mind, how the blood had dribbled down his hands and how he had kept his eyes firmly on Niall's cell phone. His actual name had been Frank Holeywell. Where had Frank been at that moment?

Niall had learned things about his background. His father was a paramedic, currently unemployed and living in Bromley. His mother worked for a Christian charity organization and lived on the other end of London, in Edgeware. Frank's parents had gotten divorced when he was fourteen, and he had obviously not dealt well with it. Soon after the divorce, he'd quit school, started and then quit an apprenticeship as a nurse, started and then quit an apprenticeship as a cook. He'd worked for a while on a construction site then started training as a cook again and stuck it out. He had quit his job a few months earlier, without explanation, and it was unclear what he had done after that. Niall planned to find out. Who had connected him with Islamist circles? How had he even come to be interested in Islam?

Niall felt miserable back in Belmarsh Prison. Catching sight of the guard who had thrown him to the floor and hurt him, his stomach lurched. The man passed him without acknowledgement, as if he had never seen him before. Perhaps he really did not recognize him; perhaps people wearing civilian clothes all looked the same to him.

"Everything okay?" asked Laura, whose talents seemed to include telepathy. Or had she picked up on the fact that his fingers were trembling, which seemed more likely?

"I'm simply imagining how it must be for someone who's wrongfully locked up in here for years. That is, if that actually happens."

"Anyone would feel nervous right now," Laura replied.

He looked at her, but she waved him off.

"I know. I'm trying to get away from the morning program niceties."

"Thanks." He and Ken set up the camera which would record the full-body footage of Farooq. With the second camera, Niall would take handheld shots and close-ups. He was glad that they had to hurry. The tension was eating him alive. What if Farooq refused to say anything to him? What if he couldn't look the man in the eye?

They were just setting up the sound equipment when Farooq was led in. Let it run, Niall signaled to his assistant, who nodded mutely. Like a boxer entering the ring, he wanted Farooq in the frame from the very first second. It was clear to him that the man would be staging every detail of his self-projection, and he did not want to miss any of it. After stepping into the room, Farooq remained standing at first. He took everything in with a calm, disdainful smile, and his body language made it clear that he was going to be the one to set the tone.

The two guards accompanying him stayed in the room, which already felt packed. The room held nothing except a table and three chairs, and the only colors in sight were gray tones. Instead of a window, glass blocks had been built into the wall. Even on the prettiest, sunniest of days, the atmosphere in there would remain dismal.

Niall happened to glance up at the ceiling at the very moment someone switched on the neon lights. Everyone squinted, as if they were seeing light for the first time after days in darkness. Ken checked the camera angle on the tripod. The faces of the guards were not supposed to be filmed. Farooq sat down, placed his manacled hands on the table, and nodded amiably at Niall.

Niall introduced everyone by name while filming Farooq's hands with his handheld camera. He then said: "Farooq, do you know who I am?"

"Of course."

"I spent a night in here, as well" Niall said.

"They arrested you, too?"

"Yes, but then they let me go."

"The system is capricious," Farooq theorized.

"How are you being treated?" Niall asked.

"I behave myself, so I'm being treated alright."

"Sure. In other words, the guards aren't beating you?"

"I'll be there when we liberate Palestine, and then I'll be able to live in my own country."

"You're currently sitting in detention. Or whatever it's called."

"Not for much longer." Farooq grinned.

"No? Have they already filed charges?"

"No."

"Do you have an attorney?"

"No."

"Have they asked if you want one?" Niall noticed the guards' growing nervousness.

"I don't need one."

"Okay. But you think you're getting out of here?"

"We will fight and win and liberate our brothers and sisters." Farooq leaned forward and seemed about to reach out to Niall. "Thank you very much, brother, for recording us. And thank you for continuing to help us today."

"How am I helping you?"

"You are. We have to carry the word out into the world. Our friends in the Islamic State are very grateful to you. Soon we will be able to free Turkey, Palestine, and other areas."

Niall tried hard to stay calm. Interviews were a new thing for him. Distinctly and loudly, he explained, "I recorded you because you killed someone. That's why you're here. How did I help you?"

Farooq grinned. "Man, you have to keep the goal in sight. It's not about me. We have to show the world what we're doing and that we're serious about it. People need to learn that we're everywhere."

"You recorded yourselves," Niall pointed out. "You didn't need me for that."

Farooq shook his head, twisting his mouth scornfully. "We saw you there, with your phone. We knew you were recording us. You'd been following us since the bridge."

"You noticed me?"

"Of course, man."

"But you didn't know I was a filmmaker."

"Didn't matter. You had your phone and were recording us, and you looked like someone who wouldn't screw it all up. The way you stood there on the bridge, looking for just the right angle. It was obvious you knew what you were doing. We need good films. Cemal said that. 'We need good films more than a good message,' he said. When we get out of here, he'll combine your footage with his. It's going to make an amazing film. He has the close-ups. It's going to be fantastic! He already knows what music he'll use."

"You have it all planned out?"

"Yeah."

"You couldn't know that I—"

"Somebody's always willing to shoot stuff with their phone," Farooq cut in.

Niall needed a moment to breathe and calm back down. He pretended to skim the notes on his phone before asking: "Had you met the guy beforehand? Did you search him out specifically?"

"Hey, man. I swear by Allah that every Englishman is our enemy."

"There are currently efforts underway in Parliament to acknowledge Palestine as an independent state. It isn't that far yet, but—"

"You are Palestine's enemy." Farooq simply kept talking. "You're friends with America. You don't want Islam to exist, you fight against it, which means that all of you are our enemies."

"You just claimed that I helped you."

"But you're an infidel." Farooq was getting angry. "You're on the wrong side."

"But you let infidels help in your cause?"

Farooq gave this some thought but obviously didn't know what to say, so he returned to his previous point. "We're going to fight the infidels, destroy your infrastructure, and push you out of our countries."

"You're English, just like me."

"You've insulted me."

"Why? You were born here, went to school here. Your parents are—"

"My blood," he interrupted abruptly, standing up, "is the blood of Palestine. And you? You're going to die. We will kill you." Chin raised, Farooq turned around and strode to the door. One of the guards stepped forward to open it.

"You're English. Who do you think you're fooling? Frank

Holeywell, you're just lying to yourself because you don't know what else to do," Niall yelled after the prisoner before he could leave the room.

Farooq paused for few seconds, then jerked himself back around and lunged at Niall. The guards grabbed his arms as Farooq screamed and struggled against them. He called on his God for help and then switched back to the curses he hoped would rain down on Niall and the guards. Niall trained his camera on the other man, filming as two well-trained men worked hard to restrain the prisoner bound in handcuffs. They pushed him against the wall and called for back-up.

Two other guards came. Then, there were four of them, with Farooq, out of control, in their midst. Niall could no longer see him, just hear him. All he could see of the guards were their broad backs. It was impossible to say whose leg, whose arm was doing what, until Farooq's yells became a whimper and the knot of men dissolved. One of the guards spun around, made a beeline for Niall, and tore the camera out of his hand.

"Confiscated," he said, quickly disappearing through the steel door before Niall could react. Two other guards pulled Farooq up off the floor and dragged him away.

Niall called after him: "Farooq? Everything alright? Are you okay?" He received no answer. The remaining guard seized the other camera, along with the tripod.

"Hey!" Ken hollered. "I need a receipt for that!"

Beth said: "Ken, drop it. We're leaving. I'll take care of everything."

Other guards showed up. "Get out of here," one of them said.

The team packed together what was left and let themselves be herded along the corridors. This time, getting out is faster than getting in, Niall thought. Last time, it had been the other way around.

In the van, he said: "I can't do this. I'm all wrong for it. I can film stuff, but I can't do interviews."

"You need to be better prepared," Beth remarked.

"I was prepared. I had no idea he was going to lose it. Am I supposed to act as if I believe the garbage he's spouting?"

"Basically, yes. You're making a documentary, not moderating a talk show. Let the people talk. If they're crazy—as most of them are—let them say whatever. You're supposed to show them as they are."

"But he—"

"Niall," Beth interrupted. "You insulted his heritage."

"Damn it, he's English."

"Farooq's mother is Palestinian."

Niall shook his head. "No. No. She works for some Christian organization. I read that last night—"

"There are Christians in Palestine. Only a few, though, because most of them have immigrated. His mother is one of them."

"Shit."

"Yes."

"Shit." He stared out the window and saw that they were in Greenwich. The last time he had driven along this stretch, he had been in a prison transport van. "I just can't do it."

"Sure, you can. I'll help you," Laura said.

"We all will," Beth added.

"I totally screwed it up," Niall declared. "We don't even have the footage of what happened back there. I'll get out. There's no point."

Ken pulled over on the side of the street. "You want to get out? Am I driving too fast?" he asked, anxiously.

"No, Ken, I meant out of the project."

"Oh." Ken nodded, put the van in gear, and merged back into traffic. "Good. I wondered." After a minute of silence, he added, "It's not true, though, that we don't have any footage."

Niall looked at him. "What?"

"I took out the memory card. It's all on there, up until he yanked the camera away from you. That's when I thought it would be a good idea to grab the card. You never know."

"We have everything? Even the part when they were beating him?"

"Yeah."

FADE TO BLACK

 Niall heard applause coming from the backseat where Laura and Beth were sitting. 📱

14

He met Carl in Chinatown for supper. "A real job?" his uncle asked.

"No, a gig."

"Did your father arrange this?"

"Don't call him that." Although he himself called him that. Carl nodded. "Sorry, my boy."

The restaurant where they were offered a fresh, modern take on traditional Chinese cuisine and claimed to have the best dim sum in the country, if not all of Europe. Every table was occupied, and a constant stream of people was being sent away. The acoustics were horrible, and the lighting reminded him of a slaughterhouse, but the guests seemed to love the place.

"It's okay." Niall poked halfheartedly at his plate. "I have to get used to it."

"I found an attorney for you," Carl remarked, pulling a business card out of his briefcase before pushing it across the table.

"What did he say? Is it worth filing a suit?"

Carl nodded. "If only to make the public aware of what happened. He says that police violence is always a hot topic. Just like police racism."

"Well, I'm not exactly a victim of racial profiling."

"Indirectly." Carl turned around and gestured for the waiter to bring him another bottle of beer. Since it was the weekend, he was the only one wearing a dark suit. All the other guests were casual, but that did not seem to bother him. He acted as relaxed as he would at home.

"Indirectly," he repeated once he had turned back toward

Niall. "They thought you belonged to some jihadist organization, and that's why they mistreated you."

"You mean that a lawsuit would have a good chance?" "Absolutely. What do you want? Money?"

Niall rolled his eyes.

"Ah, noble goals!" Carl smiled. "I'll pass that along to your future attorney. Meet him, chat, see what you can do. In your case, I would tell a couple of your colleagues from the station about it. Something like this needs publicity."

"I know that the—"

"No," Carl shook his head vehemently. "Don't start with me. Up in Bradford, there are ongoing complaints. Because of all the terrorist paranoia, the police are going after innocent people without just cause. On the other hand, somewhere else in Yorkshire, they simply stood by and watched as a well-organized band of Pakistanis raped several English girls and forced them into prostitution. They were afraid of being accused of racism because every lead they had took them to the Pakistanis. So, they simply squeezed their eyes shut and told the girls to go put on something decent."

"I read about that. What a nightmare."

"Yes."

"But you said it yourself. Pakistanis. English girls. There's more than enough racism packed in that description."

"You think so? They see themselves as Pakistanis. At least, most of them do."

"Most of them have British passports."

"And what has that done for us? For centuries, we English have traveled the entire world, conquered distant lands, brought foreign cultures back home with us. And in all this time, the Englishman has not managed to learn how to feel anything but superior." He smiled. "We're afraid of what's different from us. And nobody knows what they should be doing. Promoting other cultures, or urging them to fully assimilate?

There are discussions about whether there should even be something like Chinatown. Some neighborhoods are getting street signs in the languages of the local residents. One person argues that this helps people feel welcome and find their way around. Others claim there's no need for such measures. Learn to speak English or at least get to know English-speaking people. It's a form of ghettoization.

The reason," he said, breaking off to thank the waiter for the beer that had just been delivered, "the reason for this is that the group, not the individual, is being considered. Foreigners as a homogenous group. But that's not what they are."

Niall nodded. "Sounds as if you've given this a lot of thought."

Carl dismissed that with a wave. "You have no idea what all we see and hear over at the Ministry of Health. Gives you plenty to think about."

Niall was not interested in continuing the line of conversation or listening to what Carl might say next. He was fully aware of Carl's conservative opinions. "Thank you for taking care of the attorney."

"Of course. I'm just happy you came out of it in one piece. Still can't believe they wouldn't even let you make a phone call!"

"I wanted to call you. I knew you'd be able to help."

Carl beamed. "I'm always glad to help you as I can. How are you doing otherwise? Be honest. Want to come stay with us for a few days? We'd be happy to have you."

"How's your wife doing?"

"Susan's great, thanks. But you haven't answered my question. How are you?"

"Good. Really am."

"I can't imagine how upset you must be!" Carl waved at the waiter again, this time to order more dim sum.

"Doesn't she feed you at home?" Niall asked with a grin.

"Don't be rude." Carl grinned back. "Honestly, I love this restaurant. I would move in if they'd let me. Where were we? Upset. It has to have been a roller coaster ride for you."

"I don't know, haven't thought about it."

Carl leaned back and studied him closely. "You know what? As the years pass, I think you look more and more like Leonard."

"I can't do anything about that."

"It could be worse. People always thought he was handsome. Even today still—how old is he actually? At least seventy, right?"

"Seventy-one. Exactly forty years older than me."

"Seventy-one, and he still has his fingers in all the pots. I'm turning fifty-five, and I want to retire already." Carl laughed. "Good genes, boy. Don't complain."

"Carl…"

"Come on, I've known you since you ruined your mother's figure. I'm allowed to say that."

Niall had to laugh. "You're impossible!"

"And I like it that way. I have an amazingly dull job, so it's no surprise that I sometimes cut loose."

Now both of them were laughing.

"How are things going with the film?" Carl asked, once the soup was served.

"Great!" Niall held his gaze for a moment, but then shook his head. "Not at all well, to be honest. They confiscated our equipment this morning. We interviewed one of the attackers. He lost it, and the guards beat him up—"

"You got it all on film?"

"Yes."

"No wonder they took your stuff. Guards beating a prisoner in front of a running camera. Why are you grinning so smugly?"

"Oh, nothing."

Carl wiped his mouth with his napkin and leaned forward, conspiratorially. "Did you smuggle something out? Hmm?" He winked at him.

Niall pursed his lips but said nothing.

"Record it secretly with your phone, did you? A hidden camera that the security guards didn't notice?"

Niall shrugged cryptically. "Who knows?"

Carl sent him an admiring glance. "You're a sly one. That's all I can say." And before Niall could respond, "So what happens next? Will you be getting your cameras back?"

"Laura spent the whole day on the phone. She's the production assistant. If anyone can get the cameras back, she's the one. Tomorrow we'll pick up with the attackers' families and environments. The other one is still in the hospital, but he is ready to talk with us now. We'll have to see what comes of it. Then, I'll have to decide how deeply I want to dig."

"Exciting, huh?"

"All brand new to me."

"Are you enjoying it?"

"The reason for it isn't exactly nice."

"You know what I mean."

Niall nodded. "I'm scared, but I'll see it through."

"Very good. I'll get the check, and then we can go conquer the next bar. Deal?"

"Absolutely."

Around three o'clock, Niall collapsed on his sofa. Far from sober, he fumbled around with his phone to set the alarm. Then he discovered a text from Beth, asking him to call her back. He typed that he had only just then seen the text. He had hardly hit send when Beth called.

"Don't you ever sleep?" he asked.

"You sound drunk."

"Oh, no doubt about that. I was out with my uncle. We were in Chinatown, and then we were—"

"Niall," she interrupted him.

"What? Sorry, I kinda ramble when I've had too much to drink."

She was quiet for a moment before continuing, "Cemal Bayraktar is dead."

"Oh, crap. He didn't make it after all."

"He was improving and was transferred out of intensive care around noon."

"I was told they had him on some major meds. They probably moved him too soon."

"Maybe," Beth said. "But supposedly none of his vital organs were injured."

Niall tried to concentrate. "Doesn't fit. You suspect something, don't you?"

"Yes."

"Alright. We'll talk again later once I've slept some."

"Niall, you know what I'm saying, right?"

He focused. "You think that somebody else was involved."

"I don't have a good feeling about this."

"Oh, you can't trust feelings in situations like this. What are those shy, brittle things people are always so eager to have? Oh, I know. Facts."

"I'm not done."

"What else?"

"Farooq hung himself in his cell."

With a single blow, his pleasant, cozy feeling of intoxication vaporized. "Hung himself?"

"Yes. Did he strike you as a suicide risk?"

"I don't know. I don't understand people like him, but I wouldn't say he was suicidal. Otherwise, he'd probably have signed up for a suicide attack. Or how do things like that work?"

"He had talked about going to Palestine. Did that sound to you like someone planning to kill themselves?"

"They beat him up. Perhaps that was the final straw."

"Niall, you were in a cell, too. Could you have killed yourself in there?"

He thought about the sparse furnishings. About the furniture screwed in place, the absent doorknob. There had been no bars on the windows, not even a window latch. The ongoing suicide watch, the constant stream of people checking up on him. Niall tried to imagine how someone could manage if they really could not take it anymore and wanted to end it.

Suicide had not been an acceptable behavior in that prison. A person could possibly smash their head against the wall until they were dead; however, that approach required that they have more than a bit of luck in their death wish. One would sooner end up knocking themselves out. Or someone would realize what was going on. Farooq had not been in detention long enough to obtain a weapon. Or did he have good connections? But why would he want to hang himself?

"And they're sure that he hung himself?"

"According to the official statement."

"That went out in the middle of the night?"

"Yep."

"You can't hang yourself in a cell like that."

"I know."

"Then why have they said that?" Niall asked.

Beth inhaled deeply. "Why do you think I called you?" 📱

FADE TO BLACK
15

Looking somber, Karen Wigsley, the Home Secretary under the incumbent conservative party, was sitting in the studio for the recording of a political panel show.

"We have raised the terrorist alarm level, seeing as the odds of an attack against our country have increased," she insisted emphatically to the other panelist, opposition leader Gerald Randall, whose face twitched as if he had just bitten into a lemon. The moderator's face mirrored his.

Standing at the edge of the studio between the sets, Niall was watching the discussion on a monitor. He wondered if Randall's and the moderator's grimaces were caused by what Karen had said or by the fact that her voice sometimes edged toward shrillness when she wanted to emphasize something in particular.

"She needs a voice coach," Beth commented.

"I was just thinking the same thing. But who would volunteer to tell her that?"

"Someone who's not too keen on this life. Or whose life we're not all that attached to. Any suggestions?"

Niall tried not to laugh. He had known Karen Wigsley his entire life, but he had no desire to tell Beth that. Not unless it was absolutely necessary.

He planned to leave shortly to visit Rana Ziadeh, Farooq's mother. Yesterday, she had agreed right away to give an interview.

"I haven't changed my mind," she said when Laura had called that morning to extend her condolences on the death of her son. "If you want, come on by, but please wait until after the service."

When Niall had heard that the Home Secretary was in the building to talk about the terrorist attack, he and Beth had gone straight to the studio where the taping was being done. He had not seen Karen for a very long time, not since his father's funeral. He wondered if he should wait until the end of the taping to tell her hello. Randall, the opposition leader, was just asking Karen which measures she would recommend.

"We need to move faster and harder against those returning from Syria and Iraq. The young men who are coming back are highly aggressive and extremely radicalized, and they've been trained to kill. We shouldn't delude ourselves. They are all potential killers, and in my personal opinion, we should seize all their passports."

As could have been expected, Randall and the moderator reacted negatively to the Home Secretary's comments. She rebuffed everything they had to say.

"So typical," Beth murmured to Niall. "They sit there making campaign speeches, instead of discussing how the two terrorists just happened to die in prison on the same night."

"Nobody cares about murderers dying," Niall replied.

"I'm not saying that I sympathize with the two of them, but whatever happened has to be investigated."

"Who said that it wouldn't be?"

"It will definitely be looked into officially, but unofficially, the results are already a given. Aren't they always?"

He examined her pretty, strong face with its large, dark eyes that always seemed mad, regardless of what they saw. "Beth, I've given some more thought to this. Maybe his cell was somehow different from mine, and he actually was able to hang himself."

"Nonsense." Beth gazed at him angrily, then turned back to the bickering politicians. They had begun to debate the blocking of social media profiles and the online monitoring of suspected terrorists.

Randall laughed in bewilderment. "So, first you want to confiscate the passport of anyone based on mere suspicion—"

"Not on mere suspicion! We will not make the same mistake that a certain earlier government made after the attacks on July 7," Karen cut in abruptly.

"—and with that wipe out their identification and destroy any potential connection they might feel with our country. And the internet ban on top of that? These are totalitarian measures!"

"We are long past the scatter-shot approach from a few years ago. We need to learn from those mistakes," Randall responded. "Back then, our hysteria simply served as the catalyst behind the radicalization of growing numbers of young Muslims in our own country because they no longer felt at home here. That doesn't work! Instead, we have to make sure that the root causes behind the radicalization—"

"Yeah, sure. You seem to have forgotten who made those mistakes. You were part of that government." Karen's tone had turned snarky.

"Campaigning," Beth repeated.

"I thought they were going to talk about the attack," Niall said with a shake of his head.

"You didn't really expect that, did you?"

That's why this documentary is so important, Niall thought, though he said nothing. It would have come out sounding vain. Or naive.

"The overwhelming opinion," the moderator was saying, "among the general population, as well as what you read in the blogs and from the media commentators, is that despite this attack, sharper security measures should not be taken. Above all, measures like arms deliveries to the Middle East will not be supported by the people."

"You know, all of this is quite short-sighted." The Home Secretary leaned forward and clasped her hands around her knees. "We have to stay diligent and analyze everything very carefully…"

The political threshing continued a while longer. As Beth listened with increasing frustration, Niall switched his thoughts to another track. He turned away from the monitor and scanned the room. People were working behind the cameras, taking care of the technical issues, freshening up makeup, and refilling water glasses for the studio guests. None of them seemed to be listening, while nobody in front of the cameras seemed to care even a little about what had really happened four days before in Vauxhall Gardens or why Paul Ferguson had had to die. Or why the two attackers were equally dead.

Beth grabbed Niall's arm and pointed to the monitor: "Here it comes."

"But that's just the point," Randall remarked. "Frustrated young people, like Farooq and Cemal, without employment, without money, without opportunities have no prospects in life, but they are full of energy and have no idea what to do with it. They long for honor and recognition, but we can't offer them that. IS can, or, at least, claims it can. That's where we need to focus. We need to create opportunities and become part of that dialogue. We have to make it clear to these people that this is their home, not the Islamic State."

"So, did he understand something, after all?" Beth murmured. Unfortunately, the moment that could have turned the conversation in the right direction vanished as quickly as it had appeared. The moderator had turned to a studio guest Niall had not noticed.

"Professor Haynes, what are your thoughts on this? You recently published a book titled The Path to Jihad in which you discuss why jihad is so attractive, to young men especially."

A skinny, dark-haired man around forty, Haynes looked rather sallow and unhealthy as he held his book up awkwardly for the camera. He then repeated what Randall had said, though his version was more complicated. He talked about bullying in the schools, deficient group identities, and insufficient integration. They did not devote even twenty seconds to the attackers, and Paul Ferguson was not mentioned even once. It was all campaigning and book marketing.

Niall tugged on Beth's sleeve and pointed at the studio exit. He no longer cared to watch the show through to the end. "Come on, let's go back to the office."

"Just a second." Her eyes remained fixed on the monitor. Impatiently, his gaze wandered across the back of the stage, down the halls, and over the doors before returning to the pallid Haynes. "Who's actually responsible for picking the studio guests?"

"The show's producer."

"What is this professor doing here?"

"He's here to talk about the bigger picture. He's supposed to convey the relevance of everything and provide balance to the political message."

The studio lights were positioned such that the guests were all lit evenly and favorably. Hairstyles, clothes, the whole setup was made to look as good as possible. The faces were covered in thick layers of makeup and powder. The people in front of the cameras had to look good. Except for the professor, that is.

"It is the search for meaningful engagement," he was saying. "Let's go back a step. The western world no longer has room for adventure or true ideals. We've become weary. We don't have to fight for our freedoms anymore. We've achieved everything. The Wall fell, and the Iron Curtain is history. Where can we still fight and be heroes?"

Niall tapped Beth on the shoulder. "Does it look to you like he's not wearing any makeup?"

"Looks that way."

"Why not? The rest of them are."

"He probably refused. It's rare, but it happens sometimes." Niall shook his head. "Come on, let's go. This isn't useful."

"We could use material from this show in the documentary," Beth commented. "Or at least we could, if anyone ever said anything interesting."

Niall nodded, considering how he could incorporate the hollow commentaries.

"There's something very primitive about that, shades of anarchy," he heard Karen say. It sounded as if she had just commented on the downside of bad sex.

Haynes replied: "Fully instinctual and without much rational analysis, yes."

"And if such…people return to our country, should we just wait until they have grown rational again, Mr. Randall?"

Niall missed Randall's answer. Beth had grabbed his arm and was dragging him away. Once they had left the studio and were out in the hallway, she said: "I'd seen enough. I couldn't stand that woman another second."

"She is very…ambitious. She's always been that way."

Beth opened the door to the cafeteria and headed straight for the cooler holding the drinks. "Always? Have you been following her political career for a while?"

"You could say that."

Shooting him a puzzled look, Beth pulled out a Coke. One eyebrow still cocked, she opened the bottle, and white foam fizzed out of the neck. Beth held the drink away from her body until the froth subsided. When Niall offered no elaboration, she continued: "More than anything, she wants to become Prime Minister, which should work great for someone who enjoys scaring people about problems that aren't really as serious she claims and then jumping in with solutions for everything." ☐

FADE TO BLACK

SUNDAY
16

Rana Ziadeh lived with her husband in a house on a side street off Deans Lane in Edgeware. After Ken parked in front of the house, Niall walked back down the street a short distance to film the neighborhood. An Anglican church towered above the obedient little houses.

Farooq's mother led Laura, Ken, and Niall into her living room, which looked as if she had tidied up extra for the television crew. Even the throw pillows on the blue corduroy couch had been carefully spaced evenly apart. Niall knew at once where and how she wanted to be filmed, right there on that couch in the midst of the pillows, with the Monet print in the background.

"You may not know this, but I haven't seen my son in almost ten years." Rana Ziadeh's eyes were red from crying, but there she was, sitting up straight and composed on the sofa, not in the middle but pressed up against the armrest. The claw marks on it showed the presence of at least one cat in the house. Although the woman was not yet fifty, she was already completely gray, and her hair was pulled back into a braid. Despite the time of year, she was wearing black trousers and a long-sleeved black shirt, which was a little tight around her breasts and stomach.

"I wanted him to finish growing up with me, but Frank had other ideas, so his father got custody. He visited me during the first couple of years. Not often, but still. Then he dropped out of school, which I didn't agree with, and we had a horrible argument. He didn't want to see me after that. He also didn't come to my wedding." She looked right into the camera for a long moment. "My son wasn't at my wedding. He completely rejected me and my life. I think he hated me." Rana turned her head and gestured at Niall. She needed a moment.

Niall nodded at Ken, who acted as if he were stopping the camera. Niall had told him earlier to keep the camera running the whole time. Laura jotted down some notes.

"Is Ziadah your husband's name or…"

"No, it's my maiden name. My husband's last name is Ransley. Rana Ransley would have sounded funny." She smiled, relaxing a little. "My first marriage was a disaster, and we stayed married much too long. Ironically, I stayed as long as I did because of Frankie. I thought the boy was too young to cope with a divorce. Who knows? None of this might have happened if I had left earlier. My new husband thought I should keep my name and stay who I was. I'm not sure if that makes any sense."

"Very much so," Niall replied, before biting his lip. He had intended to avoid personal comments in the conversation. He simply was not used to doing that.

Rana looked at him curiously. "A person's name is important, don't you think?"

Niall nodded, feeling uncomfortable. He asked: "Should we keep going?"

"Oh, yes. Let's get on with it." She readjusted her position on the sofa, then looked straight into the camera before recalling that she was not supposed to do so. She quickly looked over at Niall.

"My son, Frank. I haven't seen him in almost ten years. His father would sometimes tell me where I could find him. I would sit in my car and wait there until he would come out, just so I could see him."

"Did you talk to him?"

"At first, but then he started running away. Later, I followed him some, so I could catch a glimpse of him. I stopped doing that when he turned eighteen. I simply made do with what his father told me about him. It was Frank's decision to not see me anymore. I sent him cards for birthdays and at Christmas,

New Year's, and Easter. I sent him packages, too, until my ex-husband asked me to stop mailing them since Frank just threw them away. I lost my son a long time ago. Then, I saw him on TV."

Rana stared at the floor. Niall waited for her to resume. He did not want to interrupt with stupid questions like "What did you feel at that moment?" or "Did you recognize him immediately?" He hated it when questions like that were asked. Besides that, the hesitation, the silence, was often more powerful than five minutes of running commentary.

The woman lifted her head, wiping her tears away. He had not noticed that she had begun crying. "That beard...That wasn't my son. What did they call him? Farooq? How silly! His father and I are Christians. We're both Catholic, and he was baptized in the Catholic church. My current husband is Anglican. I'm devout and always have been. I don't always agree with what comes out of Rome, but I believe in God. A loving, forgiving God. I tried to raise my son in the same belief. He was never very interested, more like his father that way. And then to see him looking in the camera and talking about Allah? How in the world did he come to that?" She had begun to weep openly, no longer trying to hold back the tears.

"Rana, Frank told me he was Palestinian."

"Yes, yes..." she murmured, fumbling for something in her pocket. Laura handed her a tissue. Rana smiled gratefully and blew her nose.

"What did you just say? Palestinian. When he was younger, he didn't want to hear anything about that. Whenever I tried to tell him something about his grandparents, about when and why they'd come to England, he'd just say, 'But I'm English. I'm like the other kids.'"

"Did he have problems in school?"

Rana nodded. "Some of his classmates thought I was Muslim. He came home one day crying because in class they had talked about where their parents had been born. Frank said his mother had been born in Jerusalem." Her eyes darted back and forth between Laura and Niall. She seemed to have forgotten all about Ken, standing behind the camera.

"I was a year old when my parents left the West Jordan area. 1967, right before the Six-Day War. My father wanted nothing to do with what was going on. He always said, "Let the Muslims and the Jews work it out between themselves." Things had gone well for his family during the British mandatory period, which is why he'd wanted to come here. He spoke fluent English, and my mother wanted her daughter to be able to grow up in a peaceful country. They spoke only English with me, and they raised me as an English girl. Then, my son came home from school, crying because the other kids were attacking him for being either Jewish or Muslim."

"What did the school do?" Niall asked.

Rana shook her head before lifting her chin and clearing her throat. "I asked his teacher to explain to the children in his class what was going on between Jerusalem, Israel, and Palestine, to talk to them about the religious differences in that area. All she said was that hers wasn't a parochial school. The children there weren't required to focus on the various religions unless they especially wanted to. And everything else they needed to learn they would eventually be taught in history class."

She turned toward Laura. "How old are you? Younger than Frank was, right? What did you learn about Israel and Palestine in school? Enough to be able to form an educated opinion about the situation there today? Enough to understand what has been happening there for the past decades and centuries?"

Laura took a moment to respond. "We mainly focused on recent history, the establishment of Israel in particular."

"That's not enough to really understand what's going on there." She fell silent, closing her eyes.

Niall gave her the space she seemed to need, refusing to press her to keep talking. With his handheld camera, he zoomed in on her hands, the plain gold wedding band. It was the only jewelry she was wearing.

Rana opened her eyes, blinking hard as she refocused in his direction, and smiled. "I'll just talk a little, alright?"

"Please."

"Back then, Frank was…You know, we had a Christian home. Frank went to a school where many of the children came from Muslim families. He looked like them with his dark hair and black eyes. He got those from me. That's why everyone thought he was Arabic, which he actually was, by half. But he was also a Christian. Above all, he was an English boy. The white children teased him, while the Arabic children avoided him. He had practically no friends. It was really hard for him. At some point, he started accusing me of things. It was my fault that nobody wanted to be his friend." The tears resumed, and she paused, breathing deeply to calm back down.

Niall asked: "Rana, can you tell us some of your best memories of Frank? What did he like to play with as a child?"

She nodded, unable to stem the tears, though her voice only trembled slightly. "He always liked to go swimming. We often went to Torquay on vacation. We could never afford an expensive trip abroad somewhere, but other families couldn't either." Rana sounded apologetic. "He really loved going swimming and was good at it. He also liked animals. For a long time, he would spend part of his weekends at an animal shelter, just so he could play with a certain dog there."

"Did he have one of his own?"

Her gaze meandered around the room, down into the past.

"My ex-husband didn't want to have a dog in the house and forbade him from bringing the dog home. One day, a family adopted the dog, and Frank refused to go back to the shelter." She stopped. "I don't remember anymore what the dog's name was. I'm afraid I was a bad mother."

In a normal conversation, it would have been Niall's duty to say something comforting, like, "You shouldn't think that!" He quashed this impulse.

As Rana realized that the typical mode of conversation was not functioning there, her smile grew nervous. "You wait, hoping to hear that it didn't actually happen. I truly wasn't a good mother, and I'm glad I only had one child."

"We aren't here to judge you. We just want to learn about what kind of person Frank was," Niall replied calmly.

She rubbed the tears from her cheeks with the backs of her hands. "I keep thinking that perhaps I was too young when I got pregnant with him. I was twenty-two at the time. It hadn't been our plan, and we weren't even sure if we were going to stay together. We hardly knew each other, his father and I, and there I was, pregnant. I think children pick up on things like that, despite how hard you try. I was much too young." She stared into the distance. Then, with a start, she stood up and left the room with a mumbled excuse.

Niall walked over to Ken's camera, swung it in another direction, and focused on the background—the wall unit with an aging television, the shelves of books. Novels, a couple of popular nonfiction titles that promised to reveal the path to happiness, various Christian books offering similar promises.

Rana returned with a box of tissues. Pulling one out, she sat back down on the couch and dabbed her eyes. The camera swung back toward her.

"You work for a charitable organization?" Niall asked.

Rana nodded. "We take care of the people in this area who have a hard time getting by. We offer legal and psychological advice, and they also receive clothing and food, toys for their children…Most of us are volunteers, otherwise we wouldn't be able to provide any of it. I work full-time as the director, and our work is funded by donations. The items and money are that is. The church supports our work." She sniffed and wiped her nose again. "We'll help anybody, regardless of where they come from or what religion they practice. I thought I had raised Frank like that, but his father…" She blew her nose once more, then looked at Niall: "You'll cut that out, right? The part with the tissue?"

Niall said: "We won't show you in a bad light, Rana. That's not our intent." If it enhanced the film, they would include a close-up of her sobbing. That was just the way it went. Then, he thought, but this is my film. I can decide if I want to show that.

"Was Frank in contact with your parents?" he asked.

"He never met his grandfather, who died shortly before he was born. That's why Frank was almost premature. I was so shocked when my father died. My mother only outlived him by four years. It didn't take long for Frank to forget all about them. He sometimes looked at photos of them, though."

"Did he want to go to Jerusalem? To see where you had been born? To see where his grandparents had lived?"

"Jericho. They lived for many years in Jericho, and then they moved to Jerusalem…It's a complicated story. He never wanted to hear about it. It seemed to be too much for him. No, he never wanted to go there. Palestine didn't interest him at all."

"He stood there in front of me and claimed he was Palestinian," Niall explained. "He sounded proud when he said that."

Rana shook her head as words failed her. She continued to weep quietly, her face averted from the camera, her shoulders shaking.

Niall threw Ken a look. He nodded. Keep the camera running. Niall asked her quietly: "Would you like to take a break?"

Still turned away, she shook her head and raised her hand. "Just a moment," she said.

Niall zoomed in on the family photos on the wall next to the door. All of them showed Rana and a man with reddish hair and pale skin, probably some years older than her. Her second husband. In the wedding photo, he had significantly more hair than he had in the more recent shots. Some of the pictures included other people, all of whom looked like they were related to him. With her darker skin, Rana stood out in each picture.

"I'm better now," she finally said.

"Are you sure? We have time."

"No, it's okay. It's just—" She noticed that Niall had been looking at the photos. "Yes, my husband's family," she said, extracting a new tissue and wiping her nose. She blotted her face with another one before sitting up straight. She propped her arm on the armrest and gazed unwaveringly at Niall: "Frank always rejected my heritage, but they tell me he was proud to be a Palestinian. What in God's name did his father do to him?"

Niall waited. She leaned forward and looked straight into his eyes.

"Are you going to talk to him?"

"We plan to."

"Then tell him something for me. Tell him that he will burn in Hell for what he did to my boy. For eternity."

As they loaded the equipment in the van, Laura remarked: "We won't be talking to his father."

"No? Why not?"

"He said he won't let himself be 'manipulated by the puppet press.' To quote."

"Puppet press, huh?"

"The Jewish one," Laura elaborated.

"Under US control," Ken added.

"He refuses to be manipulated by the Jewish puppet press that is controlled by the US? He really said that?" Niall asked.

"Uh-huh."

Ken slipped behind the steering wheel. "Where now?"

Laura checked her schedule. "Our appointment at the mosque is for three, but maybe they won't mind if we get there early. It's the mosque where Farooq went to pray before he disappeared. It's also where he and Cemal met."

"Will they give us the address for the Islamist training camp? It would save us some time," quipped Ken, who then quickly added, "That was a joke...No? Not even a chuckle?"

Laura's head popped up between the two front seats. "In case anybody actually cares, the only way we'll make any headway is if we behave with sensitivity and respect. Okay?"

"You think I'm insensitive?"

"Niall, that's not what I meant. How prepared are you for your chat with the Imam?"

"Extremely well. Thanks to the research assistants, I know everything."

"I'm serious. We're about to enter a place of worship, regardless of your beliefs. At least I'm prepared." She pulled a cloth out of the large bag she always carried with her. "Catholic churches also don't like it if you walk around with bare shoulders and legs. I respect that, and I'm not even baptized. It's the same in mosques: Cover your shoulders and legs. Women are also supposed to cover their hair."

Niall watched as she wound the cloth around her head. When she was done, she looked like she was ready to go for a ride in a convertible through 1950s Nice.

"Pretty," Niall remarked.

"That wasn't my intention."

17

"You don't have to wear that," the Imam told Laura. "Or are you here to pray?" He smiled at her as he warmly shook her hand.

"Zahid Qureshi. We spoke on the phone, right?"

Avoiding his gaze, Niall saw Laura flush darkly. Ken bit back a grin, which earned him a light jab from Niall. The Imam had been waiting for them in the cultural center's parking lot.

"Sorry to ask you to wait, but I need to take care of something quickly," Qureshi continued, after he had shaken hands with both Ken and Niall. He was wearing light linen pants and a pale tunic with long sleeves, his beard neatly trimmed. He was perhaps forty, maybe a little older. "It won't take long. Just a quick word with the press."

He pointed at the building that housed the cultural center—an ugly post-war structure, an uninspired, gray concrete block with ridiculously tiny windows. Somebody had gone crazy with a spray can across the walls. Comments like "England belongs to us," "Get lost, bloody pigs," and "Catch the next flying carpet and go home" were still legible. A group of young men and women was busily painting over the words and cleaning the windows, which had also been sprayed.

"We had an especially unpleasant incident here this morning, and I need to make a statement on it."

"Hard to miss," Niall said, his eyes still on the scrawled words.

"What? Oh, not that," Qureshi dismissed the cleaning team with a wave. "Things like that happen all the time, even though we've installed cameras and leave the lights on at night. They come anyway. No, two men disrupted our morning prayers. Luckily, nothing happened. We overpowered them before they could do any harm and handed them over to the police. We didn't plan to make a big deal out of it, but word got around, and somebody found out that the attackers were members of the English Defense League." He smiled apologetically. "Please go on inside. I've asked Serhat to take you to my office. I apologize about the wait." He waved at a young man who was working on the walls.

"Oh, please don't worry. We got here earlier than expected."

The Imam nodded amiably at Niall and disappeared inside the building as the boy made his way over to them.

"I'm Serhat." He was perhaps sixteen or seventeen, tall and thin, and he seemed nervous. "I'll take you inside."

They followed him up to the second floor. Gray linoleum floor, beige walls. Niall assumed these had once been government offices. Or a company that hadn't had enough money to improve the decor for its staff. Nobody could have really wanted the place, which was why the rent must have been reasonable and the cultural center able to afford it. Then again, maybe that was not the real story there, Niall thought. He paused to shoot the corridor behind them.

"We just moved in," Serhat remarked anxiously, brushing his fingers along the wall which was already peeling. "It doesn't look all that nice."

"Where was the center before?" Niall asked as he zoomed in on a door with an opaque glass window. A crack ran through the pane.

"A few streets over."

"Why did you move? Was it too small? Too expensive?"

Serhat hesitated, refusing to meet his eyes. "I think that someone filed a complaint." He opened the door. "Here, have a seat. I'll be right back." The boy vanished.

Niall said: "I seem to have hit a nerve."

"I'll figure out what happened," Laura declared, typing away on her phone.

Niall walked slowly around the Imam's office, letting himself soak in the space. A careening pile of newspapers, books, and papers had taken over the desk, practically burying the laptop and telephone. The walls were bare. A bookshelf waiting to have something placed on it ran along the wall across from the window.

Niall showed Ken and Laura where he wanted the camera. After taking care of that, they set up the sound equipment, while Niall took a seat on the low, overly cushy couch that sat across from the desk. Serhat returned with tea for the three of them. He set the tray down on the coffee table in front of the couch and vanished again without a word.

"They must have moved in here recently," Niall commented. "Or the Imam is just too busy," Laura said.

"Maybe so. Ken, do you have enough light?" He wanted the Imam to sit on the couch. It was too dark by the desk to film without extra light stands.

Ken set up one spotlight. The sun was shining brightly outside, but the mood inside was gloomy. The architects had obviously suffered from depression. Niall pulled out his phone and tapped the icon that would give him the latest news.

"Here it is. Attack on the mosque...by members of the radical right English Defense League...no injuries...A connection with Wednesday's attack on Paul Ferguson has not been ruled out."

"And we weren't there," Ken said sadly.

"Laura, have someone check to see if there are any cell videos or something like that online. Copy, save, check on the rights, you know."

Laura nodded and typed herself a reminder. Niall flipped through the notes that had been pulled together for him. Qureshi was obviously not getting away from his press conference as quickly as he had thought he would.

"They had to move because the neighborhood residents felt uncomfortable," Laura said. "The women were afraid they'd get killed."

"The Muslim women?" Niall asked.

"No, the English ones. There was a whole series of minor complaints. The residents clearly wanted to harass the center. At some point, the congregation gave up and started looking for a new building. There's an extensive article in The Guardian." She pointed at her screen.

"Please send me the link." Niall picked up his camera and took a couple shots of the steaming tea. He then walked over to the window and filmed the view. The building across the street housed a traditional pub. "Fish and chips for 5£" was written on the board standing on the sidewalk. Tuesday was trivia night. A couple of smokers were lingering outside the door. Retired, white Englishmen who spent their comfortable Sundays in pubs. Who were not even slightly upset by the handmade sign hanging in the window that said, "No Muslims!" It pictured a woman in a head covering, a man with a full beard, both struck through.

"We'll go over there next," Niall said, zooming in on the sign. "I'd like to talk to them." The smokers had noticed him. They stared up at him for a moment before retreating into the pub.

"Not our best friends," Qureshi remarked as he stepped into the office. "Please forgive me. Everybody's so excited, but nothing really happened."

"Two members of the English Defense League interrupt your morning prayers, and you say nothing really happened. By the way, is it alright if we keep the camera running?"

The Imam smiled. "Of course. That's what we made off with. Where should I sit? Ah, I see, you've set everything up around the couch. It really is quite dark around my desk. I need to get a lamp…"

"Does this happen often?" Niall inquired. "I mean, the graffiti, the interruption of prayers, neighbors hanging ugly pictures in their windows?"

Qureshi took a seat in the middle of the couch and waved the question off. "I'm just glad nothing happened earlier. It really could have gone badly, that much I do know. We get letters, emails, calls every day from people cursing and threatening us. On top of that, people drop by all the time to tell us what they think of us in no uncertain terms."

"This is just par for the course, then?"

"It's always upsetting and frightening whenever someone writes to us or says something or sprays the walls or drops by. After today, it's clear we need to significantly increase our security measures. I had hoped we could run an open, friendly center, where everyone would be welcome. I was naive, but it's my job to see the best in people, right?"

He flashed a smile before growing serious again. "Let's talk about Cemal and Farooq."

"They met each other through your congregation. Had Cemal been attending here long?"

The Imam nodded. "As long as I can remember. He and his family. They don't live far from here, in Streatham. Cemal's sister is attending our self-defense course, and his younger brother played in the soccer tournament we held over the weekend to raise money for residents of the Gaza Strip." He scanned the faces around him. "No, I don't just happen to know this. I checked into it after you called."

"And Cemal?"

"He came to prayers occasionally, but not regularly. I was told that his father was very strict, that Cemal was required to fulfill his religious obligations. I personally don't believe being unyielding, forcing others to do what you want, is the way to do things. I am constantly telling parents this, but I can't do much beyond that." He crossed his legs, leaning forward slightly.

"When did Farooq start coming?"

"Oh, that must have been about two years ago. I knew him better than Cemal because Farooq came to me personally with all his questions. He contacted me by email, and then we talked on the phone a few times before he finally came by. He already knew a lot about Islam and said he was Palestinian, on one side. His parents weren't all that devout, though. Do you know them? I never met his parents, but I'd like to send them my condolences."

"We came here straight from his mother's house. She lives in Edgeware," Niall said.

"There's a large Islamic center there. But if she isn't religious—"

"She's quite religious."

"Ah. But Farooq said—"

"She's Catholic."

Qureshi leaned back into the couch. "A convert?"

"Her parents were Aramaic, and they fled Jerusalem right before the Six Day War."

The Imam nodded thoughtfully, shooting a quick glance at the camera. "I wondered when the press used an English name. I thought it was because of his father. He never wanted to talk about his parents. He said that something hadn't worked out there and that he was searching for his own way. Farooq attended Arabic and Koran courses, and he often came here to pray. But also, to talk."

"How exactly did he meet Cemal?"

"He was in contact with other young men, but none of those friendships were all that close. I don't know why, but I was suspicious." Another quick look at the camera. "Should I...?"

"Please."

"It's really just a hunch, Mr. Stuart. Pure speculation on my part. And possibly strongly colored by what has happened. Hindsight is 20/20, right? I don't know if this will add anything to your film..."

"If you feel uncomfortable—"

"Oh. No, it's just..." He sighed. "Alright then. I had a feeling from the very start—truly just a subjective impression—that Farooq was looking for boundaries. He asked me why I trim my beard. I said I think it looks better, and because it's more practical. Various reasons. His response, "But it's harām." He took everything so seriously. Which is also a good thing!" Qureshi was now looking right into the camera. "It is good and important for us to treat the tenets of our religion with respect."

He continued, "Only...Farooq was looking for the radical end of things. Clear rules, precise regulations." Qureshi broke off in thought. Niall let him. He glanced over at Laura, who was impatiently drumming her fingers. Just wait, he signaled.

Finally, the Imam said, "I'm afraid he lost his respect for me after that. I couldn't help him anymore, though I tried. All of us did. We are a strong community. We make sure the wrong people don't get in."

"Which wrong people?" Niall inquired.

"The ones people call Islamists. The archconservatives. The truly extreme Sunnites. We aren't always able to recognize early enough the ones about to set out on jihad or plan a suicide bombing. We have banned a few people from the property, but I think Cemal and Farooq agreed to talk to them. We can't do anything about what happens outside this building. We can only strive to inform. In all directions." He gazed into the camera once more. "In all directions," he repeated. He then relaxed a bit and said, "Would you like to talk to Serhat?"

"Serhat? The boy who brought us here? Why?"

"Oh, I thought he introduced himself. He's Cemal's brother."

Niall glanced at Laura, who shook her head. "No, he didn't say anything."

"Serhat is rather shy. I'll get him." The Imam stood up and went to the door. "Serhat," he called, "could you please come here?" Seconds later, they heard footsteps in the hallway. Serhat stopped outside the door, as if unsure if he should come inside.

"Our condolences," Laura jumped in, walking toward him. Serhat let her shake his hand, but he stayed where he was.

"I'm sorry about what happened with your brother," Niall added, joining the two of them. "Would you like to come in?"

"You're the one who filmed it all, right?" Serhat asked, taking a little step into the room. He obviously felt intimidated in the Imam's presence.

"Where should he sit?" Ken asked from behind the camera.

"He can sit here," Qureshi answered, offering him his spot on the sofa. "I need to go downstairs anyway. Are you set here?"

"Yes, thank you very much," Laura said.

"Come sit down here, Serhat," Qureshi urged.

"No," Serhat replied quickly, as if overwhelmed by the thought of taking Qureshi's spot on the couch. "I'll just stand."

He still respects the Imam, Niall thought. Unlike Farooq. Niall proposed relocating to another room, but once Qureshi left with a friendly nod, Serhat relaxed and agreed to sit down.

"Serhat, when was the last time you talked to your brother?" Niall asked as the boy took his seat.

Serhat shifted anxiously. "I don't remember exactly."

"We aren't the police. We just want to learn more about Cemal, what kind of person he was. Whenever you don't want to or can't answer something, that's just fine. Would you like to tell us a little about him?" Serhat hesitated, so Niall continued: "I only met him once, as you already know, on that day in the park. I didn't really talk to him. I spoke with Farooq in prison, but just briefly. Your brother was still in intensive care."

Serhat swallowed. "I hadn't seen him in a long time. He just disappeared one day." The boy had practically vanished between the soft couch cushions.

"Did he live with you?"

"Yeah."

"Where did he work?" Niall asked. He knew Cemal's CV, but he wanted to hear what Serhat had to say.

"He couldn't get a job, but he tried so hard. He applied for every job he found. I know he did. For real. He filled out so many applications."

"What did he want to do?"

"He wanted to work in advertising. He got his B.A. in visual communication design from Croydon College."

"He was a graphic designer."

Serhat nodded. "He took the best pictures and liked to make little videos. They were really good. Did you check out his website?"

"No, I don't think so." Niall looked over at Laura, who was already busy with her phone. "Can you find it under his name?"

"He used a pseudonym." Serhat gave him the address. His shyness was slowly fading, perhaps because the Imam had left the room, perhaps because his enthusiasm for his brother's work was drawing him out. "He hadn't updated his page in a long time. He was—well, you know. Did you find the site? Pretty good, isn't it?"

Laura moved closer to Niall, holding out her phone for him to see. Cemal's page was up: a clean, dramatic style, unfussy and effective.

"Your brother was very talented."

"He went to college, man! I want to do that, too."

"How old are you?"

"Eighteen." He looked younger than that, Niall thought.

"Do you know what you want to study? Have you graduated yet?"

"My father says I should take a year off, wait to go to college. Experience something of the world." The thought of this seemed to worry him.

"And your sister."

"She's already in college," he said, his eyes gleaming proudly.

"Cemal was the oldest?"

He nodded.

"Why couldn't he find a job? He was talented enough."

Serhat's voice was uncertain. "I don't know, man. He said Turks couldn't get jobs in that field."

"He said that?"

"Yes, because…He did an internship with a big international advertising agency and had a great time. He worked there for six months and got to travel to Prague and Berlin and Rome. I know he did a good job. He showed me what he did, but they didn't offer him a job. After that, he just couldn't find anything else."

"Shit," Niall replied.

The boy seemed to sense that Niall had meant it seriously, and he looked at him gratefully. "You can see what he could do, can't you?"

"Absolutely. I'll look through his site more carefully later on, okay?"

"Thanks, man. He deserves that much."

Niall saw the tears in Serhat's eyes and sensed how uncomfortable it would be for him to cry in front of strangers and especially a running camera. "Let's take a break, Ken."

Ken glanced up from his camera in surprise.

"Go have a smoke. We'll pick up after that."

Ken got the message, and Laura needed no further prodding. She held the door open for Ken and left with him. Niall knew the camera was still on.

"Okay, Serhat, now it's just the two of us. I think there's something else you want to tell me, but not in front of the others, right?"

Serhat nodded, still fighting his tears.

"How are your parents doing?" Niall asked when Serhat said nothing. He also wanted to know about the plans for the funeral. If Cemal's body had been released and when the burial would take place. If an autopsy had been done or would be done. If Serhat and his family believed it had been suicide. Niall knew that he would not be asking the boy those questions. Not yet.

"They say he is no longer their son."

"Since the arrest?" He avoided any direct reference to the murder or Farooq's suicide.

"No, even before that. He disappeared for several months and didn't contact us."

"You must've been so worried about him."

"I think my parents suspected where he'd gone."

Niall waited.

"He was in a training camp."

Niall joined him on the sofa. "Cemal was in a training camp? Where?"

Serhat shrugged. "In Iraq. Listen, I don't want my Imam to find out. Or my sister. Or my parents."

"I thought they already knew. Or at least had guessed."

The boy could no longer hold back. "I kept my mouth shut for Cemal. And for Farooq."

Niall studied the boy more closely. "You mean they suspected, but you actually knew?"

Serhat nervously rubbed his palms against his pants. "I saw them. After they got back. I also have a video of the two of them where they explain everything."

"A video?"

"They told me to upload it if anything happened to them. But I can't do that. It's too much." Serhat stared at Niall, fear, but above all, pain, evident in his eyes.

"May I see it?"

"Sure. But…" Serhat hesitated as his gaze wandered around the room.

"What is it? Is there something you'd still like to tell me?" Serhat looked back at him. "You work for the station, right?"

"No, just for this project. I'm a freelancer."

"So, you work for yourself?"

"Yes."

"You make your own decisions?"

"Yes."

"Nobody is telling you what to do? Not even when the film is for the station?"

Niall could not help smiling. "It's my film. I make the calls."

"Cool."

"Why are you asking all this?"

The boy gnawed on his lower lip before leaning toward Niall and whispering. "You have to help me. MI5 wanted my brother to work for them. If that gets out, IS will kill my family."

18

"If you're watching this video, we're dead," Cemal said, beaming into the camera. "We died because we are at war for Allah. We are fighting against anyone who does not follow the true faith because they want to rob us of our faith and our land. They kill our children and rape our women. This is why, brothers, you must join the jihad. It is your duty, just as it is ours. What we do, we are doing for Allah. Our injuries do not hurt. Paradise is waiting for us."

Cemal and Farooq sat side by side, and Farooq seemed to be holding the camera. Their beards were not as long as they had been on the day of the murder. They wore black caps and black bandanas, the flag of the Islamic State on the wall behind them. With nothing recognizable in the background, the video could have been made anywhere, even in London.

"That's it?" Niall asked Serhat.

"That's some sick shit!" Serhat replied. They were sitting in front of the computer in Niall's Brixton flat, drinking the soft drinks Niall had picked up on their way over. Serhat did not want to play the video at his house, afraid his parents or sister might find out about it. He was too frightened to go to the Imam because he had no idea if he had done the right thing, and he refused to go to the station because he thought MI5 might have it under surveillance. An internet cafe was obviously out of the question. The only thing Niall could do was take him home, even though that was very low on his list of options.

"I thought he was going to say something about the Service."

"No, not here."

"Not here?" He studied Serhat. "What do you mean? There are more videos?"

Serhat nodded. "We Skyped. I recorded everything."

"You recorded your calls with your brother? Why?"

"Because he disappeared, man!" Serhat shook his head. "He was just gone! I thought I might need the recordings if something happened. If we had to go looking for him, we'd need to know where to start."

"So, you didn't make the recordings in case the police—"

"No. We don't go to the police."

"Serhat, you can't mean that." Even as he said it, Niall could still feel the officers throwing him, handcuffed, into the back of the police van before beating him. "It's their job to be there for all of us."

"I'm Turkish, nothing more than a second-class citizen to them."

"Did you hear that from your brother?"

"No, I know that myself."

"You're a British citizen."

"They don't really care. Do you honestly think they'd ask to see my ID before taking me in?"

"Do you think your brother did the right thing?" he asked the boy.

Serhat shook his head. "But I don't know what the right thing is. In the mosque, they tell us we should pray and keep talking to people until they understand us and treat us as nicely as we treat them. They say Islam is a peaceful religion, but Cemal said it's about fighting. I know that's not right, but I understand why he said he didn't just want to sit around and pray. He wanted to help his brothers who were being attacked for believing in Allah." Serhat broke off for a moment. "Or something like that."

Niall gazed at him for a long second. "You loved your brother, didn't you?"

Serhat nodded as he stared at the floor.

"He really fucked up, though. He seems to have been a nice guy and a great brother, but for whatever reason, he got himself into some serious trouble."

Serhat nodded again. "He was in a training camp in Mosul." The boy scooted over centimeters until he was in front of the computer. He pulled up a different site, typed in a couple passwords, and clicked around until he found what he wanted to show Niall. "Here's where he talks about it."

Before Serhat started the video, Niall asked: "How many of these are there?"

Serhat checked his cloud folder. "We Skyped eight times, and he sent me five videos."

Niall looked at the screen, considering the number of files that had just opened in the new window. "That's more than five videos."

Serhat shut the tab. "That's something different."

"The folder is tagged 'Cemal'."

"But it's something else."

"Serhat, either we talk about everything openly, or we can just let this go."

The boy weighed his options, clearly overwhelmed by the situation. "Man, I don't know. It's just too much." He stood up and walked around the small room, pausing in front of the bookcase to study the titles. "You have a lot of photo books, but I don't see any novels."

Niall joined him. "I don't have enough room. I use my phone to read stuff, but you're right, I don't read many novels."

"You prefer to look at pictures." He reached for a book. "May I?"

Niall nodded. Serhat pulled down one of Leonard's books and flipped it open. Elderly women in tattered rags, silhouetted against charred houses, graves already dug and ready. He quickly moved on. A half-naked girl with matted hair, caked in dirt, maybe four or five years old, peeping out from behind a bombed church.

"What's that?" Serhat slammed the book shut.

"Bosnia. Kosovo. I'd have to check."

The boy looked upset. "Why do you have something like this in your flat? War pictures?"

Niall took the book from him and set it back on top of the other books. "They're important because they document what people are willing to do to each other in times of war. Photographers who take pictures like this want to convince people that those kinds of things should never happen."

"Well, he did a good job of that."

"And you've never seen the dead and wounded in person, haven't served in the military. Despite that, you knew right away that these were war pictures."

"Well, sure. That's obvious. But nobody likes to look at stuff like that."

"My father took those photos."

Serhat retrieved the book and examined the cover. He then caught sight of the other books. "He's taken a lot of pictures. Are they all like this?"

"No, but most of them are. It was his job."

"To photograph ugly stuff?"

Niall had never thought about it that way, but Serhat was right: to photograph ugly stuff in such a way that an artistic composition was created, which actually underscored the horror all the more.

"Exactly," Niall replied. "He was a war photographer. He wanted the whole world to see the truth about war and to never forget."

"Hmm," Serhat murmured. He hesitated before putting the book back on the shelf, this time without opening it. "Is he still alive?"

"Yes."

"But he doesn't do this anymore?"

Niall shook his head. "Not for years now." He walked back to the small desk holding his computer and took a sip of his drink. He then pointed at the monitor. "You don't have to look at these anymore."

Serhat nodded in relief, as he took a step closer. He then stopped in the middle of the room and started to sob. "It's all so sick!"

Niall could see that the boy was worn and exhausted, which made him look much younger than he was. The past few weeks had to have been the worst weeks of his life. The anxiety about his brother, the secrets he had kept to himself, the worries about the rest of his family—it was too much for a boy his age. For anyone.

"Listen to me. I'll go through everything, and then we can talk again."

"I don't want the Service to do anything to us. Or IS either."

"That won't happen," Niall assured him, not because he was convinced it was the truth but because it was what the boy needed to hear. "I'll take you home now. You've done the right thing by not talking to anyone. And you were also right to show me the videos. Don't tell anybody else about them. At least, not yet. Okay? I need to watch them first."

Serhat rubbed his eyes dry. "Of course. Thanks, man."

"I'll help you, alright?"

The boy nodded, uncertainly.

Niall called a taxi, and they drove to Streatham, Serhat's neighborhood. Niall then asked to be taken to the station, as he jotted down the passwords for Serhat's cloud files on the back of a receipt. It was almost six by the time he was dropped off. Beth was in her office, Ken was in the editing room cleaning up the footage they had already shot, and Laura was torturing the research assistants, at least according to Beth.

"She makes the perfect PA," she commented.

"In other words, she's not leadership material," Niall added.

"She still lacks the right level of confidence for that."

"Because she doesn't think she's attractive, I assume."

Beth eyed him and seemed to be considering what he had said. "Why is that so important to her?"

Niall could not tell if she was being ironic or serious. "No idea. You'll have to ask her."

Beth threw her hands up defensively. "Oh, no. I don't do girl talk."

He studied her. "I wasn't serious. I couldn't tell if your question was sincere."

"Of course, it was," Beth said. "So, what are we going to watch?"

Niall stared at her for a long moment, but her gaze held nothing but anticipation. She obviously had no idea how she came across to people sometimes, he thought. He shook his head slightly before continuing, "Serhat Bayraktar received several videos from his brother via email. He also recorded some of the Skype conversations they had."

"He should get a job with the Service," Beth declared, a note of satisfaction in her voice.

"That's the next point. He claims his brother was contacted by the Service because they wanted him to work for them."

"Now that's interesting. Which branch?"

"There's no way it's true. They're gangster pipe dreams, or, in this case, terrorist pipe dreams. Serhat is trying to make some sense of his brother's actions after the fact. He thinks he was James Bond."

"So, was it MI6 that approached him?"

"Beth, you aren't listening. None of it is true."

"Are you sure?"

"Good grief, what do I know?"

Beth gnawed on a pencil before slowly continuing, "So let's take James Bond and the international crowd out of the picture. But imagine this: MI5 needs eyes into the Salafist scene. Somehow, Cemal pops up on their radar. They talk to him, help infiltrate him into the scene. Cemal acts as if he is fully committed to the cause, all the while delivering information to the Service. Perfect." She looked happy.

"And then he decapitates a corpse?"

"Well, he wasn't the one who did the killing."

"That makes it all better?"

"Maybe in that moment, it did make him feel better about himself. People can justify to themselves pretty much anything, if it helps them look at themselves in the mirror."

"And then he was just accidentally shot?"

"A cover is a cover." Beth shrugged. "Things like that happen in undercover operations. And who's to say it was an accident?"

FADE TO BLACK

Niall shook his head at both Beth and her theory. At her willingness to spin a conspiracy out of the ghosts seen by a very troubled young man. "Let's just watch the videos first."

19

Serhat could be seen in a small window in the upper right corner of the screen, while Cemal's face and shoulders filled the majority of space. The only thing that could be made out in the background was that he was sitting in a closed room with a bare wall behind him.

Serhat asked his brother where he was, and Cemal eagerly described the stages of his trip: the flight to Istanbul, the various modes of ground transportation across the country and over the Syrian border, and the journey on to Mosul.

Serhat asked, "Man, what are you doing? There's a war going on there!"

"That's why we're here."

"Shit, come back before they shoot you!"

"These are my brothers. They're helping me."

"Who? The losers you've been hanging around with the past few months? They're pretty crappy brothers, those idiots."

"Farooq came along."

"Shit, him, too? He's as crazy as you are."

Cemal glanced around, as if verifying that he was alone in the room. "Don't talk like that about my friend. We're here for training."

"Man, I can't believe it. Why did you let them get to you? You used to just pray with us to keep Father off your back. And now you're off on a crusade? Have you lost your mind?"

"You'll understand someday. Right now, you're still surrounded by infidels. I needed a long time to finally understand that. The pure teaching, Serhat. Not our father's half-hearted prayers."

"Don't talk about him like that!"

"He has no idea what it's really all about. He just pretends he does, but he'll eventually understand. And then he'll be proud of me."

"He's always been proud of you." Serhat kept rubbing his face—the desperate gesture of a boy in over his head who had no clue what to do next. "He was so proud of you, man. You went to college."

"I couldn't get a job. Nobody wanted me. You know why? Because those Englishmen—I swear by Allah—those bloody Englishmen didn't want me. I wasn't one of them. They didn't want Muslims working for them."

"You're totally crazy."

"You're still in school, but you'll learn it soon enough. They've already started treating you like crap. When was the last time they beat you up?"

"That was nothing."

"They beat you up."

"They're idiots. They beat everybody up. Once I graduate, they'll be out of my life."

"That's what I thought, too."

"Cemal, come back. You'll get shot or something. They shoot people, you know. That's what they do in war."

"The only war here is the one being waged by our brothers against the infidels."

"Until just a little while ago, you couldn't have cared less about those bloody infidels."

"Don't say that, Serhat."

"Why not? It's true!"

Sounds could be heard from somewhere near Cemal. He glanced over his shoulder and said something that sounded like Arabic, maybe a greeting.

Cemal changed the subject at once, turning to what he was learning in the camp. Training in a variety of weapons. Instruction on how to manufacture explosives. Hand-to-hand combat. He raved about how they would be making videos of everything.

"The most advanced fighters are going to show everyone else how it's done. I'll send you the links, and then you can watch. You'll come over here someday, too. I know you will. Serhat, we have to do this. It's our destiny, brother." He motioned to signal that Serhat should remain silent.

Serhat changed the subject and started talking about what was going on at school. Which teachers annoyed him. Who was making his life miserable. What was going on with the boys who regularly picked on him and refused to call him anything but "Shish Kabob." Relishing his role as big brother, Cemal offered him advice. It was obvious what kind of connection the two of them had: a close, respectful relationship between brothers who loved each other. But then Cemal remembered his new role and told Serhat that it was time to show the unbelievers what was what.

"When we get back, we will liberate London. There are so many of us already in Great Britain, but we will be united under the Islamic State."

"What? What do you mean by 'so many'?" The fear had crept back into Serhat's voice.

"Hundreds have been through the training here and are already back home. More and more brothers are coming. Sisters, too. And they will go back and make sure that our nation is freed."

Serhat shook his head, once again rubbing his face, as if he could scrub away what he had seen on the screen. As the words failed him, he just sat there, silent. Cemal, noticing how overwhelmed Serhat was, switched gears by asking him another question about how things were at school, how soccer was going. Serhat slowly pulled himself together enough to answer, though he was clearly not doing well. The shock seemed too great.

At the end, he said: "Cemal, what you're doing is shit. Come back home. Everything'll be better then."

"I'll be back in touch, brother. It's time for prayers."

Serhat shouted: "Don't pretend it's all that important to you. It never was!"

Cemal quickly interrupted him: "You should go pray, too." He then ended the call.

Cemal appeared in front of the same background in all the subsequent conversations. He sat on a plain wooden chair, the back of which was occasionally visible. Varying levels of light shone through the window behind him. The background was too blurry to make out anything like a landscape or buildings. Most of the time, the sun shone directly through the window, and in those instances, even Cemal was hard to recognize. He usually sounded euphoric, rarely letting Serhat get a word in edgewise. He talked about the path he had taken to finding the pure, true faith. To fighting for the one God.

Serhat's replies always sounded resigned: "Man, I still can't believe it."

"You can join the jihad and fight, too. You could be a suicide bomber. There are even women here who are training for that. You should see what all they can do. It's a good way to fight."

"Come back. You have family here. Mother and Father are so upset. And Dilek—"

"She's a good fighter, I know. She'll find her calling, as well. She could—"

"Cemal, come on," Serhat cut off his older brother, whose face clearly reflected his irritation at the interruption. "We're doing just fine, despite all of this. You'll eventually find a job, and then—"

"That wasn't a life!" Cemal slammed his fist down as the image wobbled. "That just distracts us from our true task. It makes us weak, and we end up growing lazy instead of fighting. The only time we can be close to Allah is when we're fighting. Only then can we…" He trailed off, apparently losing his train of thought.

"What is it?" Serhat asked.

Cemal shook his head and gestured for his brother to stop talking. He stood up and paced back and forth in front of the camera before sitting back down. "Serhat, listen to me. If we're happy—as you assume we need to be—then we are very far from Allah. And that is wrong. We should not be happy. We have to stay outraged at our enemies because that is the only way we can be truly happy. Does that make sense?"

Serhat said, "What you're saying is crap."

"Brother, you will learn." Cemal ended the call without another word.

The screen went black.

Farooq participated in another of the Skype calls. In this one, Cemal sat cross-legged on a mattress shoved up against a white wall. The corner of a gray blanket could be seen. He probably slept there. Farooq knelt next to Cemal and adjusted the screen so that the camera focused only on him. He proudly demonstrated two weapons for Serhat that they had trained with that day.

"We can take them apart and put them back together. We know how to clean and load them, and how to fire them correctly. It's not as easy as it looks. These things kick hard when you fire them. We have to practice every day aiming them well. I can already assemble and disassemble both guns blindfolded." He beamed with pride. "Do you know what's really cool? This one here—" he held up a machine gun, an M60 "—comes from America. And this one—" he picked up an assault rifle, an HK G36 "—is from Germany. We're going to kill them with their own weapons. That's so cool." Farooq looked a little crazed, like a child on her first visit to an amusement park. He lifted the rifle over his head and shouted: "Serhat, come join us! We'll conquer the world! Nobody can stop us!"

In the background, Cemal joined in the shouting.

This time it was Serhat who hung up, but as he did, he mumbled something softly before the screen went black: "You're both totally sick." 📱

FADE TO BLACK
20

Cemal had sent his brother links over Skype Chat to a variety of IS propaganda videos on YouTube. In one of them, a small group of young men with assault rifles sat under the open sky in a landscape that could have been anywhere dry and hot. An Islamic State flag waved in the background, and the men wore headscarves wound around their faces and necks in the form of a kufiya or shemagh.

Only one of them spoke—first in Arabic, then in English—calling for all brothers and sisters who were searching for the true faith to join them. He then directly addressed a certain person, informing them that the Umma—the community—had been based on his example. He repeated this three times, calling on those in the Umma to stay strong and unyielding.

He had a strong Arabic accent, but his English articulation reflected a British upbringing. In a different video with a similar setting—a small circle of young, bearded men with headscarves and weapons, the Islamic State flag in the background—a man explained the plan of attack for the upcoming days and weeks, which areas in Syria and Iraq were to be the next in line for capture.

"National borders are meaningless. They are not worthy of our attention," he declared, sounding more eloquent than the man from the first video Niall and Beth had watched. This man urged all brothers to join the Mujahideen, those waging holy war. The video had been shot from various angles. The sound quality was perfect, and the editing showed the involvement of a professional or a very accomplished amateur. Besides that, the camera work and staging were light years more advanced than the blurry video messages sent into the world by Al-Qaeda ten years prior. The man spoke very good English, and his accent pointed to a childhood spent in Yorkshire.

The third propaganda film concentrated on weapons and the men's enthusiasm. Hundreds had gathered in the dark, and as they thrust their rifles into the air, they shouted for joy. Some of them grinned into the camera as they cried out to their God. Then, tanks turning pirouettes in the streets of Al-Raqqah, pickups with antitank missiles mounted on their beds driving into the city center and firing rockets into the sky. Mountains of machine guns. Mountains of grenades. A sea of radiant young men with beards and headscarves, as far as the eye could see. The video's off-screen commentary was in English, and Niall recognized Farooq's voice. He praised the jihad as if it were a trip to an exotic vacation resort, claiming that the supply of weapons would continue uninterrupted. There was enough for everyone. Men with weapons were the symbol of earthly happiness.

After that, Farooq appeared on screen with a long beard, pale headscarf, light-colored shirt, and wide pants. For all appearances, he could have been an actor with the charisma of a rock star. He strode through the hospital, talking to the wounded and shaking hands as if he were a head of state visiting his country's earthquake victims for the benefit of the camera to subtly sway the nation in favor of a tax hike. Farooq did what he was supposed to do. He smiled into the camera and explained that all injuries, no matter how painful, would be forgotten once one's reward in paradise was granted. He called the men "heroes," the ones stretched out in their beds with missing limbs. They looked much less at ease than Farooq, their smiles forced for the camera.

The third act of the film showed scenes in a training camp. The men marched in unison past the camera, weapons in hand. Someone off-camera barked orders. Against an ongoing dramatic soundtrack, Farooq's voice described the feeling of community within the Umma, emphasizing that the path to paradise was only open to those who sacrificed themselves in battle.

When the video ended, Niall expected to see credits roll,

naming those responsible for direction, script, sound, light, and cinematography, including everyone all the way down to the grip intern. Of course, the credits never came. Because the video might have been professionally produced, but it was no fiction. What they had in front of them had nothing to do with credits and rights but rather fighting and death. Who knows, Niall thought, most of those who had worked on the film might already be dead.

A fourth video—once again, men sitting in a semicircle in front of the camera. This time, a building was visible in the background, although it bore no distinguishing details. The flag was hanging on one of its walls, and all the men were carrying weapons. At first glance, the man in the middle of the semicircle seemed to be the youngest, and his skin was the darkest. He looked much shorter and lankier than the others.

He said, "Allah does not need you to fight for Him, but you need Him. If you fight for Him, He will take what you give to Him and return it to you seven hundred thousand-fold. I know how you feel, my brothers in the West." He pointed at his own chest. "You are depressed, deep in your hearts, and you do not believe there is any honor in you. But I am here to tell you--honor belongs to the one who believes and fights for that faith, and you can find this honor in the Umma and the jihad. Brothers, come join us in the jihad. Here you will rediscover your honor, just like we have. Here you will be happy, just like we are. Come to us, brothers."

He reached into the inner pocket of his jacket and pulled out a small black book. He continued, pointing at it: "You know what is expected of you. When you die and show Allah the wounds you incurred in service to Him, He will reward you. If you fear the jihad because you think you might die, then I need to remind you that you are going to die anyway. We will all die. And then Allah will decide how He will reward us after our deaths. Those of us who have wounds that we can show Him—wounds we received fighting in His name—will be granted so much more. Do not be afraid. You will not die in vain for Allah."

The camera angle shifted and focused on a group of smiling, shouting young men, guns raised over their heads and black flags waving. Strains of heroic music and Arabic lyrics swelled in the background. "Consider our sisters who are being raped and then become pregnant. Consider our children, whose heads they cut off. This is what they are doing to our sisters and our children, and we demand that it stop. We have to fight, and when we die and our naked bodies arrive in heaven to stand in front of Allah, He will ask what we have done for Him. We will not be able to speak, to tell Him what jobs we had or what we learned in school or which degrees we earned. We will be mute, but our bodies will speak, our wounds will testify for us. And Allah will reward us when He sees our wounds. The jihad is the only thing that counts."

The camera cut back to the speaker and the silent men at his feet. "We do not need anything from this world. Everything here separates us from our Lord and God. And when we meet Him, we want to be able to show Him what we have done on His behalf. Our bodies are our only bridge to Allah."

This time, there were closing credits. The music swelled, and the voices of those on the screen faded away. They laughed and joked and chatted with each other like friends cheerfully gathered around a campfire. The weapons were their instruments, and the campfire that invited them to share their stories were the two cameras used for the filming. When the video ended, Niall felt as if he had been sitting in a dark basement for weeks without a break. He stood up and stretched before opening the door and window. Beth yanked open a desk drawer and pulled out a bag of chips.

"For stamina," she said.

Niall shook his head: "The guy who was just talking sounded Welsh."

"His Arabic accent was not very good."

The young man had stumbled in spots, but all in all, he had made a much more intelligent impression than the others Niall had seen in the videos. "They were all British, right?"

"One Irishman, probably Northern Irish. But yes. And they all have immigrant backgrounds. Presumably all from Muslim families," Beth added as she munched one more handful of chips before putting the bag away.

"Except for Farooq. Or Frank."

Beth shut the drawer very slowly, making hardly a sound as she did.

Niall continued: "I kept asking myself the whole time, why not Hamas? Why not some pro-Palestinian group?"

"Maybe they're too tame? Do you have any idea how many Palestinians have lost faith in Hamas? How many of their efforts are viewed as not radical enough? That's why you find some of them waving the IS flag these days." Beth got to her feet and walked over to the door. "I need to stretch my legs a little." She hesitated. "Why did Cemal send these specific links to his brother? There must be hundreds of films like these. Because all of them feature Brits?"

"Not sure," Niall admitted, "but I'd guess that Cemal made all of these. Filmed and directed them, did the editing. They all reflect the same creative style, and it had to be someone who knew something about camera angles, cinematography, and aesthetics. Cemal would have learned about those in college."

"So, he didn't just receive training in weapons. He also jumped right into doing PR work for them."

"That's what it looks like. If you can create a high-quality film, you have an easier time getting people to watch it. Years ago, people couldn't get enough of those jiggly, homemade-looking films. Young viewers loved them because they could identify with how real those videos looked. Now the internet is going under with those things, and professional films are back in style. You have to have more than just a good idea to stand out in this crowd. It can't look over-produced, though. Viewers want to see that somebody with training has worked on a film, even if the budget is small."

"Perfectly executed."

"Look at the number of views. Each of these films has gotten over fifty thousand clicks."

"Is that a lot, relatively speaking?"

"The other propaganda films have...Wait a sec..." Niall clicked on the other recommended videos. "These are all in the low thousands."

"Oh shit."

"Yeah."

Beth walked through the door, but from out in the hall, she called back loudly enough for him to hear: "Cemal could've been a bloody YouTube star." ☐

21

Niall opened the next document in Serhat's folder. It was a video file Cemal had mailed directly to his brother. The file name was "Kill Your Enemy." After ten seconds, Niall knew why it was called that. The film opened with a close-up of Ted Stein, the American journalist who had been beheaded three weeks before by IS. The video of his execution had been watched millions of times, despite the decision of various western media outlets to not distribute pictures. Some social media platforms had even blocked users who had shared the video.

Cemal's footage began long before the actual killing itself. The video tracked the choice of the location and the weapons, almost like it was an old-fashioned duel. It opened with three men—in headscarves and loose clothes—deep in discussion. Niall could not make out what they were saying because they were speaking Arabic. The film material was raw and unedited, which is why there were no subtitles, as there had been in the propaganda videos. Cemal, the journalist, and the three men were shown in a large, bright room, a private, almost opulent living room with inviting cream-colored sofas, armchairs, and ottomans. The floor was covered in mosaic tiles, and a staircase was barely visible in the background.

One of the three men pointed a gun at Ted Stein's head as he ordered him in English to get undressed. Stein knew that he was going to be executed, but he still did as he was told. Once he was naked, the men beat him until he collapsed. They continued to kick him, laughing. The jerky camera movements indicated that Cemal had joined in.

The man on the floor grew still. Past the point of screaming, all he could do was moan. The men stopped. Two of them grabbed him and yanked him back on his feet, though they had to hold him upright. They then wrapped him in an orange tunic resembling a hospital gown, which had been lying on one of the chairs. After binding his hands and feet, they pulled a cap over his face and led him outside.

The prisoner was tossed into the bed of a white pickup next to a mounted antitank weapon. One of the men sat beside him, while Cemal and the two others climbed into the cab. Cemal filmed the landscape en route. Niall expected to see gutted houses and abandoned streets, but what they drove through was an intact residential area. Cars passed by as people strolled down the sidewalks, talking on phones or chatting. Hardly anybody turned to look at Cemal and the truck. Pickups with mounted anti-tank weapons must have belonged to the normal street scene there. Obviously, IS had been in the area for several weeks, if not months, already.

They left the city and seemed to land immediately in an unpopulated, barren region of sand, dust, and sun. Niall could barely make out the topography. The men chatted with each other as music blared from the radio. Cemal made random comments. Due to his proximity to the microphone, he was the only one whose remarks were even partially audible. He was speaking in Arabic, but he seemed insecure in the language. The footage broke off abruptly, but then it started up again.

The prisoner was pushed off the truck bed. He landed in the dust. The man who had shoved him jumped off the truck and kicked him, laughing as he did so. He then jerked the prisoner to his feet and led him a short distance away from the truck. Cemal had begun speaking, giving instructions in a combination of English and Arabic. He told the men to go to a particular spot where he could get good camera angles.

Niall already knew the place, the images of the beheading still sharp in his mind. They would use a small rise and film it from below, so it would look like Ted Stein and his executioner were standing on a mountain summit with nothing behind them but open sky. A simple, yet effective, staging.

Although Stein did not struggle against his captors as they dragged him forward meter by meter, he kept twisting around in Cemal's direction. He could not see anything since the cap was still pulled over his face, but he could track the direction of Cemal's voice.

Stein called out: "Hey, you're from England, right? You aren't part of this. Your English is very good, but your Arabic isn't. You're not one of them. Can't you help me? What they're doing isn't right." The man behind Stein struck him and yelled something. The two in the front turned around and laughed. Cemal remained silent.

The journalist did not. He shouted: "Do something! They're going to kill me! You can't agree with that. I haven't done anything. I came here to report on the situation in the Middle East. I'm one of the good guys. Please!"

Cemal stopped walking and stammered something in Arabic, directing the others to move a little further to the right. They had found the spot. He evaluated more than one angle, searching for the ideal one. He dropped to his knees, then scooted forward and backward before finally choosing a position. He called out something Niall could not understand, and then the camera shut off.

Niall recognized the next shot. They had reached the execution. Niall paused the video, stood up, and walked around, unsure if he wanted to watch the next scene. He opened the door to see if Beth was coming back and took steps down the corridor in the direction she had gone. Beth was nowhere in sight, but another woman was striding toward him. He did not recognize her, but she nodded in greeting.

"Niall?" she asked.

"Yes, and you are…?"

"Nicole. Hi. You're looking for Beth, right? She's in the restroom, not feeling so well."

"Oh, what happened?"

"Go on in. She's over at the sinks." The woman walked on.

Niall found the women's restroom and knocked cautiously but received no response. "It's me, Niall," he called. Still no answer.

"Beth, are you in there? Someone called Nicole said I should check on you."

The door opened, and Beth met his eyes as cool and collected as ever. Yet, there was something different about her. Her eyes were a little red, and she was breathing heavier than usual.

"What happened?" he asked, staying in the hall.

Beth stepped out of the restroom. "Let's go." She moved past him, heading toward her office. He followed.

"I already started the next video. It's really rough." "Explain."

"Cemal was there when they beheaded Ted Stein."

"Ah."

"He filmed it. I haven't watched it all the way through, but they've already taken him to the execution site."

"How did Cemal get mixed up in that?" she asked as she entered her office.

The scene showed a figure in black clothes and a black headscarf, his face almost completely covered, his short shadow pointing in Stein's direction. Niall sat down at the computer and ran the video back five minutes to compare the shadow lengths. The shadows in the earlier footage were similar in length. The video had to have been shot shortly before or after noon. He was unable to guess the direction of the sun.

"Who's that?" Beth asked.

"Ted Stein." Niall was puzzled.

"Stop it. The other one."

"No idea. Just one of them."

Beth shook her head.

The man in black was holding a sword. He pulled the cap from Ted Stein's head, then stepped closer to the American. He stood with legs spread, knees slightly bent, bouncing a little.

"Pause it," Beth said.

Niall hit stop. "What's wrong?"

"Just a sec," she murmured as she tapped away at her phone.

"Are you checking your email or something?"

"Wait." Within seconds, she held the phone out to him. It showed a still from the video that had made its way around the world.

"Okay. So what?"

"Look at it closely."

It took him a moment to grasp why Beth had shaken her head. Her gesture had not been in incomprehension but because Ted Stein's executioner looked totally different in the video still she held out. There, he wore no black, but a black-and-white headscarf and sand-colored clothes instead. He also had a completely different build from the man they had just seen in the video. In frustration, Niall looked back at the computer screen.

"Is that Cemal?" Niall asked, more to himself than to Beth. "Shit, it's Cemal. I thought he was doing the filming, but he's the one standing there…"

"Did he change his clothes or something? What's it all mean?"

"No clue. Scroll back a bit. Was anyone else there in all black?" Niall ran the video back a short time but saw no one else in black.

"Okay," Beth replied. "That has to be Cemal. Hit play."

But Niall could not bring himself to do it. He hesitated. He could not bear to watch the man be forced to wait on his unavoidable death. To know that within only minutes of the film, Stein would be dead. In reality, he had died weeks ago, and there was nothing that could be done to change that.

"Damn it, I can't."

Beth looked at him, silently.

He felt a need to justify himself. "This is hard for me! I don't watch stuff like this every day. I mean, for years, my job was to film pretty landscapes. And animals. Glossy crap like that. High-end films. Discovery Channel and stuff. I can't stand here and watch a person be murdered!"

Beth was still studying him. "You think it's easy for me to take?" she asked quietly.

He realized right away that he had made a mistake, that there was a reason why she had stayed in the restroom as long as she had. She did not want to discuss it, but she was just as upset as he was. And he had implied that she was simply immune to the brutality and insanity.

"I'm sorry," he said. "Really. I just thought—no idea. Maybe a person can develop strategies that make it easier over time, or at least—"

"Yeah, you do. Because if you don't, you can't survive. But that doesn't mean it gets any easier. Images like this can destroy you. The more of them you see, the faster you come apart. I don't want to know what the mental space of someone like Leonard Huffman must be like. A friend of mine who was a war photographer killed himself after he won the Pulitzer. He couldn't stand to be celebrated for all the horrifying pictures he had taken. He felt as if he had profited from the suffering of the people he had photographed. As for me personally, I opt for the tank strategy. It turns you cynical, hard, and unfair, and I wouldn't recommend it." She spun her desk chair away from him, propped her feet up on the desk, and acted as if she were checking her email on her phone. "It's your call when we continue."

Niall was angry at himself. How could he have been so blind to think that Beth's attitude was anything more than a defense mechanism? How could he have accused her of insensitivity and then expected her to show sympathy for his fear of what came next in the film? If there was anyone who clearly had no idea how to treat other people, it was he, not Beth.

He thought about what it was that made him so afraid to keep watching. It was not only the approaching violence. He was fully aware of the facts. But the human brain was easily confused by watching things in real time. Even if one was aware something was not live, the hope still lingered that the course of events could be changed. Even though he knew the event took place somewhere else in the past, the impulse to intervene remained. As children call out to actors in a film, they are watching to warn them of impending danger.

It was the helplessness that crippled him. To be so close to the horror and unable to do anything to stop it. It brought on a wish to wake up and find himself in a completely different world. Yet, he was the one who had stood there while Cemal and Farooq had done something similar.

"Let's keep going," he said, hitting play.

The man swathed in black, who was most likely Cemal, grasped the sword in both hands and gave it a couple of practice swings. The voices of the others could be heard in the background. Cemal hesitated, nodded, then stepped back into position. In English, he called to Stein: "Alright, you're up." Niall no longer doubted it was him. He recognized Cemal's voice. Stein said nothing.

"Come on."

Stein did not move.

"Say it!" Cemal gave him a kick, and Stein fell forward, his face in the dirt. Cemal stood where he was, still gripping the sword: "I didn't kick him hard! He made himself fall, I swear!"

Two men ran into view and propped Stein back up. One of them punched him in the face and screamed at him in Arabic. Stein shook his head and did not seem to understand. The man yelled once more before hitting him again. The other man pushed him aside and planted himself in front of Stein. He said something to him, softly enough that the microphone did not pick it up. Stein shut his eyes. The man grabbed his colleague by the arm and pulled him off screen. Cemal looked at the camera. "Can we continue now?"

"Yes," an unrecognizable voice said.

Cemal resumed his position, legs apart and sword extended in front of him.

Stein looked up at him and then into the camera. He said: "My name is Ted Stein. I am a citizen of the United States, and I was abducted in Syria six months ago. The President of the United States bears the guilt for the fact that I am here and am going to be executed. His policies are causing what is happening today. They are the reason why the brothers of the Islamic State are taking extreme measures and have to fight so bitterly. I have come to the true faith and am dying as a Muslim." He sounded no more convincing than an amateur actor at his first audition.

Cemal said: "The American government could have bought this man's freedom for a ransom of one hundred million dollars, but it chose not to. This man is dying for his God and as a warning to all the infidels in his native country. We demand that the President of the United States and his allies cease their attacks against us and abandon their efforts to stop us. If this does not happen, another man will die."

Stein closed his eyes. Cemal pulled his arms back to strike.

The sword hung suspended there in the air before clattering to the ground. Stein ducked his head, and Cemal covered his face with his hands. He yelled, "Shit! Shit! Shit!" as he fell to his knees next to Stein and sobbed.

The scene went black.

Two seconds later: Ted Stein knelt in the dust, his hands bound. His executioner, this time the right one, stood beside him, holding a machete. The shadows of both men stretched long across the ground. Some hours had passed. The journalist repeated what he had said earlier, with just as little conviction as before, his face looking numb and frozen. When he was finished, he closed his eyes. His executioner uttered the same words Cemal had. You could tell from his enunciation that he was a native Arabic speaker. However, the lilt and vowels seemed to show that he had lived in Australia and had learned to speak the language there.

When he finished his speech, he stood behind Stein, the machete in his right hand. With his left hand, he grabbed the man under the chin and pulled his head back to expose his neck. In one swift movement, he slit his throat. A gurgling sound could be heard, like the sound of someone drowning. Blood spurted everywhere. The executioner slid the blade across Stein's throat one more time before letting the lifeless body collapse onto the ground. The other two men ran up and stopped beside Stein's body to talk. One of them walked off, then returned with an axe and the sword Cemal had used earlier. They continued their discussion. The man who had fetched the axe eventually picked it up and finished the decapitation, which needed several blows. Somebody off screen could be heard vomiting. Probably Cemal.

The man with the machete picked up the head and gave directions to the two other men. They flipped Stein's body onto its stomach and stretched it out lengthwise to the camera. The man carrying the head turned toward the camera and asked something. Cemal responded in English, his voice sounding exhausted and depressed. He could not stop coughing. "Further up, a little to the left, that's it." The executioner set the head down, waiting on further instructions from Cemal. Finally, everything was set up the way it was supposed to be. Still gripping the bloody machete, the executioner positioned himself next to the corpse. He proudly raised the machete over his head, and Cemal focused on it for a second before telling him it was a wrap. The camera then swung down to Stein, sweeping across the body and the head before returning to its starting point.

Cemal's voice: "That's it. We're done."

The Australian asked: "Can you make a cool film out of that?"

"Yeah, sure," Cemal replied. The scene went black.

22

"Stop," Beth ordered.

"Would love to."

"I have never felt such a strong urge to spend hours watching cute, fluffy kitten videos."

He gazed at her incredulously, hoping he was making a joke when he said: "It would be too much for you to cuddle a real cat, wouldn't it?"

"Let's not go that far." She grabbed her purse as she moved toward the door. "Alright then."

"Sure. Have a good evening, kitten videos and all."

"I meant that I needed a break. I didn't say I was calling it a night."

"When will you be back?"

"No idea." She vanished down the corridor.

Shaking his head, Niall watched her go. She had called it her tank strategy. She had said she wouldn't recommend it. Hard, cynical, and unfair. She had set off a domino effect of thoughts. How did his father cope with all this? Niall knew why he did what he did, but he had no idea how he dealt with everything. He wished he had thought to ask it earlier, though in a purely theoretical sense. The answer now seemed critically important.

Niall felt like a huge, gaping wound, aching and burning, and it made him feel nauseated. What was he supposed to do now? Why in the world did he want to tell the story of two people who were willing to chop off people's heads? If there ever had been a specific moment when he absolutely needed to talk to Leonard, this had to be it. Niall got up, shut the office door behind him, and turned down the corridor, only to come face-to-face with Leonard.

"Hello, Niall. You look like you could use a drink."

"Or two. I was just coming your way."

"How nice! You're going to Carl and Susan's, too, right?"

"Oh, crap. I completely forgot. I didn't even get her a gift," he replied, trying not to think about how strange it felt for Leonard to be invited to family gatherings. "I actually wanted to talk to you."

"Oh? About what?"

Niall studied him, how he stood there and smiled almost distractedly. Tank strategy, Beth had called it. What was Leonard's method? To lock it up and smile it away? To simply not talk about it? Niall said: "We can do that later. I need to pick up a present first."

"We'll figure it out on the way."

"Any ideas?"

Leonard thought for a moment. "She said she'd love to have a signed copy of my new book. Maybe you'd want to give her something else? Besides, she doesn't strike me as a particularly bookish person, but I don't know her as well as you do."

"Your books have lots of pictures in them." Niall grinned. "At the same time, they aren't ones she'll find all that pleasant. Are you sure that she really wants one of your books?"

"That's what she said."

"She was being polite."

"That's what I was afraid of. Hmm, does Susan have any hobbies? Secret passions?"

"China."

"China. As in dishes?"

Niall shook his head. "Could we make a quick stop at Harrods?"

"It's out of our way."

"Trust me, you'll find a whole new universe of porcelain there. And after what I was just watching, a stroll through Harrods is exactly what I need."

"Distraction?"

Niall nodded.

Leonard looked at him gravely before placing his hand on Niall's shoulder and saying: "Is that what you wanted to talk about?"

"What? No, it's not that pressing, honestly."

"Niall?"

"Hm?"

"I know what it feels like. Let's go to Harrods."

Carl and Susan lived in West Harrow, a neighborhood in the upper northwest corner of London, on a street that did not have typical rowhouses, but rather single family homes, standing free and surrounded by a few square meters of lawn. That particular evening, the quiet residential street was full of the parked cars belonging to the couple's guests. Niall noticed the black limousine conspicuously parked near the front door. A very special guest was there, Carl's ex-wife, the Home Secretary. Almost thirty years before, Niall had called her Aunt Karen. Carl and she had separated when Niall was ten and his mother was still alive. "Why are they getting divorced?" he had asked his mother.

"Karen has other interests. She is very ambitious and wants to go far in life. Carl isn't comfortable with that. He says he wants a wife who has his back, who will take care of the house and be there for him."

Niall had not understood what she meant by "has his back," and his mother had carefully explained it to him. That, and why some men thought there was no reason why married women would want to be professionally successful. "Are you successful at your job?" he had asked his mother.

"Darling, I picked this life for myself and am very happy with it. Karen wants a different life than the one Carl imagined for the two of them. Okay?"

Not too long after that, Karen had started to appear often in the newspapers and on television. Carl, on the other hand, switched from the military to the Ministry of Health and married Susan, Karen's exact opposite—naive, shy, not especially intelligent, but domestic. She was attractive, almost pretty, and a few years younger than Carl. She was fine with the fact that Carl did not want any children. To make up for it, she was allowed to keep dogs. The poodle who greeted Niall and Leonard at the door was still quite young—Susan's pride and joy, her third to date. Karen's bodyguards, who were patting down each visitor as they entered, were less thrilled. Which is why the hostess was all the more enthusiastic about Niall's gift.

"An elephant," she crowed happily before adding the small, white china figurine to an absurdly tacky collection of porcelain elephants crowded atop an antique side table. Niall avoided making eye contact with Leonard, afraid he might not be able to keep from laughing if he did.

The living room was packed. Carl had arranged for a catering service to manage all the details. Tuxedoed servers maneuvered nimbly through the crowd; full trays held aloft. If the party was like all the rest of Susan's birthdays, the guests would spend their time chatting with Carl or with each other, but rarely with her. The only difference was that, tonight, more people had been invited. Leonard was one of those not typically on the list, and he marveled at the mixture of lawyers, politicians, and business people. Niall thought he recognized the publisher of a major daily newspaper, as well as a popular playwright. Some of the men were accompanied by their wives, dressed elegantly as if for a gala event, complete with glittering jewelry. Yet even those women seemed to feel no need to talk to Susan.

"These aren't Susan's friends, are they?" Leonard whispered to Niall.

"We should talk to her. Nobody else will," Niall answered.

"Why aren't her friends here?"

"She doesn't have any. She has Carl."

Leonard shook his head slightly. He took his hostess's arm and asked her to show him around the house and garden. It was at that moment Carl discovered the new arrivals.

"Oh, Leonard, hopefully my wife isn't monopolizing you!" Carl cut in.

"I hope it isn't too much to ask if this charming young lady might give me a tour of her lovely home," Leonard declared, sounding dead serious. He turned to Susan. "Niall has told me you collect china figurines. How fascinating! Could you please tell me all about them?" The giggling Susan let herself be led away.

"What was that?" Carl asked, truly astonished.

"He wants to do something nice for her since it's her birthday."

"I've done something nice for her. I invited all these fascinating people over. Isn't it a great party?"

Niall rolled his eyes. "Don't act as if you have no idea what I'm talking about."

"But I don't."

"Let's drop it then."

Carl looked miffed. "Fine, but don't think I won't come back to this." He glanced around. "Where did the two of them go?"

"She's giving him a tour of the house, just like she said she would."

"What is there to see?"

"Carl, she's having a good time. Just let it go."

"Do I need to be worried that the old—"

"He's not all that much older than you."

"He is quite older than I am!"

"Could we talk about something else? If Susan's behavior bothers you so much, you might as well have stayed married to Karen."

"I heard my name," echoed a hard, piercing female voice. Karen Wigsley, the Home Secretary of the United Kingdom approached. Tall, slim, brown-haired—dyed, of course, because she was in her mid-fifties. Not a single gray hair was in sight. Karen was wearing dark-rimmed glasses and a navy-blue suit that fit her perfectly, accented with matching pumps and understated jewelry, as if she expected she might need to step in front of a camera at any second.

"Aunt Karen," Niall said with a grin. He knew this would annoy her. "I saw you this morning at the studio."

"Niall, my boy, if you're still wearing diapers, feel free to call me 'Aunt'." Karen gave him a peck on both cheeks. "Why didn't you come say hello? We haven't seen each other in ages."

"Should I have videobombed your interview?"

"You could have waited until I was done."

"I was with a colleague."

"Oh, do I embarrass you?"

"Just the things you say."

She laughed. "Then I said the right things. Niall, I heard that you and your father are now working together as a team."

He nodded and wanted to tell her about it, but she did not give him a chance.

"A documentary about those jihadists, right?"

Again, all he could do was nod. He did not have time to do anything besides open his mouth and take a breath.

"Knowing your father and that station, I assume this is yet another attempt to spin the attackers as victims. Right? My boy, I would have thought you'd have more sense than that. I understand you want to impress your father, but don't you think there are more reasonable projects with which you could make a name for yourself?"

"Karen, I don't think this is the—"

She didn't even bother to listen. "Look, those two criminals—thank goodness they're dead now. Who knows, they might have eventually gotten early parole thanks to difficult childhoods or something like that. Anyway, those two criminals volunteered to be trained as murderers, and they returned to our country to harm us. I don't even want to know how the poor parents of that young Air Cadet are doing. That was horrible. But those two murderers had only one goal—to hit us where it hurts. The young man was killed as a representative of each of us. It was a declaration of war on our own soil."

"Karen, the cameras aren't running."

"And you want to justify what they did," she continued, unperturbed. "I can't understand why you have to do that, Niall. Really."

"This morning, you didn't ask even once about Paul Ferguson's parents. You spouted campaign slogans."

"I did? They never give you enough time on those programs. Of course, Paul's parents received a card from me. And flowers. I think." She glanced over her shoulder as if expecting to see one of her assistants who could assure her that flowers had indeed been sent.

"How nice. Can you repeat what you said just that way when I film you?"

She waved him off. "I already know what kind of film you're making. All that liberal hogwash, out-of-touch and irrational." She grabbed a glass of champagne from one of the passing trays. "How much did you watch this morning?"

"Only part of it. We had to leave to—"

"That philosophy professor, Haynes or whatever. Dreadful person."

"The one pushing his book?"

"The one without makeup. Have you been anywhere near the Israeli embassy lately? You should check it out and shoot some footage over there for your documentary." She spat out the last word as if it were profanity, all the while standing there and looking as if she were making small talk. She even smiled. "They get together over there and scream anti-Israel slogans. I don't even know where to start with the entire pro-Gaza crowd. Do any of them have even one smidge of historical awareness?"

"I think you're getting things mixed up. That doesn't have anything—"

"I'm not mixing anything up. One of those terrible men said he was Palestinian. Hamas is too tame for people like him. Hamas! Too tame! And then those demonstrators gather in front of the Israeli embassy and—"

"Those are antiwar demonstrations, not anti-Israel ones."

She refused to be distracted. She was used to diversionary tactics and even more accustomed to ignoring them. "—in front of the Israeli embassy and demand that Hamas be let off the hook. Nobody could support that."

"Karen, it's Susan's birthday. Couldn't we talk about something else?" Niall grabbed a glass of champagne although he didn't really want one. The effort paid off—a toast to calm ruffled feathers. "To Susan, hmm?"

"Works for me." Karen sipped languidly on her drink, her eyes skimming the room with the steady calm of a surveillance camera. The voices of about fifty people hummed around her, accents cultivated in expensive private schools, all sounding like Carl's and Karen's, none like Susan's. "What did you give her?"

"A china elephant."

"Nice."

"And you?"

"Carl called me and said she was wishing for some china figurine from…um…what is that German stuff? Hutchin… something?"

"Hutschenreuther."

"That's it. How did you know that?"

Niall shrugged. "I didn't go to college, but I picked up a little general knowledge along the way."

Karen waved this off. "General knowledge? This falls in the specialist category. Anyway, she wanted some figurine from this Hutschen whatever. Something called Sun Child, a woman dancing on a golden ball."

"Sounds much nicer than a china elephant."

She laughed. "Of course, Susan didn't just wake up one morning and suddenly have good taste. He came up with the idea for her, even told me the name of the modeler, as if I'd remember something like that. The figure dates from 1933, that much I did notice. Hopefully, it didn't have anything to do with the Nazis, but you never know when it comes to the Germans. How did we get on this topic? Because of Israel? Oh well, you don't want to talk about that. I was supposed to buy that Sun Child figurine. Do you have any idea how expensive it is? My assistant told me that it would run at least two hundred and fifty pounds."

Niall nodded. "Sounds like a collector's item. My elephant didn't cost anywhere close to that."

"Exactly! And did she like it? Of course, she liked it!" Karen emptied her glass as she caught sight of someone with a tray heading her way.

Without asking, she set her empty flute on the tray and claimed a new one.

"Something tells me that you didn't give her a dancing woman on a golden ball."

"Of course not. I mean, please, I'm Carl's ex-wife. You could say that he left me for her. I'm supposed to give her a gift that cost two hundred and fifty pounds? It would look like I was jealous."

Niall could not help smiling. "Karen, you really are impossible."

She rolled her eyes. "Boy, I'll try to take that as a compliment."

"Why would you say he left you because of her? I heard a very different version of that story."

"From whom?"

"My mother. She said back then that the two of you had very different interests. It sounded amicable."

"It was." She leaned forward slightly and dropped her voice. "But he had already had something going on with Susan at that point. It wasn't all that bad, though. I had been looking around for some time, too." She smiled meaningfully and tacked a "quite a bit" to the end.

Niall raised his free hand. "Please, no details."

She laughed loudly. "When you reach my age, discretion and shame feel quite different." She leaned toward him again. "Know what? People at my advanced age still have sex. As do people your father's age, so I've heard."

"I need more champagne," Niall groaned.

"Splendid! As this country's Home Secretary, I order all British citizens to be less uptight." She lifted her flute and called loudly, "To all lovers over fifty!"

Several guests managed half-hearted cheers, but the majority simply mumbled something discreet in agreement. Susan and Leonard had just returned from their tour. The hostess was smiling, her face slightly flushed. Her eyes, thankful and full of admiration, were focused on Karen.

"She likes you," Niall whispered.

"Of course, she likes me. She likes anybody who's nice to her. She is like a puppy in a shelter, grateful for even a little scrap of attention. Speaking of which, where is that dreadful brute?"

"With your bodyguards."

"Hopefully they won't smell too doggy afterwards."

Susan joined them. "Are you talking about dogs?"

Niall answered quickly: "Karen was just telling me about the wonderful present she gave you."

Susan broke into another smile, and Niall had the fleeting impression that her eyes were damp. "Wait, I'll go get it. I have to show it to you." She blazed a path between her unknown guests and vanished.

"Please tell me what it is so I can gauge the appropriate reaction," Niall begged.

Karen gave a little sigh. "It's just a vase. I don't know why she has to be so dramatic about it."

"A vase? You gave her a bloody vase for her fiftieth birthday?"

Karen stared at him, insult written across her face. "She liked it!" Susan returned with a bulbous, white porcelain vase, over one meter tall, in which a hundred long-stem roses would have looked lost.

"Isn't it wonderful? Nobody would buy something like this for themselves. When you see a piece like that in a shop, you always think, how gorgeous, but what would I do with it?" She did not seem to notice Karen's fake little coughs. "That's why you don't ever buy one. But she gave it to me! Carl must have tipped her off." She lifted the giant vase up even higher, as if worried Niall might miss out on its details, and completely vanished behind it. "The nicest part of all is that Carl promised to bring me flowers long enough to fit in it." She beamed at Niall and Karen, clearly expecting cries of approval.

Karen turned to Niall: "You need to seriously consider whether or not you're taking the right approach with this film. You know what? You should come visit me at the Ministry. No, we should meet somewhere else. More casual. But with your team. It can't be a well-rounded documentary if I'm not in it. After all, this horrific attack falls within the scope of my responsibilities." She lifted her glass and clinked it against Niall's before tapping it against the vase. "Have a great evening, Susan. I have to go. Thanks for the champagne." With those words, she disappeared between the guests.

"Did I say something wrong?" Susan asked anxiously, setting the vase on the floor.

"Not at all. It was my fault."

"Oh, you annoyed her?"

Niall shrugged. However amusing he found Karen's sharp tongue and snide comments, however inclined he might have been to chuckle over Susan's naïveté and bad taste, there were limits. He felt the need to make up for Karen's rude behavior, "Just ignore her. You know how she can be. Once again, happiest of birthdays to you, and here's to the next fifty years!" He leaned down and kissed her on the cheek. "And the vase is great. I will buy you flowers for it the next time I come for a visit." As he turned, he found Carl standing behind him, smiling warmly and gratefully at him. ◌

23

He had intended to head home after spending a polite hour at the party, but Niall found himself caught up in various conversations with an array of people he did not know. Some of them recognized him from the news coverage, and they asked about his experiences with the Islamist attackers, out of equal parts curiosity and horror. Others had seen him on the morning talk show and asked him about the mother of the murdered Air Cadet. At some point, he fled outside, drained, into the small back garden, grateful for the fresh air and amazed at how mild the night was. He looked at the time: it was 12:30 already. He had hoped it was around 11.

"Trying to escape, too?" Carl asked, trailing him outdoors.
"Definitely."
Carl smiled: "Thank you for being so nice to her."
"Of course. Karen is just…" The right word failed him.
"I know."
"It's surprising the two of you are still so close."
Carl smiled. "You think so? I suppose it has more to do with the fact that Karen simply doesn't have time to make new friends."
"Over the past twenty years?"
"She's a very busy woman. You don't become Home Secretary overnight."
"You're probably right." Niall's eyes fell on the book Carl was carrying. "Did Susan like Leonard's gift?"
"Oh yes, she's really happy about it. A signed copy with a personal dedication—she loves it."
"Did she already flip through it?"

Carl shook his head.

"Does she have any idea what's in it?"

"Of course. Don't you start in now, too."

Niall reddened a little. "That's not what I meant."

Carl took walked out onto the lawn before stopping and looking up into the sky. "There's supposed to be an incredible meteor shower tonight. At least, that's what they said on the radio." Niall joined him and gazed up into the darkness. He had to wait some time, but then he saw two meteors, one after the other.

"Is Leonard still here?" Niall asked.

"Yes, I saw him a few minutes ago. He seems to be holding up just fine." Carl glanced over his shoulder as the back door opened. "Ah, there you are."

"I was looking for you."

"And we were just talking about you."

"Should I be worried?" Leonard asked, giving Carl a friendly pat on the back.

Carl held up the book. "Thanks again."

"My pleasure. Susan is a very nice woman."

"Yes, she is."

Leonard looked up into the sky as well. "Isn't tonight the big meteor shower?"

"We've already seen a couple of them," Niall remarked.

Leonard continued to stare up. "It's very peaceful out here, quite different from where I live in Notting Hill. The noise never stops, day or night. You can still hear it even if you have all the doors and windows shut. But I like it. It reminds me of the life going on around me." His hand shot up. "There, now I've seen one!" He turned back to the two men. "It must be over twenty years since I last saw a meteor shower."

"Over twenty years? Has it been that long since you looked into the sky?" Niall laughed.

"It's probably because I was always looking for the next shot, and the stars weren't exactly my specialty."

"Why do you remember that last time?" Niall asked. "Did your wish come true?"

"No, but it was a very particular time, back in 1991. I was one of the few photographers allowed to cover the Gulf War." Leonard hesitated, glancing back up at the sky. "It's such a nice, clear night. It must be stunning out in the country. You see so many more stars out there." He patted his son on the shoulder. "The sky over Iraq...Well, it was a long time ago."

"Weren't there some pretty strict controls over what could be reported?"

Leonard nodded. "The Americans had their own media pool, and we were only allowed to publish the things they approved."

"Embedded journalism," Niall commented.

"Yes, but that term only appeared later on."

"What does this have to do with the meteor shower?" Carl asked, sounding bored. He strolled over to the edge of the garden, where a stone bench sat under a willow tree. He sat down with a tired sigh.

"The last time I recall seeing a shower like this, I was in Kuwait," Leonard explained. "At first, I wasn't sure if they were missiles, but they were meteors. It had to be meteors because no missiles were fired that night. By that point, the war was over, which is why I remember that evening so well. It was the night I thought about just walking away from it all."

Niall was surprised. He had never heard that Leonard had come close to giving everything up. He had never mentioned it in an interview. Niall studied his father, but the older man only had eyes for the sky. Niall wondered if he could ask about what had happened back then, mentally running through the photos he knew had been taken during that time. He finally asked: "How long were you there?"

"Two months."

"There aren't many photos from that time. Was that because of the censors?"

Leonard did not answer right away. He took stepped toward Carl, who was leaning back as if about to fall asleep.

"As an embedded journalist, you spend your days and nights with the soldiers. You begin to identify with them and start to lose your objectivity, your professional distance. As a photographer, you aren't only responsible for documenting everything impartially. You also have to make sure that your pictures are clear in their message. A picture of a dying child whose leg has been torn off by a grenade? That same picture can tell different stories, depending on who is using it. That's the risk. Many photos lack meaning simply because the connotation isn't clear."

"Is that why you didn't publish many of your pictures back then?"

"They were worthless, meaningless. I beat myself up a lot because of that, and after I returned home, I swore I'd never let myself be manipulated like that again, not by the military or the government, or by terrorists or rebels."

"We need war coverage."

"Of course. I'm just saying that it's a terribly complicated position to be in, and you have to remain very diligent and aware of what is happening to you. The journalists doing it today are much better prepared. I wasn't."

Niall declared: "You have taken so many important pictures throughout your life."

Leonard laughed: "Thank you. But if I may offer a little fatherly advice, please forgive my sentimentality—regardless of what happens, the only important thing is that you stay true to yourself."

Niall nodded, a little embarrassed. "War propaganda and media manipulation have been around forever," he remarked, trying to steer the conversation back onto unemotional rails.

"Back then—as a means of justifying their involvement, which really was motivated by nothing more than oil and power—the Americans made a series of videos that supposedly showed how the Kuwaitis were being persecuted by the Iraqis. I'm not saying they fabricated everything, but they did invent some things. There were eyewitness accounts given in exchange for money, and some pretty incredible acting talents were involved. For example, it was said that the Iraqis entered a Kuwaiti hospital, where they took preemies out of their incubators and let them die.

The supposed nurse who gave this tearful report in front of the camera was, in reality, the daughter of the Kuwaiti ambassador to the US at that time. The film was made by a New York PR agency which had been hired by a Kuwaiti organization to help change Americans' opinions when it came to their involvement in the war."

Niall nodded. "I know the story."

"The famous incubator lie," he heard Carl mutter from the bench. "What a disaster."

Leonard glanced at his watch, moving back toward the house to catch a bit of light. "So late already? I'm sure you'll understand if I head home now. Carl, thank you for the invitation."

Carl stood up and shook his hand. "Thanks again. For everything."

Leonard smiled. "I'm sure I can track Susan down inside. Niall, I'll see you tomorrow. Good night."

After he vanished inside the house, Carl said: "I never would have thought he'd settle down. How long has he been with the station? When did he give up traveling from one crisis area to the next?"

"You know, he's not getting any younger, and he wants to start taking some things slower." Niall wondered how much his father's retirement from war photography had to do with the fact that he could no longer stomach all the things he had experienced over the decades.

"It's more a question of personality than age, I think."

Niall laughed. "You're talking about yourself, aren't you? Off to school at Harrow-On-The-Hill, college in London, and decades in this same house here."

"I don't like moving."

"I'm glad I don't have to walk past my old school every day. How do you do it?"

"I had a good time in school." Carl smiled. "But I understand what you mean. Only, see here, I'm on the go a lot. Conferences here, meetings there, and even if I don't have to leave the city for those, it's still stressful. I need my own space."

And a woman who has his back, Niall thought, though all he said was: "You have a really lovely home. I have always been envious."

"Oh, my boy, envy is never a good thing. You should simply feel at home here. You're welcome anytime."

"Thanks."

Carl looked back up into the sky and asked casually: "Is your film coming along well? Your—what should I call them—lead actors are now dead, unfortunately. Can you keep going with it?"

"Absolutely, especially now. We're going to check out their backgrounds, figure out their motives, interview their friends and relatives…" Niall rubbed his neck. It was time to stop watching the meteor shower. "I also want to try to shoot some footage in Syria or Iraq. I watched some videos today that—" He broke off, suddenly reluctant to reveal too much. "—that were impressive," he concluded.

Carl looked at him and grinned. "Rumors or sensible information?"

"Both. Don't worry, you'll be the first one to see anything once we're far enough along."

"Tell me," Carl replied hesitantly. "Did you talk to Karen about your arrest and what happened in the prison?"

"No."

"Why not?"

"Because I first want to talk to the attorney you mentioned to me. I haven't had a chance to call him yet."

"You should discuss everything with Karen."

"Whenever you talk to Karen about something important, it's probably best to have an attorney with you. Otherwise, you'll find yourself at a serious disadvantage."

"Hmm. Could be. Either way, couldn't she help with your film? I mean…"

"Don't bother. She basically told me tonight that I should abandon the project."

"She said that?"

"She thinks we're going to produce a sentimental piece of leftist propaganda about the poor attackers being victimized by society. Besides, she doesn't trust anything that doesn't have her in front of the camera at some point."

"Then let her have her say," Carl replied. "Why not?"

"No real reason, except that I sometimes disagree with her opinions. Especially in this context."

"It's interesting that that's what's worrying her. My concerns are quite different."

"How?"

"I'm worried some crazy Islamists are going to do something to you." Carl trailed off. He needed to say goodbye to guests who had wandered into the garden. When he was done, he returned to Niall: "I really am worried about you."

"Nothing's going to happen to me."

"Just don't go to Iraq. They don't let people like you back out again. You'd make the perfect hostage."

"Carl, we'll think about it. I'll take care of myself, promise."

His uncle eyed him skeptically. "Just don't get some idea that you need to play the hero to prove something to your father. Or anyone else. You aren't Leonard, and the situations he was in aren't anything like what IS is doing these days. Really, Niall. Be careful."

"Of course." But that was the rub. He wanted to make a serious documentary, and to do that, he needed to go to Syria and Iraq to retrace Cemal and Farooq's footsteps. And to show the world he was his father's son. Yet in reality, he was a coward, so scared he was about to wet himself. He knew Carl was right. It was highly likely he would be abducted. And as for his chances of survival—either he would live through it because somebody paid his ransom (which was quite unlikely), or he would be killed, sooner or later.

MONDAY
24

"I'll be free in shortly," the taxi driver said. Somebody was still sitting in the back.

"I already called a cab," Niall said. "I'm sure it'll be here any minute." It was past two, but he was not the last guest to leave the party.

"Yes, me. I was already heading this way."

"I'll just stay back here," Beth remarked from the back seat.

"Why aren't you getting out? You asked me to bring you here. I need to get on with my next fare now," the driver urged, a short, skinny man around sixty with an accent like an old dock worker and a voice only made possible by copious cigarettes and even more whisky.

"It's alright," Niall said, joining Beth in the back seat. "What are you doing here?"

"Leonard said you'd be here. You didn't answer your phone."

"Now what?" the taxi driver asked. "Where do you want to go? Is the lady going with you?"

"Brixton. Yes."

"Ah, is this your wife?"

"No. Could we—"

"But you'll have to pay for the trip out here, too. As long as we're clear on that."

"Sure, that's fine. But could we...We'd like a little privacy, if that's okay." Niall hoped his words came out friendlier than they sounded.

"Fine by me." The man turned back around and drove off.

They were silent for a moment, and then Beth said, "I've watched all the videos."

"You went back?"

"And you weren't there. Yes, it was really horrifying."

"I can imagine."

"After a few weeks, Cemal really got into his role as filmmaker. The off-camera commentary was sometimes provided by him and sometimes by Farooq. Whenever he spoke, he even tried to sound Arabic."

"He tried to hide his actual accent?"

"And he became more and more brutal and hardened. He even filmed himself practicing with animals. He cut off their heads, slaughtered them. It was like he was obsessed. He even hacked off somebody's hand. It looked like a European hostage, but I couldn't figure out who it was. I'm pretty sure he was the executioner in the last beheading video that went viral."

"The Irishman from the charity group who was abducted over a year ago?"

Beth nodded and folded her arms. She was wearing a t-shirt. It was quite warm, but Niall thought she looked like she was freezing.

"Serhat probably watched everything," he said. "They even talked about it." Niall rubbed his eyes. Suddenly, he felt so tired all he wanted to do was lie down. He asked the driver to open a window; he needed some air. "Maybe Serhat invented the story about the Service to cope with what his brother did."

"There's no way we can actually verify anything," Beth said. "Nobody from the bloody Service would ever talk with us. Or admit to something like that."

Niall thought for a moment. What if Cemal had been hired by MI5 to obtain information about future attacks on British soil, and it had all gone wrong? What then? "Is there any way to follow up on this theory somehow?" Niall asked.

"We could put his brother in front of the camera and see if anybody associated with him hears about it. There are also the normal channels—write various agencies and analyze their responses, although typically that doesn't turn up anything. Enough time hasn't passed yet for us to find former employees who might be willing to be whistleblowers. Maybe we could find some experts who could confirm our theories by providing supporting evidence of similar recent cases."

"It all sounds pretty vague."

"You'd risk ruining the film with conspiracy theories. At least, that's how the critics and viewers would see it. We would really need more to go on."

Niall fell silent as he weighed the options. Against her norm, Beth did not pull out her phone, choosing instead to stare out the window as if they were sightseeing.

"Karen Wigsley is insisting we put her in front of the camera," he finally said.

Beth turned toward him and almost looked amused. "She insists on being in front of every camera. Karen Fucking Wigsley has only one goal. She wants to be Prime Minister and have her spot in the history books. That way people will stop mentioning Maggie Thatcher when they want to talk about the person who has done the greatest damage to this country."

"She would probably put it a little differently."

"You know what I mean. Her press secretary has had a shitload of stress recently trying to tone down her comments."

Niall looked at her. "You mean her rather unfortunate statement about artificial insemination and lesbians?"

"'Rather unfortunate' is a pretty nice way of putting it. Besides that, she's a climate change denier. And, to top it all off, you can find an occasional, 'rather unfortunate' quote from her about foreign-born citizens or people with immigrant backgrounds. If she wants to run into an open knife, she should just get on with it. I'd stand nearby and applaud."

Niall noticed the driver was nodding vigorously. Of course, he had been listening closely to every word they said.

"I used to call her Aunt Karen years ago."

Annoyed, Beth studied him. "What do you mean? Whenever you saw her picture in the newspaper or something?"

"Don't be silly. When she and Carl were still married."

"Your Uncle Carl. The one you were just visiting?"

"Karen was his first wife. He was my mother's cousin, so I called him Uncle and his wife Aunt." Niall smiled. "That didn't show up in your research?"

"Society news isn't my area."

"Karen Wigsley falls within the political sphere."

"She hasn't been married since entering politics."

"It was a long time ago."

"Do I need to apologize now?" Beth asked.

"It's fine."

Beth gazed out the window, but this time not to watch the passing buildings. Then she turned back to him with a jerk. "I won't change my mind about this woman, just so you know."

"She doesn't think it's a good idea for us to make the film."

"She said that? At the party?"

"And she said that she wants us to interview her for the film."

"I see." After a moment of thought, she changed her position. She sat straight up on the edge of the seat, her hands pressed flat against the upholstery, as if about to jump up. "Niall, you couldn't have given me a better reason to follow up on this Service theory. We shouldn't waste any time either. Serhat didn't make it up. Cemal kept alluding to it. The Home Secretary supervises the domestic security services. I think we should go ahead and set up an appointment. What do you think?"

"Do you always change your mind so fast? It would be good for me to know, since we're going to be working together."

Her eyes were cool. "Do you want to make the appointment yourself?"

Niall sighed as he pulled his phone out of his pocket. "I'll email her." He started to type, reading aloud as he went along. "Dear Karen, it was really nice to see you at Carl and Susan's tonight. Thank you for your offer to be interviewed for my film. Would you possibly have time for that in the next few days? Love, Niall." He read it through once more before hitting send.

"'Love, Niall'—how sweet," Beth remarked.

"What? I'm just being polite."

"As long as you don't share her political opinions, I wouldn't care if you signed off with 'Cuddle Bunny.'"

"That will never happen. Neither the opinions nor the 'Cuddle Bunny' part."

"I'm not sure which one I find more comforting," Beth shot back as the taxi driver chuckled audibly.

Niall felt excluded by the unspoken alliance between the two of them. He continued, "Karen isn't very nuanced in her statements, that's true. That might be why people like her. Clear lines, unambiguous declarations. It's not my thing, but people feel like they know where she stands. And, in her own arrogant way, she can be rather charming."

The phone still clutched in his hand buzzed. He glanced at the display. "She's already written back."

"What did she say?"

"Just a sec." He clicked on the message. "We can meet with her tomorrow. She'll send us the time and place."

"Does that woman ever sleep, or why is she writing back at this time of night? It's almost 2:30."

Niall shrugged. "Maybe she really is like Maggie Thatcher and only sleeps four hours a night."

"I believe she has found a way to no longer need sleep." Beth said with her normal amount of chilly detachment, yet Niall could sense her disdain and hatred for Karen. He changed the topic. "I would like to nose around the mosque a little more to see if anyone there might have something to say about Cemal and Farooq. I still want to talk to Cemal's family and get Farooq's father in front of the camera. If he cusses us out, all the better. We will also need statements from the prison administrators."

"That'll be just like the Service. They won't go on official record about anything. Let me give it some thought. We'll figure something out…" The taxi slowed down. "What's going on?" She looked around, puzzled.

"We're in Brixton. This is my stop."

"Already? Why didn't you let me out earlier? Now I have to go back, and I don't have that much money on me."

"I don't know where you live."

Beth rolled her eyes. "Two bus stops from your Uncle Carl. The other side of the city."

"I'm sorry about that," Niall said, but Beth waved him off.

"I'll take the night bus to the station and sleep in my office."

He thought about inviting her up to his apartment. He would be able to sleep on the floor, and she could take the couch. Or something like that. He decided it was a bad idea. Instead, he paid the entire taxi fare, including Beth's share, and asked the driver to drop them off at the bus stop.

"I'm really excited about our film," Beth said, once they were outside.

"Ah, finally now?"

She made an unspecific gesture, almost like a flutter. "Especially now."

"Why?"

Beth studied the timetable as Niall looked on over her shoulder. Twenty minutes until the next bus. The only thing was that the schedule was unreliable at that time of night.

"If we can manage to get something that will harm Karen Wigsley, then we will have done something positive," Beth said calmly. "This Service rumor might do the trick. The thought of that makes me very happy." She looked at him.

Niall took the twitch of her mouth to be a smile. "Good night, Beth," he said, turning to go.

"Okay, sleep well," she called after him.

He was tired, and Beth was old enough to take care of herself. His main worry was that he no longer really knew what he was doing. Was he making a film to spotlight the end effects of failed integration policies or to topple the Home Secretary?

He trudged down the street, past the seemingly never-ending building that housed the Social Welfare Office as he thought about what had happened that day, the day before and the days before that. How should he manage everything? Beth was not the right person to talk to. She did not have even the slightest compunction exploiting his lifelong, almost familial relationship with a woman as a means of harming her. And his father? If Beth practiced the tank strategy, as she called it, by repelling negative stuff as much as possible, what about Leonard? Shopping with him at Harrods for china figurines, looking up into the sky and counting meteors—had those instances been suppression? Displacement mechanisms? Attempts to simply keep going? Efforts to cling to normalcy despite everything?

Niall was mad at himself for not simply asking him. Why had he not said something like, okay, I know the timing's bad, and we've been invited to this party, but right now, I'm not doing well and need to talk to you. That was what he should have done. It would not have been a problem with Pete, the man who had raised him and whom he had always called father. Niall still had no idea what the right words were to use with Leonard Huffman.

But Niall had the feeling that one day he would have them. As he crossed the street to his apartment, his phone went off. It was a text from Beth. "Everything's okay. Bus came a little early. Or a little late? Whatever. Talk to you soon."

He wondered if she really had no idea how he was doing. ▢

25

"It's what worked out," Laura explained patiently as Niall continued to shake his head and lean against the production van, hands in his pockets.

"Just ask me. Simply ask beforehand. That would help." His head was pounding. He had gotten less than four hours of sleep, and the sun was far too bright for him.

"Last night, Beth said it would be okay."

"Oh, okay. Well, if Beth said it was alright, then clearly no one needs to tell me anything."

"She's the producer," Laura replied, raising her hands defensively. "And she said she'd talk to you and give you the update. Work it out between the two of you."

They were parked next to the Vauxhall Pleasure Gardens, where everything had started, and they were waiting on Mrs. Ferguson, the murdered boy's mother. Niall never would have thought that talking to her so early in the film process was a good idea. And definitely not in the place where her son had been killed.

"I don't think this is a good idea at all, and to be honest, I don't want to film anything here." Niall saw Ken hurry by. "Ken, bring that equipment here and pack it back in the van."

Without a word, Ken made a beeline across the park along the trajectory Beth had just covered.

"Is this about your ego?" she asked, after Laura had whispered something to her.

"Laura, I thought you were on my side," Niall answered with a shake of his head. "What happened between yesterday and today? Beth, should I have waited with you for the bus?

I apologize for not staying with you. But I really have no idea what I did to Laura."

"Bus? You can't be serious. We're just doing our job," Beth declared serenely. "What's your problem? Laura and I made the arrangements for this shoot."

"You could have told me about this yesterday."

"There were more important things to discuss." Shading her eyes, she looked across the park. Niall followed her gaze—joggers, strollers, parents, and people walking. It was much busier than on the day Paul Ferguson had been murdered. Niall wondered how many of the people were there for the first time, just to see where everything had happened.

He said to Beth, "How could you have asked that poor woman to...here?" The words failed him, and he ended up gesturing vaguely.

"Ah, I see," Beth replied. "I thought this was about your pride. Ferguson wanted to do the filming here. I suspect she has a PR adviser. I heard she's sold her story to the Daily Mail. There'll be a sentimental article on tomorrow's front page, complete with childhood photos of Paulie."

All Niall could do was stare at her and shake his head: "And we're going along with this? Getting involved? You can't be serious."

"Sure, we can play along. We'll have a chance to comment on it however you like. You can call it exactly what it is."

"A load of shit?"

"That, too."

He nodded silently and scanned the green space. "I want lots of pictures of the PR adviser. I don't want whatever the two of them have cooked up for the camera, but I do want everything else that will be going on around us." He rubbed his face and looked over at the spot where Paul Ferguson had died. He walked along the path, then a short distance up the grass to where he had stood to film. He saw the mountain of flowers and wreaths, the stuffed animals and cardboard signs, the photos of Paul, some of them framed behind glass, others in transparent plastic sheaths. A wooden cross stood tall in the midst of the colorful mound, and several candles were burning, although their flames were practically invisible in the morning sun. Candles, like the ones in Christian cemeteries—memorial candles and a cross. A clear statement, Niall thought. He turned around and called for Ken to bring the camera. Niall remained where he was standing but pulled out his phone and filmed the memorial.

He told Ken to take some close-up shots with the camera of lots of details. The main thing, though, he emphasized—get footage of Niall as he filmed the site. A minute later, Mrs. Ferguson arrived, dressed all in black. Another woman in a dark blue business suit and high heels tried to walk with as much dignity as possible across the grass. As the two of them drew closer, Niall could see that the other woman was still quite young, perhaps Laura's age. "Stay on them," he told Ken.

"As usual?" Meaning—and keep the camera running even if you ask me to cut it off?

Niall nodded. He strode over to the camera, looked through it, and made comments about the settings he wanted. He then greeted the two women. The younger one's name was either Holly or Molly. He motioned for Laura to get a business card from her.

Mrs. Ferguson was heavily made up that day, on a scale that only actresses and broadcasters tended to reach. Her hair was carefully swept back, and Niall suspected she had recently been to a salon. Most likely, that morning. She did not look much at all like the Mrs. Ferguson who had attacked him in her despair over her son's death. Today's version was rather a soap opera variation of herself.

"I need to apologize to you," she said to Niall.

"No need to. How are you doing?"

"I'm pulling myself back together."

He examined her closely—there were dark rings under her thick makeup, and her eyelids were swollen and red. She noticed his scrutiny and added, "Well, the doctor is helping me with that."

"You're taking something for your nerves?"

She nodded. "Nothing else works right now."

"And your husband? Is he still in the hospital?" She nodded again.

"You should take a couple of days for yourself." He did not tell her she should be with her husband right now. She knew that's what he meant.

"I have to earn the money now. I hope you can understand that."

"I'm not here to judge you," Niall declared.

"But you're still thinking it."

"Mrs. Ferguson, I am so extremely sorry about what happened to Paul. I had not figured that you'd want to talk to us. That's all."

"I have to," she said, glancing around quickly. "Here by the cross, film me there." She walked over to the cross and stood next to it. "Is that alright?"

"That's fine, Mrs. Ferguson, wherever you want," Niall said, leaving his hand camera running. Ken's camera had been on for a while already. "Did you set up the cross?"

She nodded and pointed at the PR adviser. "It was her idea. My husband doesn't know anything about it." She studied the cross. "He'll like it."

"You just told me that you now have to earn the money. Did Paul give you some of what he made?"

She nodded silently.

"And your husband?"

"Unemployed. We both are." She spoke very quietly without looking at either Niall or the camera. Niall glanced at Ken, who gave him a thumb's up. The sound was okay.

"Did Paul have any siblings?"

She shook her head and stared at the cross. Niall let her take her time. She stretched her hand out toward the cross but did not touch it. With the tip of her shoe, she nudged a couple of the teddy bears lying around its base. Without turning toward the camera, she continued, "He wanted to go to college. Something with engineering. Technology, stuff like that. It was his dream.

That was why he joined the Air Force, so they would help pay for his tuition. He wanted to do that."

"I'm sure you were proud of him."

"Yes, of course."

Niall knew the reason she had turned her back to him was because she was afraid, she would start crying in front of the camera. "Do you want to take a break?" he asked.

She shook her head.

He decided to ask her something that would help her refocus. "What did you do professionally? Where did you work?"

"I didn't go to college." She lifted her head and glanced over her shoulder, uncertain about where she should be looking. She turned back to the cross. "I worked in a supermarket, but that was a long time ago. Paul was always a little embarrassed by that."

Her PR adviser came stumbling across the field. She clapped her hands and called out: "A short break? Could somebody maybe get us some coffee?" She fought her way across a molehill to Mrs. Ferguson and whispered something to her. The mourning mother immediately dropped to her knees, somewhat unsteadily, in the midst of the flowers, signs, and stuffed animals. She picked up one of the candles and looked nervously from one camera to the other.

"Is this right?" she asked.

The PR woman nodded. Niall said nothing. He just looked at Mrs. Ferguson kneeling because somebody had told her it would be good for the press, a bad PR adviser, who clearly had no idea what it meant to be filmed for a documentary, and who did not know that the moment had nothing to do with masquerades or pre-scripted statements. That the camera just kept rolling.

It was not totally fair, but it was printed in the contract that had been signed. Not everyone read the contract through completely. A good PR adviser should know these things. Mrs. Ferguson's seemed to know nothing.

Niall felt pity. He said: "Mrs. Ferguson, what are you doing?"

She looked at him with big eyes and shrugged.

"Please don't do anything you don't want to do."

She stayed on her knees and looked timidly over at the woman in the suit. "I don't want to be here at all," she murmured.

"Then why are you?"

Shrug.

"Did she tell you that you had to do this? For the money?"

Another shrug. The PR woman inhaled sharply and said, "Don't let him—"

"Mrs. Ferguson," Niall interrupted her, "this woman wants to make money off you. Go home. Or go visit your husband in the hospital. And fire her. I'm serious."

The PR woman started to protest. Out of the corner of his eye, Niall could see that Ken was recording her. He kept his hand camera trained on Paul's mother, who slowly got to her feet and trudged across the grass away from them, her head lowered. As the adviser tried to follow her, Niall said, "Leave her alone."

He did not expect her to stop, but she did. She crossed her arms and uttered a string of profanities before pulling out her phone and calling a taxi.

"I'm going advise Mrs. Ferguson not to pay you anything," Niall said to her.

"I have a contract with her." The young woman stared angrily at him out of her small blue eyes.

"Like we do with you. We filmed everything."

She propped her hands on her hips. "Are you threatening me?"

"No."

She glanced at the street as her taxi drew up. "Sounds like it."

"Under these circumstances, it would be best for us to not argue about which of us used more questionable methods, don't you think?"

With another bitter look, she stalked off and out of the park. Niall suddenly realized Beth was standing behind him, which could have been why the woman had decided to just leave.

"Great footage," she said.

"That was horrible."

"That's the way it goes if people want to be on the front page."

"It's not what she wants."

Beth shrugged before turning away. "There's no telling how she'll see things tomorrow."

Niall watched her walk toward the van. "Time to take it down," he called to the others.

He then noticed a small group of teenaged girls depositing more stuffed animals and cards around the cross. He waited until they walked away before shooting what they had left behind.

One card announced: "You are now in heaven. Your murderers are in hell," hand-decorated with a heart and an angel. The next card: "You are a hero!" with lots of hearts. Niall doubted these girls had ever met Paul Ferguson. He wondered how many of the stuffed animals and flowers had come from people who had known him personally.

He caught sight of a cardboard sign on which something had been written in black capital letters. A colorful bouquet covered the text. He pushed it aside and read: "We will avenge you. Death to Muslims!"

Niall called to Beth and showed her the sign.

"Not surprising," she said.

"Not surprising? Now what? Should we just leave it sitting here?"

Beth strolled around the improvised memorial, leaning down to look at some of the cards and pushing the flowers and teddies here and there. "Take the card with you. There'll be more like it soon enough," she said as she poked around.

"We can't just…" Niall broke off. There was no point in discussing it with Beth. He turned off the camera, picked up the sign, and ripped it into pieces.

Beth straightened up, holding a pink unicorn in one hand. She tapped the animal with one finger and watched as he tried to grind the pieces of paper into the ground.

"Feel any better?" she asked.

"No."

"Didn't think so." She set the unicorn back down beside the cross, where it looked as if it were keeping watch over the memorial. "If only everything were that simple. Black or white, dark or light." Without waiting for him, she started back toward the van.

He followed her reluctantly. She was right. Cemal and Farooq had killed people because of their commitment to a twisted belief system. There he was, upset at the people who wanted to repay an eye for an eye, who wanted to lump all Muslims together, while IS, on the other hand, was eager to do the very same thing with those they viewed as unbelievers. It felt like he was trying to defend Cemal and Farooq if only because he was at least trying to understand them. At the same time, he knew he would never be able to understand the attacking of innocent people and those who practiced their religions peacefully. If only everything was simple.

Back at the van, he asked: "Where are we going now? The mosque?"

"To meet Aunt Karen," Beth replied.

"Aunt Karen?" Laura took a seat in the back and pursed her lips. "You call Karen Wigsley Aunt Karen?"

"I don't," Beth remarked, jerking her thumb toward Niall. "He does. She used to be married to his uncle or something like that."

"Why are we going to meet Karen now? She hasn't been in touch with me yet." Niall opened the passenger door and got in. Ken slid behind the wheel and started the van.

"She contacted me," Beth commented from the back seat. "She called the station directly and made an appointment. Well, not she personally, but her office did. We're meeting her in an hour, so we have some time."

"Where?" Niall asked.

"Don't worry. We don't have far to drive."

"Where?"

Beth pointed north. "One bridge further and then the other side of the Thames."

"That's MI5."

"Yep."

On the short drive to Lambeth Bridge, Niall thought about Serhat's claim that his brother had been approached by MI5. If it were true, the whole thing had gone seriously wrong. The Service operatives had approached the wrong person, or he had simply jumped off the deep end. And now the Home Secretary was insisting that she be included in his documentary. In her position, she stood at the top of MI5. The domestic security services reported straight to her.

"Is there really no way for us to find out if Cemal was approached by MI5?" Niall asked as they reached the bridge and Ken switched on his left blinker.

Beth answered: "I looked into it. The Service always checks out the contacts of those they solicit. We could do the same, see if any of Cemal's friends or relatives were recently approached by people they didn't know. Of course, it's a relatively unreliable method. We might not learn anything."

"Let's do it," Niall declared. "Laura, can you coordinate the preliminary research?"

Laura jotted something down in her notebook. "On it," she said quickly as she pulled her phone out of her bag and started to type.

They took the first exit off the traffic circle on the other side of the bridge and drove past Thames House, MI5's headquarters, until they reached a bus bay on the side of the street. Ken pulled off and let the others out, waited for them to haul the equipment out of the back, then drove on in search of a parking space.

MI6 was only steps from where the attack had taken place, and MI5 was only one bridge further down. Niall was unsure if any of that meant anything. Irony or intent? It made him nervous.

They walked back a short distance to a narrow park sandwiched between the street and the Thames riverbank. Uniformed personnel were standing there, having already closed off part of the area for the filming. Niall, Beth, and Laura had to produce their IDs before being patted down. Their bags were searched as well.

Ken joined them a little later and had to go through the same procedure. When Karen finally joined them, she gave Niall two air kisses and amiably shook the others' hands. Her bodyguards remained in the background.

Karen's assistant had already picked the camera location. Niall's protest that he preferred to decide things like that for himself was ignored. As Karen moved toward the predetermined spot, Niall realized the rationale—the Houses of Parliament and Big Ben would be behind her, and on the other side of the river, the London Eye was clearly visible. With only a slight swing of the camera to the left, the MI5 building would be in view. Karen Wigsley had thought of everything, either she or her advisers.

The assistant informed Niall that he would not be allowed to ask any questions. The Home Secretary had prepared a statement and would say it in front of the running camera. That was all. They would have fifteen minutes.

Karen Wigsley quickly powdered her face, threw a critical glance into a small hand mirror, patted some loose strands of hair back in place, and gazed into the camera with the eyes of a professional. "Shall we?"

Niall gave her a signal. The camera was on. This time, it was Ken who was filming everything going on around them with the handheld camera.

Karen delivered her speech. She talked about a tragedy that had taken place on British soil. About the fact that it should never be allowed to occur again. That the terrorist alarm level had been raised and that further measures were being taken. That something like that simply should not have happened—two British citizens who had grown up in a democratic nation simply could not do something like the two men had. The next two or three minutes were pure campaign rhetoric. Niall was already considering where he could cut the material—how much, how little of Karen's speech was actually usable.

She reached her conclusion: "Our thoughts and hearts are with the family of Air Cadet Paul Ferguson, who became the unwitting victim of two terrorists. Terrorism always affects the innocent. Compared to war, terrorism is a significantly more unjust and dangerous threat. We will do everything we can to assure that the citizens of the United Kingdom feel safe and secure. Thank you very much."

Karen froze for a moment, then relaxed. She nodded at Niall through the camera and motioned to her guards. The assistant thanked Laura, Beth, and Niall as a black limousine pulled up as if on command to gather up Karen and her small entourage. Next up she had a meeting in the House of Commons. The police removed the security tape and opened the park again. Niall thought back over what she had said at the end about terrorism and war. There was no mistaking her statement. It was an endorsement of war. It did not matter which one, as long as it helped Karen become Prime Minister.

"That went fast," Beth said.

Niall waved Ken over. "Let's get a few more shots of Thames House, okay?"

"Niall," Laura cut in, phone in her hand.

"Just a minute. And then across the river toward MI6. Everybody already knows what it looks like, thanks to James Bond, but whatever. What I care about are the distances, how close everything is." Ken nodded and lifted the camera off the tripod.

"Niall, it's important," Laura said.

"Uh, sure, go ahead." He looked over at Laura and was shocked. She had been alright just a moment before, but her face had become twisted, her eyes huge and troubled.

"What happened? Are you alright?"

"Your father," she said.

"What?"

"He just sent a text. To the production cell." She held the device so Niall could see the screen. He took it from her anyway.

"I have been abducted. Instructions to follow," Niall read aloud. "What does that mean? Some kind of code?"

Laura mutely shook her head.

"I'll call him."

"I already did. He didn't answer."

Niall pulled out his own phone and dialed Leonard's cell. He was sent straight to voicemail. He then tried him at the office. No answer. "Did you see him this morning at the station?" he asked her.

"What's wrong?" Beth joined them.

"Leonard." Niall handed her the production phone. Laura choked down a sob.

Beth read the text and handed Laura the phone. "I saw him at the station, ran into him in the hall." She sounded only slightly more tense than usual.

"Was he alright?" Niall asked.

She shook her head. "Nothing out of the ordinary."

"I'll call the front desk." Laura was crying now.

"No." Niall stopped her. "It's probably just a misunderstanding. Let's go have a look first."

26

Niall followed Beth into Leonard's office—a large, bright, sparsely furnished room. Although it held less tech equipment than Beth's office, a gigantic screen hung on the wall. Leonard's large, black desk was one long curve, seemingly constructed from a single block of wood. No drawers, no compartments, nothing. The desk held nothing except a laptop and a phone. A minimalist group of chairs sat at the other end of the room. The walls were bare, and the only other piece of furniture in the office was a narrow bookcase behind the desk.

Books were strewn across the floor, and the desk chair had been kicked over.

As Niall crossed over to the desk, he suddenly found it difficult to produce coherent sentences. "If someone had wanted to steal something...The computer is still here. Maybe Leonard was searching for something?"

"And made this mess in the process? No. I'm calling security. The corridors have surveillance cameras." Beth dialed a number and stepped into the hall. He could hear her muffled voice but not what she was saying. Niall examined the rest of the room. The chairs had been knocked over, and when he looked closer, he could tell that the screen was no longer hanging straight.

"The halls have camera surveillance?" Niall asked once Beth returned.

"For our own safety. I'm just quoting," Beth replied.

"Sure."

"It could help us in this case. They'll let us watch the footage on my computer. When exactly did the text come in?"

"We'll have to ask Laura."

"She's talking to the receptionist right now. Let's go. We've seen enough."

Niall did not feel he could move. He stood rooted in the middle of the room.

"What's wrong?" Beth asked.

He looked at her helplessly. "Could I be alone for a moment?"

"Sure." She walked out and closed the door behind her.

Niall leaned against the desk and scanned the chaos. Somebody had been searching for something. Somebody who did not have much time, who had worked aggressively, who perhaps had Leonard in his power.

Had the film set this in motion? Had they managed to stir up too much muck? And yet, they had not really even started yet. Was IS behind this? Had they used the film as an opportunity to abduct a British journalist? I should have said no, Niall thought. It's my fault. I should have just turned it down. They might not have even made this film with someone else, or would they have? Maybe later. If I had walked away, none of this would have happened. I should have said no. For him. Although he wanted me to take it. I've done everything wrong.

He was trembling as he shuffled to the door and down to Beth's office. Laura was already there. When she saw him, she jumped up and hugged him.

"Everything will be alright," she said, starting to cry again.

Niall let her hug him, lacking the strength to return the gesture.

Laura finally let him go, and Beth said: "Sit down." She opened the email she had received from Security. "When did you get the text, Laura?"

"11:52."

"We'll start at 6:30. He always gets here early." She started the video from the security camera that was pointed almost directly at Leonard's office door. Beth ran the video forward as Niall sat down beside her and wrapped his fingers tightly around his armrests.

"Seven o'clock, nothing there…nothing…" She increased the speed. People had walked down the hall from time to time, but nobody had stopped, nobody left anything outside his door.

"Ah, here comes Leonard. It's about 7:40—" She paused the picture and ran the video back a little. Leonard strode decisively into view. He was not carrying a bag or anything else. He vanished into his office, then nothing happened.

Beth increased the speed again. Somebody else had passed his door around 8:00. After that, two women. Around 8:45, Leonard had left his office and returned about ten minutes later with a visitor. Chatting together, they went inside his office and stayed there for exactly eighteen minutes.

When they emerged, everything was different. The visitor shoved Leonard out the door and propelled him down the hallway but not in the direction the two of them had come from earlier. They were heading away from the elevator.

"Who is that?" Niall asked. "No idea. Laura?"

"Don't recognize him." She looked at her phone. "At about that time, somebody using the name Paul Ferguson was given a visitor pass." She looked up. "I have the reception list here."

"Paul Ferguson? Is that meant to be a joke?" Niall replied sharply.

"A bad one."

"Where did the two of them go?"

"No idea, but not straight back to the lobby," Beth said. "I'm calling the police."

"No!" Niall slowly got to his feet. "Not the police. We still can't be sure. And…they won't do anything. There's nothing incriminating in the video. Leonard is temporarily unavailable, so what?"

"The text," Laura mentioned.

"Could mean anything."

"'I have been abducted. Instructions to follow' could mean anything, really?" She studied him closely. "You're scared, aren't you?"

He nodded.

"We have to tell the police."

"Maybe it's all just a misunderstanding, and he's sitting at home and—" He had no idea what to say next.

"Niall," Beth said. "We shouldn't lose any more time."

He looked at her as tears welled in his eyes. "Just give me a little time. I'll go over to his apartment." Niall was already at the door when he remembered something. "Does anyone have his address?"

Laura fought her way across the crowded Central Line platform, managed to grab a couple of seats on the subway, and waited until Niall caught up with her. "You've never been to his apartment?" she asked.

"No." He gazed out the window at the people on the platform, at the station sign: Oxford Circus.

"Why not?"

Niall did not answer but continued to stare out the window, even though there was nothing to see except the tunnel wall.

"I'm scared…scared that something really has happened to him," Laura continued.

"His office was completely trashed."

"Beth told me."

Niall closed his eyes. "I didn't want to visit him. It was too much for me. His apartment, his space. Didn't want to see it. Sounds weird, doesn't it?"

"Did he visit you?"

"A few days ago, yes."

"For the first time?" He nodded.

Laura scooted over a little as two young men with giant backpacks boarded at the next station. They smelled of sweat and beer as they laughed and chatted in Spanish.

"Where did you meet?" she asked.

"Cafes, restaurants…neutral ground."

"And now?"

Niall waited to reply. He watched the noisy Spaniards, then studied the other passengers in their section. Two or three were reading on e-readers, others were messing around with their phones. Others still had newspapers or books with them. Two young black women with children on their laps were laughing together.

"Now I think I was an idiot," he finally said.
"Why don't you want to call the police?"
"Because I'm afraid to."
"Because it will make it all real?"

He fell silent. He had spent the whole time thinking about what he had done wrong, how he could fix things. But Laura was probably right. He was just deceiving himself by denying the likelihood that something terrible had happened. He did not want to lose another father.

They got off at the Notting Hill Gate station and walked down Portobello Road. Niall took in the colorful buildings with their vintage shops and the market booths engulfed in masses of tourists. The colorful cacophony radiated a certain joie de vivre. He would never have been able to guess that that was where Leonard lived. Notting Hill, Leonard had said at Susan's party, loud and lively. But Niall had still imagined a quiet old house on a side street somewhere else in Notting Hill. He had envisioned Leonard in Belgravia, ensconced somewhere among the boutiques and the embassies. Or in an ultra-modern apartment high over the city in one of the new mega-towers along the Thames.

"Has he always lived here?" Niall asked.

"I think he's had this apartment for quite some time, years and years. He told me once that he could never afford this place at today's prices."

"I thought he was rich."

"I have no idea."

Laura came to a stop in front of a blue building, the ground floor of which housed a secondhand shop for 1960s and 1970s women's clothes. She pointed to the door next to the shop's display window. "Shall we?" She rang. Waited. "He's not answering."

"Neighbors?"

Laura walked past the window and entered the shop. Niall watched through the glass as she spoke with the clerk, a woman about Niall's age with black hair, pale makeup, and dramatically lined eyes. They talked for a minute, and Laura showed her something on her phone. Niall turned away. He could not bring himself to join them—perhaps because he was afraid of what he might learn there.

The man had been in some of the worst crisis zones around the world, had voluntarily put himself in harm's way. He had survived everything—injuries, illnesses. He had never fallen into the hands of rebels and had never been kidnapped. Then, this had happened, right there in the middle of London, after he had retired?

Laura returned, clutching a key. "She has the second key. For emergencies. She said she saw him this morning. He was with someone, then she heard loud noises upstairs, as if furniture were being moved around. The two of them left around twelve."

Niall looked at his watch—a little past one. "So not all that long ago?"

Laura shook her head, "she said it all seemed pretty strange. Normally, Leonard waves at her. She's never known him to have anyone over to visit, and the other man was acting weird. He was holding Leonard by the arm and pushing him from behind."

Niall walked past her into the shop. "You saw him? With another man? Did you talk to him?"

The clerk glanced over at Laura, who had followed Niall inside. "Who's this?"

"His son," Laura explained.

The clerk's expression changed instantly. "Oh! So, it's you," she said cheerfully.

"What?"

"He would talk about you sometimes." She smiled. "Niall, right?"

"Uh..."

"I'm Katie." She held out her hand. "But to be honest, it really didn't look good earlier. I wanted to step out and ask if everything was okay, but Leonard just looked at me and shook his head a little. I had the feeling he didn't want the other man to know I was in here. The two of them went upstairs, and then things got noisy."

"What did the other man look like?" Niall asked.

She shrugged. "He was wearing a suit but nothing expensive. The kind worn by bodyguards and security personnel in the boutiques. He looked like a guard or something. I think he was Arabic."

"Arabic?"

"Yes. I couldn't swear to it, though. He was pretty dark, but he might have been Italian." She thought for a moment. "No, more exotic. From somewhere in the Middle East?"

"And then the two of them left? Did you notice anything about them?"

Katie inhaled sharply. "You could say that. He was practically carrying your father along, supporting him as they walked by. But Leonard looked over at me and raised his hand a little as if to say, stop, stay out of it." She lifted her hand with the palm facing out.

"And you didn't do anything?"

"What was I supposed to do? He didn't want me to."

"Do you think he was hurt?"

"He might have just felt dizzy!" She folded her arms. "Your interest in him is pretty recent, isn't it?"

Niall turned around and walked out. Laura hurried after him.

"Do you want to go in his apartment?" she asked.

He nodded and took the key from her.

"What was that woman thinking talking to me that way?"

"She's friends with Leonard."

"According to her."

"She has his key."

"But she can't just—" He broke off.

Laura patted his arm. "It wasn't easy for him to have a son who didn't want to have him as a father."

"For a long time, he didn't want to be my father."

"He thought it was best that way."

Niall shook off her hand and went to the door, which opened easily thanks to a new lock. The two of them walked up the narrow, steep staircase to the second floor. Niall opened the apartment door and stepped straight into a living room that would have been bright, airy, and welcoming if it had not looked as if a drunken mob on pogo sticks had thrown a party there.

He called out for his father, but there was no answer. A small, outdated kitchen and a guest restroom were behind the living room. A spiral staircase led up to the next floor. Niall looked around upstairs. A spartan bedroom held a wide bed and a bright, modern bathroom. An office doubled as a guest room. It was a completely normal apartment which had been systematically searched, centimeter by centimeter. All the closets and drawers stood open; their contents scattered everywhere. The bed sheets lay crumpled on the floor, and the mattresses had been slit. Someone had even shattered tiles in the bathroom and left the toilet tank open. The couch and chairs in the living room were upside down, their undersides cut.

There was no longer any doubt. Leonard had been kidnapped. Why had Niall not agreed the moment Beth had wanted to call the police? What had made him think he could find his father if he just went looking? Valuable time had been lost and it was all his fault.

"The police?" Laura asked, her voice wavering.

Niall nodded.

27

The kidnappers had still not called by evening. There were no ransom demands, no video claims of responsibility, no proof of life. The police went through the CCTV footage, questioned potential witnesses, and did what police generally do in these situations. There was a strict news blackout on Leonard Huffman's disappearance.

Niall got home shortly before midnight. He stretched out on his bed and concentrated on Leonard. Maybe the situation had nothing to do with IS and the documentary. Had his father agreed to go along with that man? He could have easily asked Katie downstairs for help, but he had chosen not to. Was he trying to keep her out of it? Or was it because he was not in serious danger? But then why was he not calling?

What kinds of motives did the abductors have? Niall ruminated. Money was always a big one, but no demands had been made. Could that be a good sign or not? Maybe Leonard had owed money somewhere and was unable to pay it back. Yet somebody should have made contact already, he felt certain. Maybe Leonard had taken incriminating photos. Maybe he had tried to pick up the wrong woman, and her husband had lost it. Damn it, he thought. Why would someone who did not want money kidnap another person? Nothing made sense. At the same time, everything ended in the certainty that Leonard was actually in great danger.

Niall felt more acutely than usual how little he knew about his father. The only things he knew were the public facts everyone else interested in Leonard Huffman knew. Born in 1945, his Jewish parents had fled the German Reich in the 1930s and settled in London, where they eventually met and got married. Leonard was their only child. People had claimed that his Jewish heritage had sensitized him to the world's injustice, but Leonard had always said, "If that were actually true for all Jews, or anyone else whose ancestors experienced pain, misery, persecution, and hatred, this would be a very different world. That's not the reason."

Leonard criticized Hamas just as much as the Israeli attacks on Gaza, and whenever he was asked about his position on war, regardless of which one, he would simply urge both sides to make peace. He always claimed it was not his place to decide who was guilty or who had started things. His maxim was: War should not

exist. There is not a single justifiable reason to go to war. He was often asked: Not even in self-defense? "There's no such thing as a defensive war," would be his response, "a just war. War occurs when one group attacks another. With words, with actions. Stop trying to beat each other up."

These statements dated from the eighties, and at some point, he had simply grown tired of repeating himself. In later interviews, he just said, "All I do is repeat myself. I have already said everything I need to say on the subject. You can see the rest of it in my pictures." Who would abduct a man like that? Niall was puzzled.

Once it had become clear the day would end without a ransom demand, the police had eventually asked Niall if it was possible that he was extorting someone.

"Blackmail? Where did you get that idea?" Niall asked.

DI De Verell did not even try to respond. His next try was, "Could he be trying to get away from someone?" Niall had asked De Verell to talk with the people from the station, with Leonard's friends. Anyone who knew him better than Niall did. The DI had looked skeptical.

The Anti-Terrorism Unit had been put on alert for an Arabic-looking man who had had an appointment to meet with Leonard at the station and who had called himself Paul Ferguson, who then went with—or forced—Leonard through the city, and who possibly trashed his office and his apartment. And who took him away when he was done. The police told Niall: "It would be best if you just went about your work as usual. There is absolutely nothing you can do at the moment."

But how was he supposed to just work as usual? He wondered. Even if he would have been able to pull himself together enough to focus on the shoot, the police had confiscated all their footage. The station's attorneys had been unable to stop them. Backed by the stipulations of the anti-terrorism legislation and the fact that the country's alarm level had been raised to its highest stage, the police had spent the afternoon gathering mountains of documents, hard drives, memory cards, and other material, which they carried out of the building, though not before forbidding everyone from discussing any of it with anyone.

"We're just supposed to report on the weather while you violate the freedom of the press, threaten journalists, and abuse your power?" the station director had yelled at the officer-in-charge. "And all in the name of the war on terrorism? What kind of assholes are you anyway?"

All he'd received was a cool answer that he was welcome to come along with them if he wished to file a complaint. This was the moment Niall realized the full extent of the terrorism paranoia. Every one of them was a suspect. Absolutely every single one of them.

They would not be able to continue filming. Whatever they shot would be confiscated right away by the police. Was that what the kidnappers had hoped to achieve? Not money, but the shutting down of the film to prevent the release of the footage? Was there something out there he had not uncovered yet? Or had he filmed something so damning that somebody was doing everything they could to make sure the footage vanished?

But was the person in question not worried that the police would stumble across whatever it was when they were viewing the film? So perhaps the trouble was not with what Niall had already discovered but what he would eventually stumble across.

That was why he had to keep going, he resolved, unofficially, without the police knowing about it. He had to figure out what he was up against. Then he would know why Leonard had been abducted. It was the only way to help him.

Niall's next thought was that they wouldn't kill him. If they killed him, the research would continue. Whatever they were trying to hide would then come to light. Right? Perhaps it had nothing to do with stopping the film but with money and attention after all, he decided. If IS had managed to abduct Leonard Huffman, the world would sit up and notice. Maybe it really was that simple.

Niall stood up and opened his laptop. It took him a minute to find the video that had come to mind. Cemal had sent it to his brother as well, but Niall had not watched it, just read about it. It had gone viral two weeks before, and all the media outlets had covered it.

He started the video. It showed an IS prisoner in an orange shirt, like those worn by the others right before their executions. But in this video, everything was different. The video had not been shot outside, but inside. The lighting had been carefully planned. To the trained eye, the camera angles looked like ones set up by a professional. The video had been cleanly edited, and there were Arabic subtitles. The man in the video looked haggard and exhausted. His eyelids were reddened, as if he had a minor infection. His lips were cracked, and his teeth were brownish and spotted, but his gaze was firmly fixed on the camera. It was Oliver Chisholm, the British journalist who, according to a recent announcement, had been abducted almost a year and a half before.

"My name is Oliver Chisholm. I am speaking voluntarily, without the threat of violence or punishment. This is the first of several messages for my family, friends, colleagues, and the entire Western world. Above all, this is for the people of Great Britain and the United States and for their governments. I am a journalist and photographer, and I have been here for seventeen months. My government was notified about my situation, but they have done nothing to fetch me home. Like the US government, my government does not care what happens to its citizens. Other governments take care of their people. They negotiate with the Islamic State and secure their release. The US and Great Britain will not. All they have had to do was pay the ransom, and I could have come home to my family. This is not what they did. This not what they ever do.

Over the next few weeks, I will explain why that is the case. There is a plan behind it. My family and friends are not even allowed to talk about the fact that I'm here. They are supposed to keep it a secret, so nobody will know that my government is willing to let me die. That will not be happening, not yet, because I plan to expose the truth about Great Britain and the US's secret agenda. After two highly unpopular and ultimately lost wars in Iraq and Afghanistan, these two governments need material that they can falsify and distort to manipulate the media and deceive their people. I have converted to the Islamic faith, and I now support the Islamic State to the best of my ability. My messages should be heard and understood by all unbelievers around the world. I will send another message soon."

Chisholm spoke with a soft Scottish accent. He did not stutter. His gaze never flickered anxiously. He hardly blinked and made no nervous movements. If there were a textbook case of Stockholm Syndrome, he was it. He did not mention liberation but instead talked about being fetched home. He said nothing about hostages, ransom, or extortion. He made no mention of abduction. Instead, he focused on a secret agenda the two governments were pursuing. Neither Great Britain nor the United States were willing to negotiate with terrorists, and they were the only governments that refused to do so. If you started tracking the money, the abductors had worked out a pretty lucrative business model, and that was not all. In those days, he suggested, anyone of either nationality ran the risk of being abducted. Enforcing secrecy about these abductions had become standard practice. They stirred no panic among the populace. There were no public discussions about whether the government should have even considered making ransom payments. There were no false signals to the abductors.

Niall sat back down on his bed. British and American journalists, of course—how many had they already taken? Nobody outside the intelligence services and the government knew with certainty. Now, with Leonard Huffman, IS believed they had finally abducted someone for whom the government would be willing to pay. They wanted to extort the government. They also presently had a professional for their propaganda videos and photos, as well. They were cynical and cunning. His first assumptions had been right. Niall felt dizzy. He barely made it on his feet and into the bathroom before he started vomiting.

That night, he dreamed he had traveled to the Golan Heights along with his father. Together, they were filming how soldiers on both sides were beheading each other, and Leonard kept calling out, "Again, again! The light wasn't right!"

After two hours, he woke up, fully clothed and freezing. Although he had not pulled up the blankets, he was drenched in sweat. He wondered why he was awake. A dreamy memory floated to the surface, something Leonard had said to him a long time before, "You have talent. And you know your way around the technology. It's all there. The only thing you're missing is inspiration, the inner spark. The dedication."

Niall's response had been, "I used to have that inner spark, but then you showed up."

This was how they had talked to each other. Now, he felt horribly guilty for repeatedly, harshly rejecting Leonard, the man who refused to give interviews but who had tried so hard to talk to him, as if to make up for all the lost years. As if now that he was old, he wanted to pass along to Niall something more than just his genes. What other reason could he have had to do the project with him? Niall looked at the clock. It was 5:30. He wanted to sleep more, but then he noticed his phone was blinking. A text. He hoped it was from his father. He did not recognize the number. The text had been sent shortly after two o'clock.

FADE TO BLACK

The text said, "My brother Serhat has been arrested. They claim that he kidnapped your father. Please call me when you read this. Dilek Bayraktar" 📱

ZOË BECK

TUESDAY 28

Niall gripped his coffee and watched Beth as she tried to convince the woman behind the counter that all she wanted was hot water without anything else and, if she had to, she would pay the price of a cup of coffee.

"Why does she want to meet us here?" Beth asked, once she joined him at the table. "Is Starbucks really a good place to chew out the people you blame for your brother's arrest?"

"Starbucks is at least a good place to finish waking up." He drained his coffee. "Good morning, by the way."

She just nodded. "Still nothing from Leonard?"

"I would have told you otherwise."

"Shit." She pulled a tea bag out of her purse and stuck it in the hot water before glancing back at Niall. "Don't ask."

"Didn't plan to." He stared out at the street. A group that looked nothing like tourists had gathered on the opposite sidewalk and was gradually growing larger.

Dilek Bayraktar had called him right after he had texted her around 5:30. "I'm sorry about what happened to your father," she had said. "But my brother didn't do it."

"Thank you. I don't think he did. I've met him."

"Good. Let's meet at nine at the Starbucks on Kensington High Street."

"When, today?"

"Yes, in about three hours. See you then." Dilek had hung up without waiting for a response.

His first impulse had been to ask Laura to come with him, but then he had decided it would be better to take Beth along, maybe because he wanted to spare Laura, since she was so upset about Leonard's disappearance. He'd had no idea what to expect. Beth was…more hardened, he'd reasoned. Above all, she had picked up on the first ring. He could still hear her explaining her tank strategy to him. Even though he knew exactly what she meant, he could not help imagining her at the wheel of a tank. Beth would have been able to drive a tank and talk on her phone. Beth, without requiring much explanation, had agreed to meet him that morning at Starbucks shortly before nine.

"That's the Israeli embassy over there," Beth remarked, and it sounded like an explanation. He looked at her questioningly, and she pointed through the window at the growing crowd. The first of them were already holding signs: "Stop the bombs! Free Gaza!" "Gaza should be free!" "End the siege!" "Stop the killing!" "Down with Israeli apartheid!"

"I only looked away for a second," Niall said. "Where did they all come from? Are there always so many of them, or is today a special day?"

"There are daily protests at this point, but today there's supposed to be a march from the embassy down to Downing Street. According to the organizers, there were about a hundred thousand demonstrators last time. They want to hold these marches once a month or so until peace returns to the region."

Palestinian flags had started flying as the crowd sloshed onto the street and blocked traffic. Niall studied the people themselves—women and men, many—though not all—who seemed to have Arabic roots. Some of the women were wearing headscarves. Many in the crowd were young, but not all. Niall was unable to make any snap generalizations about the group in terms of the age, gender, or ethnicity of the protestors.

Soon, more distasteful slogans were appearing in the mix. "Zionist warmongers! Stop the Holocaust in Gaza!" had been painted in white on a black poster. Someone else was carrying a cardboard sign that showed a swastika and the Israeli flag joined by an equal sign. Some of the demonstrators stepped into the coffee shop to get something to take with them. There was constant coming and going.

"This was not a good call on her part," Niall commented.

"She wants to join the demonstration."

"You think so? Oh, I think she's here."

Dilek Bayraktar had sent him a picture so he could recognize her. She was wearing a Palestinian scarf knotted around her neck but not her head. Dilek had long, straight, almost black hair that she wore loose around a round face with large, watchful eyes. She was dressed in shorts and a white t-shirt on which she had written "Freedom for Gaza." Of course, she planned to join the demonstration.

"Here you are," she said in greeting, holding her hand out first to Beth. "Dilek, hi."

"Beth," Beth said. "This is Niall, but you already know him. Somehow."

The small standing table had already been maxed out with two people. With three, nobody could move, but Dilek did not seem to mind. "Where is the camera?" she asked.

"The camera? I thought we just wanted to talk. About Serhat. And my father."

"Exactly. I want you to film our conversation. You're still making the documentary, right?"

"You're here because of Cemal?"

She looked frustrated. "No. Well, maybe, in a way, but I wanted to talk about my little brother first."

Niall was getting impatient. "And why would I film that?"

"So that no one can misquote me. Don't you get it? My brother is in prison. I can't risk somebody putting words in my mouth, too."

He looked at Beth, who was watching Dilek with open sympathy.

"Alright. We can do that."

Dilek set her phone on the table. "I would first like to make a statement. I will also record the audio." She looked at Beth. "It's okay with me if you want to film it with your phone. I'll start as soon as you're ready."

Without releasing her cup, Beth grabbed her own phone with her left hand. She held it up and tapped the screen with her thumb before saying: "It's on." Dilek gazed into the small device, and for a moment, she looked uncertain. She reached into her pocket and fished out a crumpled piece of paper and smoothed it out on the tabletop. Niall saw that she had jotted down several talking points in a clear, decisive script.

Dilek took a deep breath, exhaled slowly, and moved her feet apart to stabilize her stance. "Last night, the police came to our home and searched it. They said they had a warrant, just as they'd had a few days before, after Cemal's arrest. They claimed that a man had been abducted, and since Cemal had been in contact with our little brother Serhat during his time in the training camp, he was under serious suspicion. The man who had been taken was the initiator of the documentary about our brother Cemal, and obviously Serhat wanted to stop the film from being released."

She paused and looked at Niall. "Thanks to the anti-terrorism legislation, he has no right to legal representation, no right to an arraignment, no rights at all. Since last night, my little brother Serhat, who has never done anything to anyone in his entire life, is officially a non-person. If that were not the case, he would still have some basic rights. Serhat is eighteen years old, and at this very moment, he is presumably sitting in one of the worst prisons in England."

Dilek broke off again. She studied her notes and turned the paper over, but the back side was empty. She looked satisfied. She lifted her eyes back to Niall. "Mr. Stuart, I would be grateful if you could speak with the police and tell them that my brother had nothing to do with your father's abduction. I know that this situation must be very difficult for you, but I also know that you can understand my position. His ideas are very different from Cemal's. Please, Mr. Stuart, help him. Thank you very much." She concluded her statement with a nod at the phone.

"Do you want me to keep filming?" Beth asked. "Absolutely," Dilek replied. "So, Mr. Stuart?"

"I will definitely speak with the police," Niall said. "I don't think your brother had anything to do with this. Not at all. And… I'm truly very sorry. I'm sure that everything will get figured out soon, and they will let him go." He could not help thinking about his brief stay in prison. He felt a little sick when he thought about them doing to Serhat what they had done to him.

Dilek shook her head. "They can hold him for twenty-eight days without filing an indictment."

"I promise I'll do what I can."

She gazed at him doubtfully. "What can you do? What can I do?" She seemed to deflate, her moral outrage evaporating, at least for a moment. "Last night, I decided it was a good idea—the only right one—to talk to you. Now I think that they'll just do what they want. There's nothing we can do, nothing in the world."

Niall wished he was able to take her hand and comfort her, but he refrained.

"Listen, we both have to do what we can." He recalled something. "I know an attorney who might be able to help. He was recommended to me in case I wanted to file a complaint against the police and the prison for excessive use of force."

Dilek looked at him with interest, the tension, the moral strength returning. "Do you have his name? That would be great."

Niall rummaged around in his wallet. His uncle had given him the man's business card, but he'd had neither the time nor the necessary peace of mind to actually call him. He found the card stuck between two supermarket receipts and handed it to the young woman.

She read it and then asked: "Do you know him?"

"No, his name was given to me."

"By whom?"

Beth leaned forward. "May I?" She picked up the card but set it down almost right away and looked at Niall curiously. "Yes, I'd like to know that, too."

"Is something wrong with him?" Niall asked.

The two women started talking simultaneously. Dilek threw up her hands and gestured for Beth to continue.

Beth took over: "He represents white, middle-class men, as well as white, upper-class men when possible. He's definitely not somebody for Dilek's brother. He wouldn't even talk to Dilek."

"If you used him as an attorney, his strategy would focus on you being a white middle-class man with no prior convictions," Dilek added. "An Englishman to the twentieth generation and all that. It is always so nicely formulated: a respectable citizen, an honorable member of society. He isn't even slightly interested in pointing out the flaws in the system."

Niall's astonishment grew. "How do you know that?"

"Member of the conservative party. Good friend of the—" Beth paused. "Good friend of our Home Secretary."

"Never heard of him."

"The two of them don't necessarily attend the same parties, but people say they are very close, politically speaking."

Dilek said, "One of his most high-profile defenses involved a banker accused of embezzling funds to help finance the British National Party. That was only two or three years ago."

"That was him? Are you sure?"

Beth nodded, as Dilek continued, "I also recall a rape case against a radio host. What was his name? You know who I mean. He was even kicked out by one of the most conservative private stations because he was too far right. A complaint against him was filed by a black prostitute who accused him of raping her. He also hadn't paid her for something or other. Our upstanding Mr. Attorney got him off easily."

Niall remembered the case from three years before. The radio host had been declared not guilty due to a lack of evidence. The attorney had ripped the young woman to shreds. What value did a prostitute's word carry? How could one place any worth in the sensibilities of a woman who had sex in exchange for money? How trustworthy could a woman be who did not even hold a British passport? Niall wondered why in the world his Uncle Carl had thought it was a good idea to recommend the man. Because of his success rate? Because he was friends with Karen?

"You should have a chat with whoever gave you this name," Dilek added.

Niall gazed at her, then Beth. "I'm sorry, I had no idea. I didn't recognize the name and haven't had time to check into him. Please accept my apologies."

Dilek nodded in silence. Her eyes wandered out to the demonstrators in front of the Israeli embassy. She seemed sunk deep in thought.

"Are you going to the protest now?" Beth asked.

"Yes. Sitting at home and crying with my parents isn't helping Serhat."

"For political or religious reasons?"

The eyes Dilek turned on Beth were angry. "Political, if you must know. I am marching for peace and against the war. I'm not saying that Hamas' hands are clean, but Israel has the upper hand. And whoever has the bigger weapons decides not only the war, but also the peace."

"So, you'd also go to Hamas and tell them to stop their shit?"

"Of course!"

Beth pointed outside. "Some of your fellow demonstrators look like they'd like to go up to Hamas and tell them they're not hardline enough. When are you going to start killing more Israelis?"

Dilek and Niall looked out at the street. A black IS flag could be seen among all the calls for peace.

"Oh, shit," Dilek murmured.

"Does that not support your cause?"

"No way. Crap, they'll ruin everything."

"I also think the swastika puts a damper on things, too," Niall added.

"It isn't nice, but sometimes you have to be extreme to get heard," Dilek said. "But the IS flag shouldn't be here." She seemed to be honestly upset.

"So now what?" Beth asked.

"See for yourself." Dilek was suddenly the one pointing out the window. A lot of protesters were shoving and cursing at the carrier of the IS flag, and a fight broke out on the sidewalk. What had started as a harmless tussle quickly escalated into a massive brawl. The demonstrators who had lined up at Starbucks to pick up coffee dashed back out into the street. The police materialized from nowhere, and the fight was quickly dispersed. However, the combatants just moved further on before continuing where they had left off.

In the meantime, the street had filled with people, and cars could no longer pass through. The police flooded in from all directions. Niall assumed that they had roped off the street. He had never witnessed firsthand how quickly panic and violence could escalate in a large crowd. One of the baristas ran to the door and locked it. She then returned to the counter, her eyes glued to the front window. A protester careened into the window right next to Niall. Niall stared in horror at the face distorted by pain and grotesquely flattened against the glass. Four policemen stood behind the man, who was about Niall's age. Two of them kept him pinned against the pane, while the other two beat him with their cudgels. The police wore bulletproof vests and helmets.

Dilek cursed under her breath. They had become the only ones in the coffee shop besides the baristas. "Can you let us out?" Dilek asked the woman who had locked the door.

"Not until it's over. I can't risk them getting in here and destroying the place."

"Is there a back exit?"

"It lets out on the back courtyard."

"Great, we'll take it."

"The courtyard is locked most of the time. Besides, I don't know how the insurance will take it if—"

"Unlock the door," Dilek demanded firmly, cutting off the excuses. The barista fell silent, obviously recognizing the young woman's natural authority and resolve. Niall was certain that the conversation would have become more complicated if he had been the one asking to use the back exit.

Two minutes later, they were standing in a small alley that let out onto Kensington High Street. Protesters and police officers dashed past them. The riot was still in full sway. Frightened pedestrians who had not managed to slip out of the danger zone were pressed up against the street facades.

"We have to get around all of this," Dilek said. "I know these streets. Just follow me. You want the next tube station, right? Me too. I have no desire to get caught up in this shit."

"Dilek, did you really have no idea what your brother was up to?" Niall asked as they walked along.

"Cemal?" She waved it off. "He was frustrated. He was always playing the 'I'm a victim and everyone hates Turks' card. He tended to do that even before anyone had said anything against him. Cemal was eager to see racism everywhere and couldn't have cared less about politics. Just felt sorry for himself, didn't have a clue. If he had come to a protest like this," she jerked her thumb back over her shoulder, "he'd have had no idea what the people on the street were for or against. Religion didn't matter much to him either." She stopped. "And then he suddenly started praying five times a day and grew a beard."

"Didn't you think that was suspicious?"

"Sure, I did, but it made our parents very happy. They said: 'Our boy finally appreciates our religion.' I thought he was bored because he didn't have a job, that it was just a phase. Then he disappeared. We didn't know where he was. Honestly, we didn't. We never suspected he'd do what he did."

"What did your parents say?"

She continued walking: "After Cemal's death? Father said: 'Our wars were long ago. Nobody wants to see those times return.' That's what he said." She stopped again and looked at Niall. "That's how we were raised. Just because my parents are Muslims doesn't mean they're jihadists from some mountain village who can't read or write."

"Dilek, nobody said they were. That's what Cemal thought, right?"

She sniffed. "Yes. Probably. It's just that I…oh, forget it." She turned away from him and hurried on. She said nothing else until they were back out on Kensington High Street, near the roadblock on the relatively calm side of the chaos: "Since his death, I sometimes wonder if maybe he was right. Maybe people really did bully him. Maybe they bully me, too, but I just don't notice because I'm stronger and more self-confident than he was. I had to assert myself much sooner than him. As a woman, you always have to take a stand if you want to make anything of yourself." She threw a glance at Beth. "Your colleague knows what I mean. She isn't someone who slept her way to the top or who relies on a man."

Beth cocked an eyebrow: "Not in this life."

Dilek smiled. "Let me tell you something: I don't want my brother to have died in vain. I know now, better than before, that it is my duty to help the people in this country wake up, so they can see what all is going wrong."

"By being part of an anti-Israel demonstration?"

"It was supposed to a peace protest. But—" Something distracted her. She paused, mesmerized by a small knot of people who seemed to be casually strolling down the street. Beth followed her gaze, and Niall tried to make out what Dilek had noticed. Dilek resumed her commentary, though she spoke faster, "Not anti-Semitic. But anti-war. Pro-peace. I owe that to my poor, deluded brother. And in terms of Serhat, could we maybe get something on TV?"

"I wish I could," Niall said.

"Then do it, damn it!" Dilek looked as if she wanted to slap him.

"Dilek, I'll do what I can. I'll talk to the police right away. Okay?"

She looked him, gentler, with something like gratitude in her eyes. "Really?"

"My word of honor."

"That means something to us, your word of honor," she replied.

"To you?"

She laughed briefly. "Now I'm the one starting. To us Turks. You know what I mean."

"It means something to me, too," Niall declared. "As soon as I hear…"

She nodded. "I hope your father is released soon," she said quietly. She then turned and walked toward the roadblock.

Niall looked around for Beth, but she was nowhere in sight. He called her phone.

"Kensington Church Street," she said in lieu of a greeting. "Wait, give me a second...Okay, now. Dilek was watching guys that were acting weird, so I followed them."

"Why?"

"Because they were up to something."

"What were they doing?"

"Well, they didn't have any machetes with them, but I could smell gasoline when I got closer. They've now gotten directions to the New West End Synagogue on their navigation apps."

"How do you know that?"

"I heard them. They were using a voice recognition app."

"They probably don't want to go there to pray, do they?" Niall started walking quickly in the direction he assumed Beth had gone.

"They're wearing anti-Israel shirts."

"Shit. Call the police?"

"Do it. I'll make sure not to lose them."

"How far is the synagogue?"

"Fifteen minutes. Ah, and tell them that today's Tisch'a beAv."

"Who?"

"Tell them that today's a Jewish festival day, and the morning service will be full." He heard her take a deep breath. "A good day for an attack."

29

Niall caught up to Beth before she turned down the street where the synagogue was found. She pointed ahead at a small group of four young men in bright shirts and one very pregnant woman, strolling along leisurely in no clear hurry, with no obvious destination, not all that differently than Cemal and Farooq.

From a distance, Niall thought the synagogue was a Christian church. It was a red brick structure with Gothic Revival elements which were, in reality, Moorish in origin. The five walkers slowed down and came to a stop. Beth dragged Niall down a side street next to the synagogue, a good spot to watch what was happening outside the building.

"Did you call the police?" Beth asked.

"Yes, they're on their way. It'll take them a little while, since they're understaffed, thanks to the protest."

"It's as if they planned it that way," Beth mumbled, mostly to herself. "The entire London police force is busy with other things."

"Beth, wait. These people aren't wearing anti-Israel t-shirts, and they don't look as if they've just come from some crazy protest. The woman is pregnant."

"They changed their shirts on their way over."

"But the woman is pregnant! What if you're wrong about them? You only caught sight of them as they passed us."

"Dilek was nervous."

"It wouldn't take much to make her nervous. Her one brother is in jail, and the other one is dead, so come on. They could just be tourists. See, they're taking pictures." The five of them were staring at the building, and two of them were taking selfies with the synagogue in the background.

"No, they aren't tourists."

"They might want to go to the service."

"I saw them eating and drinking."

Niall stared at Beth. "So what?"

"Today's a fast day."

His arguments were dwindling. "Has the service already begun?" Beth nodded.

"I'll call the police again." He dialed the emergency number and moved away down the alley, so no one could hear him. The woman who answered his call calmly assured him that they were taking his concerns seriously and that somebody would be dispatched as soon as was possible. He was not to put himself in harm's way but was instructed to stay calm and wait.

Beth motioned him back over. "Niall, they have accelerants with them. I just saw a bottle, in one of the backpacks. You have to believe me."

He gestured reassuringly. "The police are on their way. We're supposed to wait and not do anything stupid." He hoped that his everything-will-be-fine tone would get through to her, but Beth simply rubbed her eyes. Niall saw tears in them. Beth's lips quivered. She was crying.

"What's wrong, Beth?" he asked softly.

She took a deep breath. "Their faces, the look in their eyes."

Niall glanced over at the five young people who were still standing in front of the synagogue and chatting. The woman took a sip from a bottle of juice.

"Beth, I'm not sure what you saw, but all I see is a juice bottle. Besides, the woman's pregnant. What woman would—"

"That's one of the usual tricks," Beth interrupted him, clearing her throat. "She's wearing an explosive vest under her clothes. The men's clothes are too tight." She grabbed Niall's arm. "That's probably why Dilek looked so surprised when she walked by them. She recognized the woman from earlier but saw her without the huge stomach. Dilek realized right away what they were up to. Don't you get it? The woman's the bomb. The men will spread gasoline everywhere to maximize the damage."

"How in the world did you come up with that? It all sounds so—"

"Niall! I know what a suicide bomber looks like. Trust me."

The group started to move, climbing the three steps to the building's entrance. "Now!" Beth dashed across the street.

"Beth, we have to wait for the police!"

But she was already tugging open the heavy wooden door before it had shut behind the others. Niall cursed and hurried to catch up with her.

He found her standing in the foyer, peering into the synagogue's worship space. When she noticed him, she gestured for him to be silent and still. He gazed over her shoulder at the gigantic space with a colorful mosaic floor, gleaming woods, lots of gold, and Hebraic script on white walls. The pregnant woman was standing in the middle of the room, her right arm uplifted and a cable running from her hand to her body. A sea of heads surrounded her, all men, all in kippahs. A cacophony of voices screamed. Some were already on their feet and trying to escape.

"Don't move! Be quiet!" the woman ordered. "If anyone leaves this space, I'll press the trigger. Sit down."

The voices died away, and the splatter of liquid could be heard, then the shuffling of feet. Those who had tried to run returned slowly. Subdued whimpering came from various corners of the room, swelling slightly before dwindling to whispers.

"Silence!" the woman repeated.

Niall pressed himself tightly against the wall, afraid she might detect him, and Beth cowered close to him. Her eyes were closed, and she seemed to be concentrating hard on something.

He threw a cautious glance up to the gallery, where he could make out two other group members. One of them was spraying something from a couple of bottles, while the other was gradually emptying another canister. The women sitting up in the balcony lowered their heads, trying to shield their faces best as they could.

Beth had been right. The service was packed, every seat taken. How many people could there be? Niall wondered. Five hundred? Seven hundred? Some of the women being sprayed uttered high, terrified cries. The woman in the pregnancy vest slowly circled the lectern.

"Shut up, or I'll push the button."

"They're going to do it either way," Beth whispered without opening her eyes. "They want to gain time to spread the accelerant everywhere, so the entire synagogue will go up, even the women's gallery. No one is meant to survive."

"When will the idiot cops get here?"

"Too late."

"Then there's nothing we can do, is there?"

"Not quite."

"Not quite?"

"Kill the woman before she can set off the bomb."

She was right. It was just that that was impossible. The woman had moved to the opposite end of the space, near the Torah ark. Niall was no longer able to see the men. He turned to Beth, whose eyes were still shut, but something had changed. She had tensed her muscles, like a lioness about to spring. He glanced back inside. The woman was now on the other side of the lectern.

"What is she doing?" Beth asked quietly.

"She seems to be walking around the room."

"A lap of honor, in farewell."

"Beth, what are you going to do?" Niall whispered. "Let's get out of here. It's a police matter."

"There are at least eight hundred people in there. If you want to go, then go." Beth pushed him aside and dropped to her knees. She stared with round, watchful eyes into the interior. The woman had almost finished her lap back to the lectern and was less than two meters away from them. Niall suddenly realized that Beth was clutching a jackknife, and before he could try to stop her, she sprang into the worship space, directly at the woman, and knocked her to the ground. He heard cries, gurgling. Beth yelled: "Get out, all of you! Now!"

Niall managed to slip inside before people started flooding out. Gripping the bloody knife, Beth was standing over the woman, whose pregnancy vest had been torn askew. A deep, gaping wound ran across her throat. Her eyes were wide open, as was her mouth. She was perfectly still. Beth's foot was pressed hard against the woman's wrist, the one attached to hand holding the trigger. The trigger lay beside her hand, its cable leading over her arm and to the explosive vest under the stomach apparatus.

"Beth," was all he could say as tears trickled down her face.

"We have to get out of here," she said, although she seemed unable to move. Up in the women's gallery, four fires ignited at practically the same moment. The men must have set them. The flames raced along the line of accelerant, spreading in all directions. The worshipers were far from safety, especially those still in the gallery. In their panic, they were clogging up the narrow staircase, stumbling over each other on their way down.

Niall looked at the dead woman's pregnancy vest. What would happen if the fire reached the explosives? He grabbed Beth's arm and hauled her down the aisle behind him. She offered no resistance, and they were soon swept up in the crowd trying to push its way through the foyer. Niall slipped his arm around Beth, pulling her tightly against him. The people surrounding them were screaming and shoving each other, as flames licked their way down the gallery. More shrieks. The fire had caught up to its first victims.

Niall needed a moment to register why the crowd had come to a standstill. The clot was in the foyer, where the women were descending from the gallery. The knot suddenly dissolved, and Niall along with Beth and the others were hurled outdoors. He could feel himself stumbling over something, over someone, who had fallen. Out on the open steps, Beth almost slipped out of his arms. He yanked her back upright and dragged her along.

The police had tried to block the street to the right and left of them. The fleeing people had already overrun the barricades as the officers milled around between the screaming people. Fire engines, ambulances, patrol cars covered the street. Some people collapsed outside the synagogue, while others vanished down side streets. First responders forged their way into the building.

Beth seemed to have lost her ability to stand. He took her across the street and leaned her against a wall, his arm tightened protectively around her shoulders.

That was when the first burning women spilled out onto the pavement from the synagogue. They dropped onto the ground as the firefighters rushed over to beat out the flames with blankets. More fire engines screeched up, followed by more ambulances, as even more first responders stormed into the synagogue. Hoses were unrolled as the sirens grew louder.

Then, they heard the explosion. A dull bang, and it was over. The building did not collapse. The shock did not reach the adjacent buildings. There was only the dull bang. The entire street fell silent, almost ghostlike. Conversations died as all eyes turned toward the synagogue. Time froze for several heartbeats until a new surge of bodies burst through the door. Paramedics, firefighters, injured worshipers.

Niall then noticed that Beth had drawn closer to him. He looked at her and patted her arm.

"We're safe. Everything's alright." Of course, nothing was alright. But they were alive.

A paramedic stopped beside them. "Do you need help?"

"No, we're good."

"Your wife is bleeding." He pointed at Beth's hands.

Beth did not respond. Niall said, "I'll take care of it. We'll be okay. Others need you more than we do." The paramedic hurried on. Niall pulled off his shirt and wiped Beth's hands. Her clothes were covered in splattered blood.

"I have to get out of here," Beth whispered.

"Do you need a doctor? Should I—"

"No, I have to get out of here. Now."

"Why? I don't understand. Here there's—"

"Police. I need to leave. Please. Anywhere."

"Beth, I'll get you something to drink, and—"

"I killed a woman."

"Yes, and saved hundreds of lives. You're a hero! How did you do that?"

"I'm leaving, now." Beth moved away from him, pushing through people to the street, away from the synagogue, in the opposite direction from the one they had come from an hour earlier. Beth's pace and resolve seemed to grow with each step she took. It was hard for him to keep up with her. He tried to talk to her, but she ignored him, swatting at him at one point to signal that he was to shut up. She never looked at him even once, just hurried away. Then, she turned left at an intersection and came to a stop in front of a small shop. "Could you buy me some water, please? And some tissues. And shower gel or soap."

He went inside as she waited outside in the glaring sunlight. After he bought the things, she walked on in search of a quiet alley, where she washed her hands and face, drinking what remained of the water. When she was done, she leaned against a wall and finally looked at Niall. "Thank you."

"For what?"

She swung the empty bottle slightly.

"That's nothing. Thank you. For that unbelievably brave—"

"I need new clothes," she cut him off.

"What's wrong? Why are we running away? You—"

"Portobello Road is around here somewhere. I think it's to the left at the next intersection." She set off without even glancing at him.

He followed, shaking his head. He could not understand what she was thinking, but how could he? She had done the most courageous, amazing thing he had ever seen. She had defused a human bomb and saved hundreds of lives. Killed a person. With a small knife. She had simply walked in and killed the woman. It had looked like something out of a movie.

Beth was walking very quickly, and she turned at the intersection. It was a residential area with no shops, but the street then crossed Portobello Road. They came out just steps from Leonard's apartment.

"You'll need to change your clothes, too," she told Niall.

"Beth, I'll do whatever you ask, but you have to talk to me and tell me what's wrong."

"I need new clothes." She stopped and looked around, her eyes weary, pleading.

Niall said: "Do they have to be new ones, or would used ones work?"

"Used ones?"

He pointed at the secondhand shop directly across the street from them. ◻

30

Katie from the secondhand shop gave them the key to Leonard's apartment and sold them some clothes for Beth, no questions asked. She probably thought they were a couple.

Everything in Leonard's apartment was still covered with the fingerprint powder. Beth looked around, uncertainly. He had told her about what had happened, but it was the first time she was seeing it for herself.

"What were they looking for?" she asked quietly.

"Beth, why don't you go upstairs and take a shower? You'll feel better afterward. I'll clean up down here a little. Or something like that."

She nodded and disappeared up the stairs. Niall started with righting the overturned chairs and closing the drawers and cabinets. He then went into the kitchen to get something to drink, but all he could find were juice and milk, coffee and tea bags. He had hoped for something a little more potent. He searched through the rest of the apartment and continued to straighten things up as he went. By the time Beth came from the bathroom in her fresh clothes, his alcohol hunt was still fruitless.

"All I want is water," she said, stepping into the kitchen to fetch a glass.

It felt totally absurd that in their particular situation, he was in his father's apartment. Niall sent a text to De Verell, asking if there was anything new to report. The response was almost instantaneous, "No, what about you? Why are you in his apartment?"

He looked around, astonished, scanning the room for a camera before realizing that the building was being watched from the street in case the kidnappers returned.

"Just happened to be in the area. Nothing new from my end. No one has contacted me." De Verell did not answer.

"What are we doing here?" he asked Beth as she appeared from the kitchen and sat down on the sofa between the slashed cushions.

"I had to get out of there."

"The hospital would have been the better place for us. I'm worried about you."

"I'm just fine," she said, draining the glass.

"You just did something incredible."

She shook her head.

"Wouldn't it be a good idea to take a sedative and...talk to someone?"

Another shake of her head.

"Beth, why did you have a knife with you?"

She shrugged. "Always do."

"Why?"

She did not answer.

He watched her and considered how to arrange the puzzle pieces that had been coming together since the attack at the synagogue. "You're Jewish?"

She nodded.

"Grew up in Israel?"

"Born and educated there."

"Military service?"

Beth nodded again.

"They say it's the hardest military service in the world. Lasts three years, right?"

"Yes."

"I've heard that after those years, lots of people go to Goa and try to block everything out with drugs. As much as they can."

"You're pretty well-informed."

"Did you go to Goa?"

"No, I came to London and went to college."

"You don't have an accent."

"I went to an international school. My parents speak English. I'm a fast learner and good with languages."

"Did you learn that in the military?" Niall asked.

"Languages?"

"How to kill people with jackknives?"

"Anybody can kill a person with a jackknife."

"And yet, no one else did."

"No one else had to decide if they're just going to watch eight hundred people die or if they're going to do something about it."

He had no idea what to say to that. They both said nothing for a while. Niall avoided looking at her. He shut his eyes, but at once saw the burning people stumbling out of the synagogue, the woman with her throat slashed, Beth's foot on her hand. He opened his eyes and stared at the black television screen.

"I thought I needed to hide. That's why we're here," Beth said.

"The police already know."

"That I—"

"No. That we're here. They're watching the apartment, of course." He looked over at her. She had pulled up her legs and rested her forehead against her knees. "Beth, I called 999 before the attack. They'll be able to track us down either way. I don't understand why you felt you need to hide. You saved hundreds of people. It was an emergency. Or self-defense. Whatever you want to call it. Both, probably."

Beth leaned back, laying her head on the couch frame as if it weighed a ton and her neck could no longer support it. "Niall, do me a favor and don't say anything to the police."

"And how do you think I can manage that? Didn't you hear me? I called the bloody emergency services."

"And I told you to, too. Oh, shit."

"You did the right thing."

"During my military service, I kept praying that I would never have to kill someone. I left Israel because I was afraid that someday I would need to. That was exactly the kind of situation that gave me nightmares—a suicide bomber and I would be the only one who would be able to stop it. We acted out scenarios like that, but that was twenty years ago. I truly thought it was all in the past." She got to her feet and walked upstairs. He heard her go into the bathroom. She returned with her phone.

"There's now a hashtag for the attack: #nweterror." She clicked through the tweets. "People were even tweeting from inside the synagogue, begging for help."

"That's why there were suddenly so many emergency workers there. Anything about you?"

She nodded. "And it's already spreading to the other media. 'The police are searching for the unknown rescuer.'" She refused to look at Niall. "I don't want this."

"Other people would be throwing themselves at the media's feet to get their fifteen minutes of fame," Niall pointed out.

"You understand where I'm coming from."

"Sure," he answered, though he really was not certain that he did. The media had wanted to celebrate him as a hero, despite the fact he had not been one. He had done nothing except film a murder he had been unable to prevent. He had had every reason not to want to be on the front page of anything.

"A video claim of responsibility is already up online." Beth sat down on the armrest of the chair he was sitting in so they could both see her phone screen.

Two bearded men, sitting in front of an IS flag, were speaking directly into the camera. "We no longer believe in the possibility of a political solution to the Palestinian crisis with Israel. Hamas has failed. The PLO has failed. We believe in liberating Palestine with Islamic State troops. We will support the Islamic State and join the fight against Israel everywhere around the world. If you are seeing this video, we are dead. We have taken hundreds of Jews with us, just like the Israeli government kills hundreds of us every day. We regret nothing." The two of them murmured something in Arabic.

"Yes, the two of them were there," Beth confirmed.

Niall had no idea if he had ever seen the men or not, but he knew he would hear soon enough on the news if the men from the video had been among the synagogue attackers.

"What about the woman?" he asked.

"Men are taken more seriously, which is presumably why she isn't in the video."

Niall rubbed his face. "Do you think they had anything to do with Cemal and Farooq? Two attacks within a short time. In the same city. Both with ties to IS."

She shrugged. "Maybe. They might have just wanted to take advantage of the media's heightened sensitivity."

"Anybody setting a packed synagogue on fire in the middle of London will get their attention."

Beth pocketed her phone. The clothing she had bought in Katie's shop was, technically speaking, menswear—wide trousers, a plain shirt. Niall thought they looked great on her.

He wondered how she managed to process things. Only an hour before, she had been on the verge of collapse. Now that she had washed off the blood, showered, and changed clothes, she was back to being the old Beth. She said, "People get much more scared when attacks occur close together. They no longer think that something is a singular event but that it can happen anywhere at any time. After this, people will hardly leave their homes anymore." ▯

ZOË BECK

WEDNESDAY
31

Around 4:00, Niall eventually gave up on trying to sleep. It was already growing light outside, so he decided to head over to the station.

He got there about 5:30, and Beth was already in her office at her computer. She greeted him like normal, as if the day before had never happened.

"Any news?" she asked.

He nodded. "I was on the phone a long time last night. Then, De Verell came over to my place. He knew we had been in the synagogue, and he wanted me to tell him what I'd seen. I described the five attackers as best I could."

Beth looked at him. "And?"

"That's all."

"He was satisfied with that?"

He described the conversation that had taken place in his apartment between him, DI De Verell, and DI Gilpin. They had asked, "How could you tell those people were up to something?"

"I was probably just hypersensitized," he'd told them. "I heard someone say that only a week ago the woman had shown no signs of being pregnant, and that's what made me suspicious."

"Someone?"

"I overheard it on the street. Then, they changed their shirts, and I couldn't miss the smell of gasoline around them. They were chatting about heading over to the synagogue and used some app to get directions."

"You were that close to them?"

< 238 >

"Yes, I followed them all the way to the synagogue, which is where I waited for the police. I called 999, but when nobody showed up after a few minutes, I went inside. It was total chaos in there, people were trying to get out."

"But you weren't alone. Somebody was with you."

"Oh that. Yes, my co-worker. She was horrified. We had no idea what was going on. We offered to help, but the first responders said it would be better if we got out of the way. So, we walked around to a bit. It was the kind of thing you need to work through."

"And you ended up at your father's apartment."

"And we ended up at my father's apartment. Yes."

Niall told Beth that the inspectors had seemed to accept his story. Gilpin had even thanked him. He had had to give them Beth's name and number, but if they had not called by then, perhaps nothing else would come of it. Or at least, not right away.

"Or maybe in five minutes. We'll see," Beth replied, followed by: "Thanks."

"Sure."

"No, really. Thank you."

"We'll call it protection of confidential sources."

Her lips twitched upward. "That's a very creative interpretation. The police would call it making a false statement."

"We'll see."

"You've become rather brave."

He did not think he had ever seen Beth truly smile to the point of lighting up her face. For a moment, she did, albeit briefly.

"I've been through Twitter and Facebook. There's—"

"You didn't sleep at all, did you?" he interrupted her.

"A little. I found posts on Twitter and Facebook, but no photos."

"I'm just amazed anybody stayed calm enough to pick up their phone and post something."

"There you go—brave people," Beth said. She pointed at the monitor. "The Prime Minister has already asked the telephone and social media companies to cooperate with the intelligence agencies.

Niall sat down, scanning first one screen, then the next. His eyes traveled from the computer to the keyboards, the laptop, the speakers flanking the monitors. Hardly any light was glimmering through the north window. Just a minute before, he had walked through the morning sunlight and had believed, for a moment, that everything would turn out alright, somehow. Sitting in this dusky, artificially lit room, he knew nothing would be alright. He thought about how happy he would have been if the intelligence agencies did, truly, know everything.

Then, they would know where his father was and who had abducted him. Total surveillance and the total abolishment of privacy—how quickly and willingly he would have tossed his basic rights out the window and accepted their violation by a democratic government just to save one person. His father.

He stood up. "I need to get some coffee."

"Get me one, too."

"I'm going to take a short walk and get myself something. I'd like to be alone for a while."

"Of course." She nodded, turning back to her computer and the reports she was reading about the synagogue attack. "We can incorporate these into the documentary, if we ever get back to it," she murmured.

Niall did not answer as he walked out of her office. There was nothing new from his father. He had discussed that with Gilpin and De Verell the evening before, as well. He had still not received any demands. He had no idea what was going on and was very worried. Were the police doing anything? Or was every officer in England focused on the terrorist attacks?

"We've set up a task force that is doing nothing else except searching for your father. At the same time, we think there might actually be a connection to the attacks," Gilpin had explained. "However, this is not the only lead we're following up on, either." The cascade of words hardly had begun to explain why they had not made the slightest bit of progress.

Niall walked past the recording studios. A tall, sturdily built man in a suit stood in the corridor, talking steadily into his headset. Niall recognized him as one of Karen Wigsley's bodyguards. Niall stopped and pointed at the studio door, "Hi, is the Home Secretary in there?" The man studied him before apparently recognizing him and nodding curtly. Niall opened the door and slipped inside.

Karen and a moderator were sitting in front of the backdrop for the news broadcast. The moderator was in the middle of a discussion about possible arms deliveries to Israel. "That would not be a popular decision at this point."

Karen's reaction was momentary silence, a response that was never expected from her. Just as the moderator was about to continue, Karen jumped in: "What I am about to tell you is something I haven't discussed yet with the Prime Minister. It might, uh, even cost me my job, but it's worth the risk. So, Leonard Huffman has been abducted by members of IS."

"The Leonard Huffman? The photographer?" the moderator cried.

Karen nodded once before continuing, "We're still waiting for a ransom demand, even though we aren't in a position to pay it. However, this time I want our citizens to be aware early on of what has happened. More than anyone else, Leonard Huffman has shown us the reality of the war zones around the world. His photographs remind us, over and over again, that war is the most horrifying thing people can do to each other. But sometimes, you don't have a choice. Sometimes you have to risk the lives of a few people in order to save many. Sometimes you have to attack in order to defend yourself. The Islamic State has challenged us, and we must react."

"What do you mean? We were discussing arms deliveries to Israel. How does Huffman fit into that picture?"

Karen grimaced. "Three incidents in less than a week, all orchestrated by IS. Two attacks, one abduction. Almost a hundred people have died; many others were injured. The attacks targeted the British government, as well as the state of Israel. Huffman is Jewish, and he was working on a documentary about the men who killed Paul Ferguson. This has sent a very clear message." She glanced at her watch and then at the moderator. "I'm afraid I must head back now. Thank you for your time. I need to go see if I still have my job." Karen smiled grimly before stepping off the set.

Niall stared at the empty seat she had just vacated.

"We're still waiting for a ransom demand," she had said. Niall was unable to help thinking about the video of the kidnapped Oliver Chisholm. Everything was suddenly so clear to him that he was amazed he had not seen it all much earlier. What had made him think that he would be the one to receive instructions from the kidnappers? Why should they contact him, the son, when they could jump straight to extorting the entire British government?

Niall ran out of the studio into the corridor where the bodyguard had been standing, but he was nowhere in sight. He dashed to the exit, and there she was, standing with her bodyguards, advisers, and assistants. Niall pushed through them and grabbed her by the shoulder.

"You've heard from him? How is he doing?"

He was yanked away from her, and his arms were twisted behind him as something closed around his neck. Everything went black, and the last thing he saw was Karen yelling something at him. But he could not hear what she was saying before he passed out. ▢

FADE TO BLACK
32

Carl dropped by Niall's apartment early that evening. "And you can't go out at all? It's so nice out."

"Sure, I could. I just don't want to." Since returning home, Niall had hardly moved off his couch. Circulation, they had said. Too little sleep, too much excitement. It could even happen to a grown man. Niall had simply passed out when Karen's bodyguards had grabbed him.

Even though he was uninjured, the man who had put him in a headlock might have briefly cut off his air supply. In any case, the paramedic had been convinced that he was just fine and that all he needed was a little peace and quiet. Afterward, Beth and Laura had taken him to the tube station, making sure that he got on board and stayed there.

Niall had asked Carl to come by because he wanted to know what was up with Karen and how he could gain access to her. He did not believe her claims that she knew nothing about where Leonard was being held. Beyond that, he wanted an explanation from Carl as to why he had recommended the slimy lawyer to him, although Niall suspected he already knew the reason.

"He's a friend of Karen's. And his success rate in court is unbelievable," Carl countered. "I just wanted to do something nice for you. Should I see if I can find someone else?"

"No thanks. I'll take care of it myself as soon as I have the time. I'm honestly not sure what I would achieve by filing a complaint. Or if that is even the right course of action." He studied Carl, who was slouched gloomily in his chair. "What I'd rather know is what is going on with Karen."

Carl cleared his throat before leaning forward and picking up his cup of tea. Then, he talked. About Karen and her political ambitions. Karen and her impossible behavior. Karen and her extraordinary arrogance. How the Prime Minister might force her to resign. How the Foreign Secretary had to be furious. The entire country had been turned upside down by her incredible revelation. And yet, the voices were slowly growing louder—had she maybe been right? Should they be defending themselves? Should they be supporting others who were also being forced to defend themselves against the butchers that called themselves the Islamic State?

He shifted to what had been going on in Israel. The threat from Hamas. The declining support from the international community. How there was another enemy on the scene—the Islamic State, which supposedly fought in the name of religion. National boundaries did not matter to them, at all. Palestine would be incorporated into the Islamic State, and Israel and all Jews would be annihilated. In IS's opinion, Hamas was weak and insufficiently engaged in promoting the one true faith. While Carl talked, Niall just laid, eyes closed, wishing he was alone.

"You're not listening anymore, are you?" Carl asked. "I hope you don't mind if I wrap this up. I need to get home soon."

"Oh no, sorry about that. I was just thinking about Leonard."

"I wanted to distract you a little."

"I know. Thanks."

"What were you thinking about? Want to talk about it?"

"I was thinking that Karen might've been contacted by the kidnappers and was being blackmailed."

"No!"

"I thought they might have pressured her into revealing that they'd abducted Leonard."

"You don't think that anymore?"

"No. I mean, I don't really know. But I do know they're constantly sending out video messages, trying to reach the public at large. Why would they take the trouble to go behind the scenes in this case? It doesn't fit their MO."

Carl said nothing as he thought and drummed his fingers on his knee. Niall continued, "Why don't they do something? What could they possibly want? I just don't understand."

Carl replied hesitantly, "Niall, I don't want to worry you, not more than you already are, but maybe they haven't contacted anyone because they're still in transit."

Niall looked at him as he let the words sink in. "Shit. You're right. I hadn't even considered that. They're still on the move. That's got to be it." It was practically impossible for someone to get off the island with a hostage those days. All the harbors and airports were under tight surveillance, and the controls had been heightened. They would never be able to slip out on an international flight, and even an escape by ship was nearly unthinkable. So, they would have to go by land. The only possibility was via the Channel Tunnel between Dover and Calais. There, vehicles were loaded on board a train, which would certainly have been a good choice for hiding a hostage. They would manage it somehow. Then they would continue by land. It would take them several days to reach Syria or Iraq. How long? Niall sat up and reached for his phone on the lamp table. He pulled up a route planning app.

It was approximately two thousand seven hundred miles from London to the Syrian border. The straight drive time—forty-eight hours if one did not stop and was lucky enough not to run into any traffic jams or passport checks. They would presumably swap out the drivers, since there had to be more than one kidnapper, Niall reasoned. They might be trying to drive straight through; they might be stopping at night. The drive would take at least three days, he thought, and if they had to make detours or took their time, they might need up to a week. The direct route would take them through France, Belgium, Germany, Austria, Slovenia, Croatia, Serbia, Bulgaria, and Turkey. Once on the continent, the first passport checkpoint would be at the Croatian border. The Schengen Agreement would be in force until then.

They would naturally take the land route, which was why they had not been in contact. They were still in transit, he realized.

They would have to drive all the way across Turkey before reaching Syria. And then? How did the Islamic State secure its borders? Checkpoints, and whoever had no justification for entering their territory was executed on the spot?

Carl made a half-hearted attempt to distract Niall from these lines of thinking, but he finally gave up and left. Once Niall was alone, he wished that he had company and had not let Carl leave. He was still stretched out on the couch, staring at the ceiling with no idea what he was to do next. He got up, walked around, opened and shut kitchen cabinets, opened and shut bathroom cabinets, and still had no clue. He sank back down on the couch and paged through his father's photo books, scanning the pictures for the hundredth or two-hundredth time.

Bodies of young men being tipped off the bed of a truck into a mass grave in Bosnia. Falkland girls in colorful dresses, their eyes squeezed shut in fear as heavily armed British soldiers marched past.

Emaciated Somali refugees barely on life's side of death, flies already perched on their bodies, carrion feeders lurking in the background. Child soldiers from the Ugandan Lord's Resistance Army gripping weapons taller than themselves, sitting proudly on their dead victims.

Niall set the volumes aside and thought about the countless photos that had not found their way into books or other publications, like the one of the other Niall who had died in Leonard's place. It was around 4:00 when he was jolted awake by the sound of his phone going off. A text. Sender: Leonard. Message: Check your email.

He did. They had sent him a video from Leonard's email account. The staging was not as slick as in the films Cemal had made. This was simply a single camera with Leonard talking straight into it. He was also wearing an orange cloak or overalls, but it was hard to tell exactly since the camera was pulled in tightly on his face. Hardly any of the background could be seen.

Leonard said, "Niall, my son, I'm doing well. Please don't worry about me. I will now tell you exactly what you need to do. Follow my instructions to the letter. Go to Jacobson's. You will have to verify your identity there, and it will only work if you go in person. I have given you full power of attorney, did that a long time ago already. They will provide you with access to a safety deposit box there. You must photograph the entire contents of the box and email it to me. After that, go straight home and wait for further instructions. Please do exactly what I've told you to. I—"

Then, an abrupt cut. The scene went black, and nothing else followed. That was all there was. Jacobson's, a private bank. Niall wanted to watch the video again, but when he clicked on the link, all he received was an error message. They did not want anyone to analyze the video. He cursed himself for not having paid closer attention.

Niall considered his options. Should he tell the police? Beth and Laura? Carl? He looked up the bank's hours. They were not open before nine, as he had suspected. But then, he found a phone number that was answered around the clock. "Naturally, we are available to our customers at any hour of the day or night," read the website. He glanced at the clock. 4:15. He dialed the number.

ZOË BECK

THURSDAY
33

Around six am, the streets in the city's financial district looked like a ghost town. Niall took a moment to orient himself. Perhaps he had taken the wrong exit out of the huge tube station, he thought, but then he caught sight of the Bank of England, which, like Jacobson's, was located on Threadneedle Street. Niall followed the road until he stood in front of the bank. A contemporary construction sandwiched between classical neighbors, but not an aggressive nod to the modern age, it was rather a fusion of elements from its surroundings. It harmoniously blended into the venerable facades around it. The sun was still casting long shadows, and it was gloriously cool, although the air carried a faint hint of summer. If only it could stay like this, Niall thought. He wouldn't complain if someone found a way to stop time. The city could stay asleep, and the chaos in his mind could freeze. No noise, no rush, no people.

Well, almost no people. A slender, blonde woman in a pantsuit smiled at him and held out her hand in greeting. She was around forty, about the same age as Beth though vastly different in appearance and demeanor. Her hair and makeup were perfect enough for a photo shoot, and she wore immaculate clothes with overt charm. The woman spoke with a bright, private-school-educated accent and exuded a professional demeanor that was not overly chummy or borderline effusive. Niall felt uncomfortable. He had showered, of course, but he had not shaved. And fresh clothes might have been more advisable than grabbing whatever had been lying around on the floor.

Her name was Rachel. Either he did not pick up on her last name, or she never gave it. Although she was not the one to whom he had talked on the phone, she knew exactly what to do. She was also extremely discreet—not a single word about his father's abduction or any other personal comment was mentioned. She said nothing beyond what was required by the matter at hand. Upon entering the lobby through the marble entrance, he noticed that besides an array of electronic security controls, swarms of security personnel were on hand. He could see that the black-clad men were armed, but he felt some consolation from the fact that they smelled of nicotine and coffee, and that they looked a little tired. Human, he thought, not like this Rachel, who was rather superhuman in her perfection.

Rachel handed over his ID at a security checkpoint, which bore little kinship to those in airports. He was patted down, x-rayed, photographed, compelled to sign every form imaginable, and finally allowed to enter the bank. The ground floor more closely resembled an exclusive club than any bank lobby he had experienced. But all he'd ever had was an average account in an average bank. There had been no reason for him to be on the receiving end of cups of coffee or newspapers. Rachel explained to him that the administrative offices were located on the upper floors while the safety deposit boxes were kept underground in the vaults. She had everything set up for him, and she dutifully apologized for the extensive security measures, which were especially stringent on one's first visit. She then offered him a cup of coffee, which he declined, before leading him to the deposit box in the company of two security guards.

The three bank employees left the room before Niall opened the box. Then, Niall raised the lid, looked inside, and thought for a moment it was empty. It took him a second to make out the brown envelope flat against the bottom of the box with "Niall" printed on it. After lifting it out, he positioned himself so his body blocked the envelope from the security camera.

The flap was sealed with a special sticker. He ripped it open, expecting to find documents, a letter, something. Anything but a photo of Niall. The other Niall, lying there after having caught the bullet that had been supposed to hit Leonard. Blood-soaked, dead.

Niall set the photo back in the box and examined the inside of the envelope more closely. It was empty. He shook it, held it up against the light. But it remained empty. He picked up the photo, clamping it along with the envelope under his arm as he ran his fingers over every centimeter of the deposit box's interior. Using his phone's flashlight, he illuminated the small space before shutting the lid and stepping into the hallway to ask Rachel if there was another box. Or if someone had been able to remove something from that one. She responded negatively to both questions before asking if there was anything else she could do for him. His time here had obviously run out, and she had better things to do.

Niall understood the subtle hint and said that he needed to send an email but would then be done. Rachel accompanied him to the club area, which was still ghostly empty, like a deserted hotel bar. He sat down in one of the heavy, dark leather armchairs and took photographs of the envelope and picture, which he then emailed to his father. As he was slipping the photo back into the envelope, he noticed that something was written on the back. An archive number, perhaps. He took a picture of this as well and sent it off. He was done. He said goodbye to Rachel, nodded to the security guards, and stepped onto the street, where the sunlight was still casting long shadows, though shorter now. It was also much warmer outside than it had been in the bank, which had reminded him of a cold, desolate tomb. He was deeply inhaling the London city air when a taxi drove past. He savored the stench, the garbage, the life that surrounded him as he returned to the tube station, through the turnstile, down the never-ending escalator, and deep underground. As he walked, he realized something. He was back to waiting.

The only message to reach him during his return trip was from Laura. Apparently, Beth had had a long talk with the station manager the day before, and he had given them the green light to continue with the documentary. "We will get our material back," he had announced grimly.

After that, Beth had asked Laura and the research assistants to put feelers out at the mosque, as well as at Cemal's university and the ad agency where he had interned. They had managed to find two young men who had been close friends of his before Farooq had become his best and only friend. Laura had also thought to make inquiries about Serhat. He was not currently being allowed any visitors, neither his family nor an attorney. The only information the family had was what was being voluntarily shared with them by the police. What they were saying was that the boy was doing well, but they needed to check out his potentially suspicious activities.

According to Laura, Serhat's sister was spending all her time running from one newspaper to the next, trying get the injustice against her brother on the front page. Unfortunately, they were only interested in discussing her other brother, Cemal, the one about whom she did not want to talk. The good word that Niall had put in for the boy with Gilpin and De Verell seemed to have been for nothing.

Niall decided not to go straight home but to head over to the TV station. He texted Laura that he wanted to meet with the two new contacts as soon as possible. It would at least give him something to do while his father was still missing. Before reaching Oxford Circus, he received a text from Carl asking if there was any news.

All Niall wrote back was, "No." Should he tell him about his visit at the bank? What would be the point? The kidnappers' video was no longer accessible online. At the same time, he wanted to talk to someone who understood him and who would possibly be able to help. He ran into Beth in the reception area. She had just walked in and was clutching her keyring, her bag slung over her shoulder. She did not look either sleep-deprived or stressed. He had no idea how she did it.

"It's early," she said. "You look like shit."

"Interesting date with a charming blonde. It was a short night."

She studied him before evidently deciding he was lying. She rolled her eyes and pushed the elevator button: "Why aren't you in bed asleep?"

"I'd prefer to work."

"The man upstairs is going to make sure we get our material back. At some point, anyway."

"I know. Laura wrote me. Something about new people for us to interview. You authorized her to look into it."

The elevator arrived, and they got on. Once inside, Beth examined her reflection critically. She seemed dissatisfied, although she looked like she always did.

"What will happen if worse comes to worse, and we can't get our stuff back?"

"In that case, you might not get paid."

"What about the others?"

"They're all salaried."

"You, too?"

"Of course."

"Alright. Sounds like a manageable risk from my end."

One corner of her mouth crept upward. "Very good."

The elevator came to a stop, and they walked down the hall to her office. "Did you catch up on your fluffy cat videos last night?" he asked.

"Until dawn." Beth opened the door but stood frozen on the threshold. He ran into her, having assumed that she would step into the room as soon as the door swung open.

"What—"

She raised her hand to cut him off. Niall looked over her shoulder. "Someone's been in here," she said.

"Probably the cleaning crew."

She shook her head. "They don't mess with the computers."

"To dust them?"

"The computers aren't on. I never turn them off. Sleep, yes, but not off."

"Sometimes they turn themselves off, for updates and stuff. Maybe that's what happened?"

"No, they always restart."

"Maybe something affected the entire computer network. Some kind of system maintenance?"

She slowly shook her head before reaching for her cell phone and calling the front desk to ask if she could be sent the surveillance footage from her hallway from the night before. She listened for a moment without saying a word, then stuck the phone back in her bag.

"What?"

"For about one-hour last night, the cameras failed to record."

"That doesn't mean—"

"It does, Niall."

"Don't jump to conclusions." He tried to push past her into the room. "Watch the footage anyway, and—"

She blocked his way. "Niall, last night, somebody was in my office and on my computers."

"Who could that have been? The police?"

"They already took what they wanted from us."

"Leonard's kidnappers? Someone who knew the bomber?"

"People like that riot."

"Who then?"

Beth did not reply as she continued to study her office.

"This is getting silly. Let's just go in and—"

Beth pulled him back into the hall. "Let's go somewhere else, some café or other."

Ten minutes later, they were the first and only guests in a small café on a side street off Oxford. "Show me your phone," she said. He set it down on the table. "Turn it off."

"No, Beth. I won't. I have to leave it on in case the kidnappers contact me. I—"

"Turn it off. You can turn it right back on again."

He looked at her doubtfully but did as she asked. While they were waiting for the phone to power back up, Beth asked, "Have you recently had to charge the battery more often than usual?"

"Yeah, but I've been on the go a lot more over the past few days than I usually am."

She pointed at his phone. "Does it always take so long to turn off?"

"No idea. I never turn it off. Why?"

She placed her hand on the phone and said softly, "I suspect someone has tapped your phone. When it starts back up, switch off the GPS and the mobile data link."

"But I just told you that I—"

"And give it to me, so I can see what all is running on it. I might find something."

He shot her a skeptical look. "Beth, I think you're a little confused. I'd rather not use a word like paranoid in this case."

"Just do it."

He shook his head in irritation, typed in his password, and handed her the phone. She clicked through the apps and settings, asked questions, and looked worried.

"I'm not up on all the latest stuff, which means I can't really be sure. I've set everything back to the factory settings, and I limited the data access for those apps that seemed strange to me." She held the phone out to him. "Just be careful."

"Swell. Did you change any passwords while you were at it? Will I even be able to access my emails and stuff?"

"Don't be a baby."

"What about yours?"

"I turned it off. I'm going to buy a new one."

"Wow, you're really serious about this. Some people might think you're delusional. Who would want to tap our phones?"

"The intelligence services," she replied.

"Why?"

"Because the two of us have popped up in connection with three alleged terrorist attacks. You, especially. At least one of our intelligence services is bound to have us on their radar."

"And you think it might have been agents who searched your office last night?"

Beth nodded.

"You really need to get more sleep," he declared. It sounded spiteful, though he had meant it to sound considerate. Niall gave a startled jerk as his phone beeped. "Your paranoia seems to be contagious."

It was a message from Laura. Cemal's former co-worker did not have time to chat with them until the day after next. He was in Prague to give a presentation. A former friend from the mosque, however, had time just then. Where should she send him? He was sitting at Victoria Station.

"Here," Beth ordered.

"Here? Not at the station?"

"Absolutely not. They could listen in on us there."

"But not here?"

"They don't know we're here, do they?"

"This is a public place, more or less." He looked around. They were still the only guests, and the server was spending a majority of his time outside, smoking.

"I feel safer here," Beth remarked.

"Good grief. Please find somebody to talk to. A professional. It sounds like you're suffering from PTSD. I mean you just—"

"Shhh!"

Niall fell silent.

"Tell Laura to get over here and have Ken bring the equipment." Beth glanced at her watch. "They should be able to get here in about fifteen minutes."

He nodded, typed out a note and sent it, before looking back at Beth. "You really do need to take better care of yourself," he remarked.

"Any news? About Leonard?"

"No. I mean…I…" That was the moment Beth's paranoia completely washed over him. He wondered what would happen if somebody were listening in and heard him tell Beth about what he had found in the safety deposit box. What if Beth was not everything she claimed to be? He could not help thinking about Mossad.

"Well?" she urged when he still seemed at a loss for words.

He shook his head. "I feel like shit. I keep thinking it's all my fault."

"That's the news?"

"There is no news. I just wanted to complain a little."

"Why don't I believe anything you've just said?"

"Because today you're behaving really weird."

"Don't you trust me?"

He shifted his weight nervously in his chair. "Beth, please. There's no news, okay?"

She pointed at the envelope that he was still carrying with him. "What's that?"

"That? Oh, I just need to mail it."

"Your name is on it."

"Yeah."

She studied him and waited. Ignoring her probing gaze, he sipped on his coffee and stared out the window as if watching for Laura and Ken.

34

Beth stood up, obviously put out by his refusal to tell her anything about the envelope. But, he thought, what business was it of hers? She asked at the counter if it would be alright for them to shoot film footage there. Ken and Laura arrived and set up the equipment, and Cemal's friend also appeared, slightly sweaty. Although it was only nine-thirty in the morning, he was clearly suffering from mild stage fright at the sight of the cameras. Niall explained the project to him and tried to soothe his nerves. Laura read him the usual legal notifications, calmed him down a little, and bought him something to drink. Then, they were set.

Niall was not ready to talk with the young man, so he flew through the notes Laura had jotted down for him. "Yassir, you knew Cemal from school, right?"

"Yes." He threw a searching glance into the camera and ran his fingers through his hair. "Was that alright? Or should I do something different?"

"Don't look at the camera if you can help it. Try to act normal, relaxed. Just chat with each other," Laura said. "This isn't a feature film."

"Okay," Yassir replied, a tad disappointed. "I don't need makeup, do I?"

"No." More disappointment. "Oh well, maybe it's for the best," he murmured.

Niall tried a different tactic to get him to loosen up. "What do you do professionally, Yassir?"

"Oh, I'm a doorman. Different places around town." He nodded emphatically before recalling something. "Oh, not in clubs or bars. A doorman at hotels and boutiques, places like that. I work for a management and security company that services luxury establishments of all kinds." The last sentence sounded like something he had memorized.

"And where do you live?"

"In Clapham. I have my own flat," he said proudly.

"Do you still go to the mosque regularly?"

"Not as much as I used to. Most of my friends aren't there anymore. Somehow everything's different now, since…well, for the past few years. People treat you funny if they find out you attend a mosque. Our Imam is alright, but as soon as you tell people you attend a mosque, you can tell they start wondering if they should call the police."

"Really?"

"Uh, yeah."

"Kind of uncomfortable."

"You could say that. I just want…Well, I like to learn things, and they offer stuff at the cultural center. Classes, you know. I was never good in school, and now I want to make something of myself. The Imam says it's not too late."

"No, it isn't."

"Yeah, makes sense. But I don't go there as much anymore."

"How long did you know Cemal?"

"Since grade school. Forever."

"Were you close?"

He shrugged. "Chums, sure. But Cemal was always smarter than me. Much smarter. At some point, you get tired of that."

"But you saw each other at the mosque."

"Yeah, and we talked, of course. Until he got weird. Everything was shit, and the world was out to get him. I asked him, 'What's wrong with you?' And he said, 'This is a shitty country. I can't get a job because I'm Turkish.' And I said, 'You're talking crap, old man. I have a job, and my parents come from Egypt. What's the difference? If you're right, I shouldn't have a job either.' Do you know what he said to me?" He leaned forward, tapping his finger on the tabletop. "He said: 'They need us for all the menial jobs, but I'm overqualified for those.'"

Yassir continued to drum the table. "He pretends to be all high and mighty, claiming he's overqualified. And me? The low-paying jobs are fine for somebody like me. I don't do shit jobs, okay? I wear a suit to work. Black suit, white shirt, tie. I always polish my shoes. But he called that menial work. After that, I didn't want to have anything to do with him."

"I understand."

He seemed to have forgotten about the camera. "Listen, I'm going to tell you something. We parted ways after that, and our friendship ended. At some point, Farooq—that's what he called himself—showed up, wanting to convert to Islam. At first, he made a nice impression. A little serious perhaps, but still okay. The two of us got along just fine until he and Cemal started hanging out, and then it all went to hell. They screwed up and listened to one of those guys who hang out on the street sometimes and hand out flyers. Holy war, true faith, you know. It was way too much for me."

"Did you talk to anyone about it? Your Imam, Serhat, someone else?"

Yassir shrugged. "What for? Everybody knew about it. You don't need to discuss stuff everyone already knows about."

Niall studied Laura's notes and considered what his next questions could be. Basically, he had already had everything. Nothing there added anything new to what he already knew, but voices like this were important. They were authentic.

"May I ask something?" he heard Beth ask behind him. Niall turned around, annoyed. "Yassir, did anyone ever approach you with questions about Cemal? A stranger? Someone who seemed odd in connection with him?"

He shook his head but seemed to be giving her questions some thought. His eyes wandered aimlessly without coming to rest on anything. "The only odd one was Cemal. Overqualified, what a shitty thing to say. Should've gone and fucked himself. Sorry about that. No, nobody ever asked about Cemal. Just about Farooq."

Niall and Beth stared at each other. "Who?"

"No idea. They were just suddenly there, friendly, you know. Asked about the mosque and stuff, then wanted to know if I knew Farooq and what he was like. I said, 'Guys, I don't know him all that well, and even if I did, I wouldn't chat about him with someone who just walked up to me on the street.' Who did they think they were anyway? Then, they left. But they were polite and apologetic."

"They asked about Farooq?" Niall repeated.

"Yeah, man, that's what I just said. I don't think you're all that overqualified, are you?" Yassir laughed at his own joke. "But the lady on the phone said that we were going to talk about Cemal. I don't know all that much about Farooq. So here I am, sitting in front of the camera, and all I can say is that I don't know and can't talk about that. That's shit. Let's get back to Cemal. What do you still want to know?"

"Do you know his brother Serhat?" Niall asked.

"That's insane, isn't it? What's he doing in jail? His sister Dilek said that's where he is. But why? That boy is alright. His sister, sure, politics and all that, but not Serhat. He doesn't make any waves. What in the world are they thinking?" Yassir's eyes widened, and he suddenly pointed at Niall. "Now I get it. It's all about your father, isn't it? They say that Serhat helped kidnap your father. What kind of crap is that?"

"I know that Serhat had nothing to do with it," Niall replied.

"Then tell the police!"

"I already did."

"Then why won't they let him go?"

"I don't know."

"Dilek said she'd get him out."

"Hopefully, she won't do anything rash."

"Dilek gives a lot of thought to stuff. She's always overqualified, even more than her brother." Yassir nodded, satisfied with himself. "She does some pretty incredible things."

"You admire her?" Beth asked.

"Yeah!"

"You don't find the way Dilek dresses or how she lives to be in violation of your religious convictions?"

Yassir propped his hands on the table and shoved his chair back a little. "No. This is twenty-first century London, not some village a hundred years ago. Anyone who thinks otherwise is just messed up." He pointed at himself. "I understand that. Cemal was too overqualified to get it. The Imam says that what Cemal did was backward and dumb, dangerous, and horrifying to Allah."

"Smart man, your Imam," Niall said.

"Yes. But Farooq used to say that he wasn't teaching true Islam, and Cemal was right with him on that. He started saying he was shit, too."

They chatted a little more about the mosque, the move, the mess with the neighborhood residents. Yassir had nothing new to add, and they brought things to a close. They thanked him for his time and packed everything up. Niall checked his emails, but there were no new messages.

He suddenly remembered what his father had said about going home as soon as he was done at the bank. Niall had thought he had just said that to end his instructions. "Go home," as in, go somewhere. Don't just stay at the bank. But what if he had meant it directly, literally? If that was the case, he had screwed up and squandered hours ignoring an important part of his instructions. Had he put his father in even more danger? What if something had been dropped off for him there? Or—if Leonard was waiting for him?

"Everyone, I need to go home," he said.

"For how long?" Laura asked. "We still have a pretty long list of things to take care of. I mean, we can do that now, or not?" She glanced at Beth for backup.

"We can discuss them at my place," Niall said, immediately regretting his words. As usual, his apartment was a mess, and he was unsure if he really wanted the others to see how he lived. "If it's not inconvenient? Or maybe just later?"

"Preferably today," Laura said, flipping through her notepad.

"We really need to talk," Beth concurred as the other two went on ahead and she and Niall took care of the bill, leaving a generous tip. "Our theory was off. The Service didn't approach Cemal. It was Farooq."

"What does that change? It doesn't matter whether it's Cemal or Farooq, does it? We still have no proof, just Yassir's vague claims. Without corroboration, his story could mean anything."

Beth said, "I thought at first that Cemal was the executioner in the later videos. But I've watched them enough times that I now suspect it was Farooq."

"And if Farooq was the one approached by the Service…"

"If it did, the Service sent an executioner off to spy for this lovely country." ▢

35

As they got off at the Brixton tube station and forged through the crush of people on the platform, Niall longed for the city's morning chill. It seemed much too hot to the others as well, none of whom were saying anything. Although it did not take even ten minutes to reach the ugly apartment block Niall called home, Ken's clothes were drenched by the time they got there. Laura kept furtively wiping the sweat from her forehead, and Niall fanned himself with the envelope from the deposit box. Beth was the only one who did not seem bothered by the heat.

Nonetheless, she lagged her three co-workers, and eventually Niall told the other two to go on ahead while he joined her. They had reached the movie theater by the time Beth came to a stop.

"What are we doing here?" she asked. "Why are we all coming to your place?"

"You don't have to. It's just that I have things I need to do at home. I…" He had thought up a couple of excuses on the ride over, but they had evaporated in the heat.

"What's going on?"

"Nothing. I just forgot something, and…"

"It's about your father, isn't it?" He shook his head, feigning disbelief. "What about that envelope? Is it from him? I recognize his writing. Did he send it to you today?"

Niall acted as if it only just occurred to him that it was Leonard's handwriting. "This here? Oh, no, it's just an old envelope. I'm reusing it. I hadn't even noticed." He was a terrible liar. He stopped and looked helplessly at Beth as she put her hands on her hips.

"Out with it."

So he told her everything. The video, the trip to the bank, the envelope. He explained that he had believed he needed to go back to his apartment because Leonard had specifically said to go home.

She listened and shook her head, "And all of this without telling anyone. Splendid idea."

"Who then? I no longer know who to trust! Should I have called the police? Or you?"

"You should've at least—"

"And then you would've driven me crazy with your paranoid theories," he added resentfully.

Her feelings obviously hurt, she spun around and resumed walking. "I see. It's my fault."

Niall felt instantly guilty. "Beth, please. I had no idea what I should do. I thought it would be best if I didn't get anybody else involved." She walked on without saying a word. "In any case, I'm hoping there'll be a message waiting for me at home."

Beth rubbed her forehead. "Why would they make you go on such a wild goose chase?" she asked skeptically. "They communicate with you via internet videos. They're not going to drop things off at your door." They had reached the apartment house by now. Laura and Ken were waiting for them beside the entrance.

"Show me the photo," Beth said.

"Sure, once we're upstairs."

"In front of the others? Show it to me now."

"I need the bathroom," Ken called.

Niall sighed and tossed him the keys. "Fifth floor, but don't take the elevator. It smells. We'll be right behind you. I just need to…" He waved helplessly at Beth. Laura understood the gesture and followed Ken inside. Once the two of them had vanished, Niall sat down on the low wall that surrounded the patch of grass and pulled the photo out of the envelope.

Beth did not take it from him. "Who's that?"

"An American journalist who saved my father's life. 1981, the tank battle of Susangerd. Leonard was only wounded, but the other man died after being shot in the head. That's why there's so much blood. His name was Niall, and I was named for him."

Beth studied him, no warmth, no sympathy in her gaze. Only cool, analytical assessment. "What does this have to do with Leonard's abduction? A clue? Is this about something that happened in 1981? About Iraq or Iran? Was there a letter with it?"

"No letter, no clue. It's a previously unpublished photo. It has to mean something, presumably, but I'm not sure what. That's why I was waiting all day and why I'd really like—" He never got any further than that, thanks to a thunderous crash. He spun around, unsure about the direction from which the explosive-like sound had come. That was when he saw people pouring out of his building and screaming for the fire department. Beth sprinted for the entrance, while Niall followed her at a somewhat slower, more uncertain pace.

"Don't! There's a fire in there!" somebody yelled in their direction.

"Which floor?" Beth called back.

"Fifth."

Beth dashed toward the stairwell with Niall at her heels. He caught up to her on the stairs. Although he was not as fit as she was, his fear for Laura and Ken drove him on. Three young women passed them between the third and fourth floors, rushing downstairs screaming.

At the fifth floor, Niall paused, wheezing, at the fire door that separated the stairwell from the hallway that led to the apartments. He could see an inferno on the other side of the glass. Two people were lying on the corridor floor. Niall flung open the door as the heat and noxious smoke assailed him. He realized too late that by opening the door, he was feeding the fire, and the flames crept closer to him. But they were still far enough away. He grabbed the man lying right in front of him by the shoulders. Beth lifted his legs and helped Niall carry him to the stairwell.

Niall ran back and wrapped his arms around the second figure. It was Laura. Gasping and coughing heavily, he dragged her out by himself while Beth held the door open for him. She took Laura from Niall and lay her down beside the other man who was moving a little, groaning and choking just as severely as Niall. Beth checked Laura's pulse and breathing as she yelled at Niall: "Where's Ken?" Entering a third time was out of the question. There was no more air, just searing heat, and Ken was not there anyway, otherwise Niall would have seen him. Regardless, he stretched his hand toward the fire door but collapsed in a fit of coughing. He sank down onto the top step as he heard the shriek of sirens.

He watched as Beth tried CPR on Laura, shaking, and screaming at her as she rhythmically pumped on her chest. He heard Laura's ribs crack. He heard the footsteps and voices of the men and women streaming past him from the floors above, dragging bags and suitcases stuffed with the things most important to them. Finally, he heard footsteps and voices from below—firefighters and paramedics.

He tried to crawl toward Beth and Laura, who were only two meters away from him, but he never made it that far. All he could do was watch Beth scream and fight and sob. All he could think was how strange it was to see Beth crying once again, cradling yet another dead woman in her arms. He did not make the connection between the body and Laura until someone grasped his shoulders and propped him upright while trying to talk to him. Then he understood that the girl was dead, and he too began to scream, to weep, struggling to make his way back to his apartment which blazed like the fires of hell, where somewhere Ken had to be. He wanted to search for him and save, at least, him. That was what he told the person who was holding him back before a mask was pressed onto his face. He could no longer see what was going on with Laura and Beth. He inhaled what they gave him, wishing he were dead, and continued to cry.

They took him outdoors. He could barely recall how they managed to get him down the stairs. Did they help carry him, or did he walk down on his own? At some point, he found himself sitting beside Beth in an open ambulance, one among many.

When he started to blame himself for what had happened to Laura, for not being able to rescue her because he had gotten there too late, Beth told him that there was nothing he could have done for her. He had no idea whether he should believe her or not, so he started rambling about the seconds that make the difference between life and death. Beth patted his shoulder and tried to comfort him.

He asked about Ken. The paramedics told him that the entire building had been evacuated, and nobody was left inside, at least no one still alive. They did not say that Ken had to be dead because his body was in the middle of the fire. They would only be able to recover him once the flames were completely extinguished. No one would risk life or limb for a dead man. Once it was clear to the head of operations that it was Niall's apartment that had exploded, he asked the usual things. Were there perhaps gas canisters or flammable or explosive materials in the apartment, something they might still need to take into consideration? Beth answered for him, explaining that it was likely a case of arson. The chief believed that he was reassuring Niall when he told him the police were on their way and they would get everything sorted out.

Niall began to laugh and was unable to stop until Beth firmly wrapped her fingers around his arm. So, that had been the message, he thought. That had been why he was supposed to go home. That was what had been waiting for him. His father had sent him there.

"Beth, could you do me a favor?" Niall asked once they were alone. He was breathing more freely again, felt relatively calm.

"What?"

"When the police come, tell them you want to speak with De Verell. They need to pretend that I'm dead, just for one day, for the media. That'll make the kidnappers think they achieved their goal."

She studied him for a moment before nodding. "Okay."

"I'm leaving."

"Where are you going?"

"I have an idea."

"That you don't want to share with me."

"I'm not sure."

"Not telling someone what you're up to hasn't worked out all that great for you."

He shook his head. "I'll be in touch soon. May I use your card for the tube?"

She pulled the ticket out of her wallet and held it out to him.

He nodded and got to his feet. As he looked at her, she suddenly seemed fragile and forsaken. Exactly like he had just been feeling. He hugged her quickly like a good friend about to leave on a long trip before disappearing among the ambulances.

36

London was miserable when it was hot. The city was also unbearable when it was cold, foggy, or rainy. Under windy conditions, it was impossible, but it was especially wretched when it was hot, since that was when it stank of foul river water, warm sewage, and old garbage. Or reeked of sweaty bodies, cheap perfume, fatty foods, and beer.

At present, it was a day like that. Mid-August, over ninety. As the asphalt baked, mirages shimmered over its surfaces. Niall decided to stop by a pub on his way to the tube station. He ordered a glass of water, went to the restroom, washed his hands and face, drank the water, and ordered another. As soon as the first article announcing that he was "presumably among the fatalities from the bomb attack in Brixton" was posted online, he left and took the tube to Oxford Circus.

Annie was sitting in her gallery cafe, attentively studying an array of garish photographs. She wore large glasses with thick black rims, and her black hair was pulled back in a braid. Without saying a word, Niall pulled out a chair and joined her. She looked up in astonishment, smiling as she recognized him.

"Niall," she said, immediately turning grave. "How are things with your father? Any news?"

Niall shook his head. She took off her glasses. "I'm so sorry. Have the police—"

"Annie, I need your help."

"What can I do?"

He looked at her before quickly glancing away. On his way over, everything had seemed so clear, so logical. Annie would help him, since she was the one who had shown him the photo. Just then, he had no clue where to start.

"I just lied to you. There is news."

"What have the police said?"

"They don't know about it."

She fell silent, waiting.

"The kidnappers sent me a video in which Leonard told me to go to a particular bank and request access to a certain safety deposit box. He wanted me to take out what I found inside, photograph it, and send the shots to his email address. Once I did that, he said I would be given more instructions. What I found in the box was the picture of the other Niall. The dead Niall." He studied her, but she did not react, was seemingly just as perplexed as he was.

"What does this have to do with his abduction?"

"I don't know."

"Was there a letter? Some kind of note?"

"No."

"Nothing at all?"

"No."

"And then?"

"So, I waited, but nothing happened. Until I began to wonder if he had meant for me to follow his instructions literally. He had told me to go home and wait for further instructions, but I didn't do that. I went to the TV station and didn't go home until hours later."

"And then..."

"A message was indeed waiting for me. It didn't reach me though, but two of my colleagues instead. In the form of a bomb. My apartment exploded the moment they opened the door."

Annie's hands flew up to her mouth.

He looked at the clock. "Two and a half hours ago."

"What are you doing here then?"

"Someone wants to see me dead, but I'm not, so I left."

She nodded slowly. "And now?"

"Whoever intended to kill me thinks the attack was a success, at least for now. I need to find out who did that before they realize I'm still alive."

"How can I help?"

"What is it with this photo?" he asked. "There has to be a link somewhere."

"I told you everything I know."

"Do you think somebody wants to make sure this disappears?"

She thought for a moment. "His wife is no longer alive. Leonard told me that, must've been four or five years ago."

"Children?"

"I don't know. Sorry." She absentmindedly gathered the prints lying on the table into a neat stack and stuck them into a portfolio.

"Wait," Niall said.

She hesitated.

"May I have a look?" He carefully picked up one of the prints and turned it over. A series of numbers was printed on the back of the photograph, like the one he had seen on the picture of the dead Niall.

"These are your archive numbers, right?"

Annie nodded.

"Does every gallery do this?"

"Each one has their own system, but yes, it makes sense to…" she trailed off. "What is it?"

Niall was searching for something on his phone. He had lost the envelope holding the photo, probably when he had run up the stairs. "I took a picture of the back side of the photograph. Here. See? There it is."

Annie stared at the screen, squinting. She slipped her glasses back on and looked closely. "Yes, that's my numbering system but not my handwriting."

"Not your handwriting?"

"No, it looks like Leonard's."

"Are you sure?"

"Yes. I'm at least positive it's not my handwriting."

"Why would Leonard or whoever write the archival number?"

"No, it's not the number tied to that photo."

"You can't know all the numbers by heart."

"I know my system. One of Leonard's photos from the eighties would have a much lower series number."

"I don't get it. Why would he write the wrong...Oh." He looked at Annie, and they both had the same idea. Without another word, they stood up and walked through the shop to the back door, taking the stairs up to Annie's office. This time, she let him accompany her to the archive. She did not have to hunt long to find what had been filed under the number.

"Your father obviously put together this little scavenger hunt. The number on your print is the one assigned to this envelope. It is sealed and has your name on it. Go ahead and open it." She turned toward the door. "I'll wait outside."

He hesitated, then nodded. She shut the door behind her carefully, as if a loud noise might have caused the entire archive to collapse. Niall glanced around. He needed to sit down. Or at least lean against something. He could feel the tension from the last few hours, the sleep deprivation, the sadness, the excitement. His knees felt shaky as his pulse raced. Just turning his head made him feel dizzy. He finally decided to sit on the windowsill. There were no chairs in the archive, only cabinets and more cabinets, and shelving units arranged in dark, narrow rows. The window was darkened to block the sunlight, and the room temperature was intentionally cool, due to the sensitivity of the photo paper.

Niall examined the envelope. It had the same seal, the same notation on the front. His first thought was what if Leonard mixed up the envelopes? But in that case, the wrong archival number on the first print would make no sense. He tore open the envelope, as he had already done once that morning, and reached inside. This time, what he pulled out was a picture he had never seen before. And he was certain that except for himself and his father, there was only one other person in the world who also knew what was in this photo.

He studied the picture for a long time, examining all its details closely to verify that he was not mistaken, to assure himself that it was an actual photograph and not a fake or a montage. As he had done earlier, he checked to make sure there was nothing else inside the envelope, but this time, there were negatives. Since there was no contact sheet, he held them up to the light, checked them quickly, and stuck them back into the envelope, keeping out the photo. He turned it over and read: 19910301. No archival number, just a date: March 1, 1991.

He scrutinized the photo one more time, hoping he would spot an obvious clue that he was holding a fake even though he had seen the negatives. The photograph showed a naked man on his knees. His hands were tied behind his back, and he was bent so far forward his face was touching a filthy floor. His mouth was opened in a scream of anguish. Another man was standing behind him, a man in uniform, in British uniform. He was holding a gun, the barrel of which was rammed into the anus of the man cowering naked and handcuffed on the floor. The man in uniform was grinning. Not into the camera, just grinning. He was enjoying what he was doing.

A picture can be deceptive, Niall reminded himself, since it can capture for eternity, and therefore distort, a moment in time. However, this picture left little room for doubt. The man in uniform had shoved the barrel of his gun into the body of his victim. It did not matter if he pulled the trigger in the next second or not. This form of humiliation, of abuse, of intimidation, was horrifying, regardless of the connection between the date and the war that had just ended. Even if it was the only crime perpetrated by the man in uniform, it still made him a war criminal, a man who assaulted prisoners. At least, one prisoner.

Niall tried to recall how Carl's military career had ended. Niall had been a child during the Gulf War, but had his parents ever talked about it? Or had the story simply been that Carl had decided to make a career change? There was no way anybody except Carl and Leonard knew about the existence of the photo, which was why there was no spectacular story about Carl quitting the military and taking a job in the civilian sector. Niall imagined Leonard pressuring Carl to leave the military with the threat of going public with the photo and Carl agreeing but living through the decades in fear that Leonard would someday blackmail him again.

Was Carl behind Leonard's abduction? Had he used the uproar around the murdered air cadet as an opportunity to throw everyone off track? What if there were no Islamists behind the kidnapping, just Carl? Had Carl assumed that this photo was locked in the safety deposit box? Would Leonard have knowingly sent Niall to his death if he had known about the bomb? And why then? Why was Carl so desperate to get rid of the photo just then of all times? Because Leonard had confronted him with it again, Niall guessed. What had Leonard demanded of him? What had been so important that he would have been willing to place his life—and that of his son—at risk?

Niall had no idea, but then a vision of Karen floated to the surface of his mind. Karen, who had been married to Carl back then. Had she known about it? Had Leonard threatened to tell her about Carl's past? What would that have achieved? He was missing something. Niall tried to rearrange his thoughts, but he kept coming back to Karen. Karen, the Home Secretary who presumed to do and say things that were the purview of the Prime Minister or the Foreign Secretary. Karen, who talked about taking military action.

Carl and Karen had gotten divorced shortly after the Gulf War, and Carl had married Susan. But Carl and Karen were still friends. Connected by friendship. A man who worked for the Ministry of Health and the Home Secretary. A film about Islamist terrorists. The abduction of the man behind the film project. A man who possessed material that could be used to blackmail the man from the Ministry of Health. But why? It made no sense to Niall.

One more time from the top, he rehearsed. Leonard had wanted Niall to uncover the story behind the attack. The reason why Paulie Ferguson had been murdered. Religious fanaticism. Radicalization. MI5. The Service, which reported straight to the Home Secretary. The Service, which had been interested in Farooq. The Service had recruited an executioner, a butcher.

What did Carl have to do with this? Nothing. In which case—Niall left the archive.

Annie was waiting for him in the corridor. She looked at him anxiously and sensed that something had happened, but she did not ask. He handed her the envelope and said, "Seal it back up, and hide it somewhere."

Niall walked past her, down the stairs, through the shop, and out into the bright sunlight. It had been freezing in the archive, and the summer heat slammed into him like a wall. Not the first wall of the day, he thought. The asphalt was baking. London was unbearable at that temperature. Niall turned back toward the gallery, considering how it was where he had met his father for the first time. Back then, he had found him without even trying. He would find him again that day.

37

Niall walked to Piccadilly Circus, past the closed bars and theaters, continuing down side streets, which despite the bright sunlight seemed dark and cool, as if the night would never completely release the buildings. He bought a baseball cap and a pair of sunglasses before letting himself be caught up in the tide of tourists and swept down to the Thames. He took a seat at the bar in a dark pub within sight of a TV and ordered a cup of coffee.

According to news coverage, he was presumed dead. Broadcasters discussed the possibility of the attack being linked to his father's abduction, before turning to the war. The US had already dispatched fighter jets, and the Prime Minister had just announced to the press that nothing stood in the way of a British military intervention against IS. The reporters mentioned that other countries would be involved in the strike, but they did not say which.

Nobody cared anyway. The only nations that counted were the US and the UK, Niall thought. The little brother followed in the footsteps of the big brother, the 51st State of America! The reporters showed the results of the recent public opinion poll about the military strike. Since the murder of Paulie Ferguson, support for the war had increased, spiking significantly over the past two days.

The attack on the synagogue had resulted in other perspective changes. The majority of those polled now expressed support for arms sales to Israel, whereas before the attack, only one-quarter of respondents had favored it. The last question on the survey related to Hamas. Over half of those surveyed believed that Israel and Hamas should join together to fight IS.

FADE TO BLACK

They wanted to arm an entire region that had spent decades sunk in war. Tanks that had once been delivered to Qatar or Iraq by the Western European nations or the US were now in the hands of IS, as were armored vehicles and heavy artillery pieces out of Russia. Weapons from the last Gulf War. American helicopters. Munitions from Saudi Arabia. All governments denied these sort of reports. The official story was that IS had grown rich from running an extensive protection racket and had acquired their weapons through well-plotted raids, rounding out their collection through the black market. Most of the officers were allegedly former members of the Sunni military under Saddam Hussein. Or Syrian army deserters. Now, more weapons were going to be funneled into the Middle East for even more wars. The government press secretaries claimed that there was no other solution to the conflict. IS was too aggressive and would not be stopped any other way.

When wars came, they were never motivated by religion or the value of human life but by economic interests, Niall knew. By coastlines and ports, oil reserves and access to strategically important sites. War waged in God's name was a lie. It always had been, despite what some poor idiots, the ones being used as cannon fodder, believed. How convenient that Paulie Ferguson had died so shortly before the decision had to be made about Great Britain's involvement in this war! How unbelievably convenient, almost providential.

Niall knew Leonard's clear, unwavering opinion about these matters, just like everyone else did, "There is not one good reason to go to war." That had been his sole mission, the one that had driven him around the world to show people what they were doing to each other. Why would a man with his ideals choose not to go public with the horrifying photo of Carl and his victim? What agreement had the two men reached? And what had happened to convince Carl that it was necessary to kidnap Leonard?

Niall ordered another cup of coffee and a glass of water as an announcement ran along the bottom of the screen. "Breaking news: The photographer Leonard Huffman has been released by his abductors." Niall exhaled deeply. He felt his body relax, then he started trembling uncontrollably. He pushed the coffee aside and ordered a whiskey before pulling out his phone and skimming news sites. It was the same news everywhere, more details to follow.

His father was free. So they said. It was exactly what he had expected to happen. He imagined Carl threatening Leonard, his old acquaintance, demanding to know where that photo of him was. And Leonard saying that it was gone. Carl might have responded that he knew about the safety deposit box and presumed it was there. Leonard would have offered to prove it wasn't." Could it have been like that? Had they sent him to the bank to prove that a different picture was in the box? Had Carl decided to kill Niall to make sure that he never discovered the truth? If so, why would he not just kill Leonard? Then the thought came once more that Leonard had perhaps knowingly sent him to his death. Go home. Go die—something did not fit.

Carl would not have released Leonard if he had known that Niall had found the photo. Niall needed to wait until his father was in safety, and that was what he would do. Drink his whiskey, wait, and stay dead for everyone else. About an hour later, he searched his pockets for money, found another ten-pound bill, and ordered something to eat. The barkeeper casually asked if he was allergic to the sun or if he was avoiding his wife.

Niall said, "Both."

The first pictures of Leonard appeared when he was about halfway through his meal. As Leonard stepped out of an unmarked police vehicle, a mob of journalists quickly engulfed him. He was weeping because he had just learned his son was dead. To the barrage of questions, he described his abductors as ethnically Arab, and said that they had described themselves as Salafists and had talked about the Islamic State. He had never left London, but they had discussed taking him abroad and killing him there if their demands were not met. He was then taken into the building behind them, which proved to be a hospital. Niall recognized Detective De Verell. He wondered if De Verell had told his father the truth. Perhaps they had let him believe that Niall was dead, so he did not have to pretend to be heartbroken and risk spoiling it all.

But did Niall really think the investigators were that cold-hearted? To not tell a man that his son was still alive, knowing he believed he was responsible for his death? Niall had to admit the answer to those questions was yes. At least Leonard was free, he thought. Carl had gotten what he wanted. He believed the photo had been destroyed. Leonard had been suitably punished, and Niall was out of the picture, as far as he knew. Niall would be unable to ask any more questions or find any more pictures. The damage was contained, and the documentary would never be finished.

The documentary. The one about two young men who had learned how to kill people in a training camp. One of whom had likely been recruited by the Service to infiltrate the Salafist scene. Niall finished his meal and left. It was a long way to Harrow, and there were things he needed to take care of along the way.

38

Susan screamed when she saw him. It was a scratchy, rather choked screech as she covered her mouth with her hands. Niall could tell that she had been crying.

"You're alive!" She threw her arms around him.

"Yes." He tried to gently slip out of her embrace, but she just pulled him more tightly against her.

"Niall, I'm so happy! You're alive!" He felt warm tears trickle down his neck.

"Susan, it was a misunderstanding. I'm so sorry you were worried." He could feel her shake her head against his shoulder. She hesitantly loosened her grip, and he was able to gently push her away. "Is Carl here?"

She nodded with a little hiccup. Niall strode past her into the living room where Carl was waiting. Niall stopped in the doorway and studied the other man. Carl would know that he knew everything, or maybe not everything, but enough. Niall could tell that Carl had not reckoned on seeing him again. De Verell had followed through.

"Who do you work for?" Niall asked. "MI5?"

Susan had followed him. "Carl, he said it was a misunderstanding. Isn't it incredible? He's not dead!" When nobody said anything, Susan realized that something was off. "What's wrong?"

"Your husband works for the Service," Niall said, not taking his eyes off Carl. He heard Susan gasp.

Carl laughed. "My boy, you must be feeling just fine if you can make jokes like that. Come on in and sit down. Have you seen your father?"

"On TV." Niall did not move. "I waited until then."

"Those Arabs finally let him go. You must feel so relieved. You really don't want to sit down?"

"How long are you going to keep this up?" Niall asked.

Carl glanced at his wife. "Susan, would you be a dear and get Niall something to drink? What would you like? It's probably too warm for whiskey. Anything sound good?"

Niall said nothing while Susan stood there helplessly, trying to inconspicuously wipe the tears from her cheeks.

"Then I'll pick. Susan, I have an idea. We have some wonderful Riesling in the pantry."

"But you prefer—"

He interrupted his wife. "Darling, the one I told you about. We've been saving it for a very special occasion. Do you remember the one?"

She thought for a moment and then nodded.

"Good. Make sure it's cool enough. It should be just the thing in this heat. Besides, we have something to celebrate, don't we? Niall, returned from the dead! And Leonard, back in one piece. Too bad he isn't here."

Susan hurried to the kitchen pantry. Niall heard her searching among the bottles.

Carl walked over to Niall, hands in his pockets and a smile on his lips. "Come on. Let's go sit down and talk about everything." He grabbed Niall's elbow and shoved him toward the couch.

Niall refused to sit down. "Did you do Karen a favor by turning everyone in this country into a racist? Or did she do you a favor by holding that strange speech about the necessity of delivering arms to Israel? Are you trying to further your own career inside your...framework, or does she need your support to become Prime Minister? Maybe you both need each other."

Carl slowly shook his head. He did not sit down, either. "Niall, it really was too much for you, wasn't it? But now we should celebrate the fact that your father is back in one piece."

Niall heard Susan messing with glasses in the kitchen. She gave a sharp cry as one of them hit the floor, quickly calling out that everything was alright. He watched as Carl smiled dreamily at his wife's clumsiness. Niall said, "The more I think about it, the more certain I am that Karen's the one under your control."

Carl shook his head smiling, "A self-confident woman like Karen? How could you even think something that absurd?"

"Yes, nobody would ever suspect it. I believe you have something over her. You want to know why?" He paused, for effect, not because he expected Carl to answer. Carl seemed to be more focused on his wife sweeping up the glass shards in the kitchen than he was on what Niall was saying. "Because it makes no sense the other way around. If she had known about the photo, she would have ratted you out a long time ago, just to get you off her back. Someone like Karen can easily find new people willing to do her favors."

"Which photo?" Carl let his words fall nonchalantly.

"You know the one I'm talking about."

"My boy, this really has been a rough day for you." As he heard footsteps, his face brightened. "Susan, darling, did you bring three glasses? What's this, only two? No, no, you must join us!" Susan set down the bottle, wine bucket, and glasses before returning to the kitchen.

"You want her here so I won't talk about the photo, right?" Niall asked. Susan returned with the third glass and a corkscrew.

"Screw top, darling." Carl smiled as he caught sight of what she was carrying. "It no longer says anything about the quality of wine. The most exquisite wines come with screw tops these days, and the cheapest stuff is bottled with corks." Carl poured the Riesling into the three glasses. He lifted his glass, "Niall, my boy, we're toasting the fact that everything is over, that you're still alive, and that your father has come back safe and sound from the hands of his kidnappers."

Susan was the only one sitting down. She picked up her glass, glancing uncertainly back and forth between the two of them. "Niall, what's wrong?" she asked quietly. "Take a sip."

Niall's eyes remained fixed on Carl. "Susan, it would be best if you left us alone for a bit." She stood up.

"She stays here," Carl said.

"You really want that?" He thought he recognized something derisive in Carl's gaze.

"What's going on here?" Susan asked, her voice shrill.

"I wasn't joking earlier. Your husband isn't who you think he is. He doesn't drive to the Ministry of Health in the mornings but to a certain office in Thames House. I also know that he was behind my father's kidnapping."

An astonished cry. "How can you—"

"He and Leonard have known each other for over twenty years."

"Yes, he told me that—"

"They were together in Iraq in '91. Carl got off on abusing the POWs, and Leonard took a photo of it." Carl waved this off with a smile.

Susan cried in horror: "Carl, say something!"

But Carl just grinned, holding his glass and apparently waiting for something.

"Leonard caught him doing it one time," Niall continued, "as he rammed the barrel of an assault rifle into a prisoner's ass. The man was kneeling naked and cuffed in front of him. He was already subdued and humiliated, but that wasn't enough for Carl."

"That's disgusting, Niall!"

"Don't tell me. Tell your husband."

"I can't imagine that Carl—"

"I saw the photo, Susan."

Carl was still calm. "Niall, you must have been mistaken."

"No. I saw the photo," he repeated. "Carl, you're finished. The photo is still out there, and Leonard showed me where it was, but only after you'd abducted him. Otherwise, I probably never would've known about it. It was a situation like this, I assume, that made you try to kill me." He ignored Susan's whimpering. "The only reason I'm here is because I want some answers from you. I probably won't get them, but I wanted to at least try, before—" He considered how to put it.

At that moment, he could feel what it was like to have power over another person. Not just through physical violence, but through knowledge, the possession of information. He felt both relaxed and dominant, untouchable and strong. Niall sat down on the couch, leaned back, and crossed his legs. "The photo, my dear Carl, still exists, as does the negative. Of course, I won't tell you where they are, but even if you knew, even if you could possibly destroy the negative and all the prints at this very moment...Even then..." He let the sentence dangle.

Carl nodded. "You mean, even then it would be too late. What did you do?" He spoke quietly and firmly, his wine glass in one hand, the other draped loosely over the back of a chair.

"I took pictures of it, of course. Of the entire photo, distinct details. It's all digitized now. Not quite as good as a scan, but it should be good enough, I think."

"Where are the files now?"

"Where should they be?" Niall picked up his glass, sensing something like victory. "Online. Mailed to my co-worker's account."

"The lovely Israeli," Carl said with a nod.

"You knew that?"

"Obviously."

Niall smiled before finally taking a sip. The Riesling was cool and dry, perhaps a little too sour for his taste. Before that point, his suspicion that Carl worked for the Service had just been a theory without any concrete proof. Finally, Niall believed a stable foundation had replaced the shaky ground he had been on.

"Beth's account," he said. "But that in and of itself wouldn't be especially earth-shattering, would it? The photos are also on my blog. That's what I did before coming over here. I'm the man whose father was abducted, the son of Leonard Huffman. If I die, lots more people will be interested in my blog, and they'll find the photos. They're out there, Carl. You can't get them back. Someone will find them and make sure they make the rounds, even if the originals aren't around anymore. It's over."

FADE TO BLACK

Carl raised his glass and toasted first Niall, then Susan. "To us. We could have been great men." He drained his glass in a single gulp. Susan sat beside Niall on the couch and sobbed, obviously completely lost. "Drink, my love," Carl urged. "You'll feel better afterward." She obeyed him, as usual.

Niall did not like the wine much, and he was just setting his glass down on the coffee table when Carl collapsed. Susan jumped up to go to him, but she stumbled, groaned, and also fell to the floor. Niall felt an unpleasant heaviness behind his eyes, followed by a wave of nausea. As his eyelids closed, the world turned red and black. Confusing images floated before him, of Beth, of Laura. At least Laura was still alive there. He saw both women running across a street. Somehow Leonard materialized in front of him, trying to tell him something, but Niall could not hear him. He fell helplessly into a deep, dark sleep.

39

For the second time that day, Niall found himself in an ambulance. He was lying down, and someone had put him on an IV drip.

"He's awake," a paramedic declared.

DI Gilpin, as blonde and cool as ever, climbed into the ambulance and nodded. "You were lucky," she said.

"What happened?" The taste in his mouth was revoltingly sour, as if he had vomited.

"How are you feeling?"

"Nauseated. My head and throat hurt." Apparently, he really had thrown up.

"Good thing you didn't drink much. They still had to pump your stomach, though." He tried to remember. The wine, the "special occasion" Riesling Susan had been told to find.

"How are Carl and Susan?" he asked.

Gilpin shook her head.

"I'm sorry about Susan," Niall said. "She had no idea what was going on."

"You have your co-worker to thank for this."

Niall followed Gilpin's gaze out into the darkness beyond the ambulance. It was glaringly bright inside, so it took his eyes a few seconds to adjust. He recognized a police car, the coroner's vehicle, and a hearse. A woman was leaning against the patrol car, smoking. He had never seen Beth smoke, but it was definitely her.

"She found the photo of Carl Davis in her inbox and came straight out here. When she saw what was going on, she called us." Gilpin paused, perhaps to consider if she should tell him everything. She continued, "She broke into the house and poured saltwater down your throat until you vomited." Gilpin now smiled. "I think she likes you."

Niall coughed and changed the topic. "What did Carl put in the wine? I mean, it had to be in the wine."

"Don't know. We're waiting on the lab results, which might take days."

"Can I go..." He had wanted to say, "go home," but then he recalled that he no longer had one. "Where am I supposed to stay?"

"We can arrange for a hotel if you like, for a couple of days." She looked at him. "I'm really sorry about all this." She sounded sincere.

"It's okay." He turned toward the paramedic. "Can I get up?"

She checked the IV bag, which was almost empty. "Do you feel up to it?"

"Yes."

"Remember to drink a lot over the next few hours."

"Okay."

He sat up carefully, pausing long enough for his circulation to start up again. Everything went dark for a moment, but then it was back to normal. He slowly got to his feet, climbed out of the ambulance, and took a step, DI Gilpin at his heels.

"Would you mind giving me a little space?" It came out harsher than he had meant it to. She raised her hands defensively and walked over to her partner who was just coming from the house.

Niall made his way over to Beth, who offered him a cigarette. He shook his head. "I feel sick enough as it is."

"You really look like shit." She studied him through narrowed eyes, shaking her head. "Green really isn't your color, at least not in skin tone."

"Thanks a lot." He leaned against the patrol car next to her. "And thank you."

"We're good." She dropped her finished cigarette and stepped on it. "You should go lie down."

"Sure. But where exactly?"

"A hotel?"

"Gilpin said the same thing. Might be a good idea."

"Leonard's?"

"Maybe a better idea even."

"Ask him. You have some things to discuss anyway." Of course, they did, Niall realized. Niall had not seen him since his release, and he had no idea if anyone had told Leonard that his son who had been dead was no longer dead. Or if he had known all along.

"I assume it's the middle of the night."

"Not quite that bad. It's eleven."

"Want to come along?"

Beth was just about to light another cigarette, and she shook her head. "No, this is your thing. I'd just be a third wheel."

"I wouldn't be here if it weren't for you. Come on."

She puffed away and took her time before answering. "Alright," she said finally. "Somebody has to look out for you." She almost smiled, but then grabbed her bag and rummaged out a piece of gum. Not for her, for him. "Here. Until you can brush your teeth."

He took it. "I don't think I have a toothbrush anymore."

"It's amazing what you can buy these days."

He looked at her and laughed. She grinned but stared fixedly at the ground. Niall had no idea what to say next, so he hugged her. She grudgingly pushed him off.

"Let's not get carried away," she murmured.

"Niall," he heard Gilpin call.

He turned in her direction. "I'd like to go see my father. May I go now?"

"Niall, I—we—need to talk to you."

He watched her and DI De Verell walk toward the patrol car. Niall said nothing, but he could sense that something was wrong. He had no desire to hear whatever they had to say. He had already been through so much.

"It's your father," De Verell said. Holding an iPad in one hand, he opened the passenger door with the other. "We should sit down. Beth, you too, if you'd like." Once all of them were in the car, De Verell held out the iPad so Niall could see it. "A video message for you."

Niall started to shake. "Has he been kidnapped again?"

De Verell shook his head wordlessly and hit play. The video showed Leonard in his office at the station. Niall guessed that he had set the camera up on a tripod about two meters from where he sat. Leonard looked happy and calm, his office neat and tidy. Niall's heart slowed back down as he saw him.

"Niall, my son, I need to explain a few things to you. I wanted you to make the documentary so the connection between the one attacker and MI5 would come out. More specifically, the link to Carl. To be very clear: The two young men were ordered to carry out that attack. I'm not sure if the entire agency knew about this or not, and there's no way to really know. It was Carl's intention to stir things up more in the Middle East. The greater the tensions are in that area, the more important his position is in MI5. He wants the government to send more weapons there, mainly to Israel. His goal is for Great Britain to become Israel's primary ally, more important than the US. If he succeeds at this, he will become the most powerful man in the nation.

For years, the mood in Parliament has not worked in his favor, which is why he leveraged Karen. I wanted to stop him, but I couldn't just go to him and say: 'Remember the photo, you have to stop.' I needed proof. I thought that through the film, everyone would find out about what he was planning. He told me I had to stop you. I said I wouldn't, and you know the rest." Leonard stopped, pressing his lips together and glancing away from the camera, but then he continued.

"Niall, I have made some pretty bad decisions in my life. I should have published the photo of Carl a long time ago. Not doing that went against my principles, my entire philosophy. Even back then, he knew how to manipulate people. It wasn't just a coincidence that he left the military and went right into the Service. How do I know that? There were only two people who knew what had really happened. Karen and me. But that's another story." Leonard hesitated again, taking a deep breath. "Back in Iraq, he told me he knew about you. It was all still a secret, because we—your mother and I—wanted to protect you. He said, 'You don't want anyone to know, and do you know why it's best if nobody does? Because otherwise the poor lad might be in danger. Imagine what would happen if someone kidnapped him just to get to you, to force you to not publish something. Wouldn't that be horrible?'" Leonard let the words hang there but didn't look away from the camera.

"If you care about something, if you love anyone, that makes you vulnerable to blackmail. Especially if you have secrets. These are both true for me. Please go to the police. Go public with my confession. Someone has to stop Carl." He rubbed his face and stared into the distance for a second. "Niall, I've realized today that I've done too many things wrong in my life. I can't continue knowing what has happened because of me and my decisions. There's no court through which I can fix things; there's just the two of us. I can't bear for you to see me again, and that makes me a coward. I let myself be blackmailed, and I failed to do the right thing. You almost died because of me, and that would have killed me. I will end things now. Niall, I have always carried you in my heart and always loved you the best I could. I am very proud of you." The scene went black.

FRIDAY
40

"When did you get this?" Niall asked as soon as he could speak. They were all still sitting in the patrol car, except for Beth who was leaning against the trunk and smoking again.

"He made this video before Carl Davis died. He didn't know you'd posted the picture of Davis online. I assume this was his version of a suicide attack. He wanted to prove what kind of person Carl really was."

Carl really had manipulated everyone. Susan had not known what kind of person she had married, and Carl had taken pleasure from that. And Karen? Perhaps he had helped her along her career trajectory and had demanded various favors in return. Like he had that time. He had had no problem turning his ideas into action.

Gilpin nodded. "There is an MI5 file on every politician. Nobody outside the Service knows what's in those files."

"Karen doesn't know what's in hers?"

"Even if she never did anything that would make her susceptible to blackmail, her file could be stuffed full of lies. These files have nothing to do with facts, just speculation."

"Intelligence services around the world are in a position to mold the past to fit their agenda. They just repeat their invented truths until people actually believe them," De Verell replied.

Niall had always believed Carl, the cheerful, helpful man who had been occasionally irritating in his conservatism. He never would have thought him capable of these actions. Yet now he knew that Carl had been delusional and arrogant enough to believe he could shape the future of the country, and people had helped him to do that. Had nobody been willing to stop him? Besides Leonard? Perhaps there had been others before him who had simply not survived, Niall wondered.

They helped Niall out of the car and led him back to the ambulance. He agreed to take something to help with the shock. Beth stayed with him. She did not hold his hand, but she occasionally patted him on the shoulder while mumbling encouraging platitudes. He fell asleep in the ambulance and woke up hours later in a space that looked like a hospital room. Fortunately, it was a private room. Beth was fast asleep in the visitor chair.

Niall saw three cell phones sitting on the nightstand beside his bed. One was large enough that it was almost a tablet, presumably Beth's new device. It was turned off. Next to it were his phone and Beth's old one. He picked his up and pulled up the internet. He wanted to know what the media were reporting about Leonard's death. And Carl's. And if he was now being treated as alive or dead in the news.

He regretted the decision. The only good news was that Cemal and Dilek's brother, Serhat, had finally been released. He could find nothing about Carl, only a mention of a murder-suicide that had taken place the night before in Harrow.

His father's farewell video was nowhere online. The Home Secretary had issued an official statement that the rumors about the Service's connection with one of Paulie Ferguson's murderers were completely baseless. She talked about conspiracy theories and how the internet was fertile ground for such nonsense.

As for Leonard's death, the story was that he had been unable to cope with his abduction and the terrible things he had experienced at the hands of his kidnappers. He might have even blamed himself for the deaths of two of his colleagues, it was speculated, as well as his son's near escape from death. Obviously, his abductors had been able to influence him, since shortly before his suicide, he had spouted crazy theories.

The synagogue, Niall thought. Had Carl been behind that attack, as well? Or had that just been a coincidence, an attack inspired by Paul Ferguson's death? Would they ever know? What had De Verell said? The intelligence services were in a position to mold the past to fit their agenda. No, they would never find out. He ran a Google search for articles on the synagogue attack. There were still no leads on the person who had disarmed the suicide bomber. The reports were pointing to "uncertain events during the attack." Niall glanced at the sleeping Beth and smiled.

Since he had last checked, the death toll had risen to ninety-four. Two older victims had succumbed to smoke poisoning. Eight hundred could have died. Beth had saved over seven hundred people, and nobody would ever thank her for that. She did not want them to.

Niall set his phone back down. He noticed that he was crying. He had tried to hold back the tears, but finally, he gave up. Beth woke up and looked at him. "Oh, I must have nodded off. Don't read the news." She gathered the phones off the table.

"Too late," he said.

"You really can't be left on your own."

"Serhat's out."

"Yes, that's good."

"We should call him."

"That was the plan."

"And check on how Dilek is doing."

Beth nodded. "But not at five in the morning."

"Don't you want to go home? You'd sleep better."

She considered his suggestion. "There's nobody else out there who wants to kill you, right?"

Despite everything, he had to smile, but then he realized she was serious. "Go home," he said. "Thank you for everything."

"Get yourself a new phone. They're definitely listening in on this one. Like I told you when they trashed my office, the Service has its fingers in everything."

"Carl is dead."

"Who knows who's sitting on the other end and listening."

"You really are paranoid."

"Yes. It helps sometimes." She stood up and walked to the door.

"I'll pick you up later, and then we'll go see Serhat."
"Thank you," Niall repeated, but she was already gone. ☐

FADE TO BLACK
THREE WEEKS LATER

At 01:00:00:00, an image of a woman wearing a hijab fades in. She was shot from the waist up, mid-range, against a white wall.

"For years, I have fought for freedom and equality in my country. I always believed that Great Britain was my homeland because I was born there and had a British passport. But nobody ever accepted me as British, not me or my brothers." Cut to a full side close-up. "My older brother Cemal felt so alienated that he joined the jihad. He killed people because he was convinced it was the right thing to do. He took a stand for his beliefs, and he died in a British prison." Cut to a full-frontal close-up. "He did not just die. He was killed by British police officers, just like his friend Farooq. Because of a different crime, my younger brother was arrested without justification. No attorney, no accusation. He survived days of beatings in prison. He is only eighteen years old." Cut to a mid-shot. "Until a little while ago, I believed that my big brother had made the wrong decision to join the jihad. I now know that he made the right one. I will follow in his footsteps. My name is Dilek Bayraktar."

At 01:01:27:38, the scene fades to black.

Zoë Beck writes, translates (fiction from English), and co-directs with Jan Karsten the publishing company CulturBooks. She studied English and German literature in Giessen, Bonn, and Durham before becoming a creative producer for international film productions. She now lives in Berlin, and her books have been published in nine languages to date.

CPSIA information can be obtained
at www.ICGtesting.com
Printed in the USA
BVHW081212230123
656676BV00004B/13